Now, published for the
first time anywhere, her most
extraordinary novel

JACQUELINE SUSANN

YARGO

This is Jacqueline Susann's
first novel, completed in 1956 and
only recently rediscovered.
Although never previously published,
it was a story which always had
a special place in her heart.
Here, from the author of

Valley of the Dolls,

The Love Machine

———and———

Once Is Not Enough,

———is———

YARGO

Yargo is spellbinding, romantic—
the story of a beautiful woman
who was kidnapped by the
most attractive man she had ever met—
a man from outer space...

THE STORY BEHIND
JACQUELINE SUSANN'S

YARGO

Written during the early 1950s, Jacqueline Susann's *Yargo* "thoroughly reflects the romanticism of the young Susann and is written in a style inimitably her own," Marc Jaffe, Bantam's president and editor in chief, has said of the novel. "There is an innocence and idealism about it, as well as a hopeful message about the strength of human love that many readers will find touching and appealing."

Irving Mansfield, her husband, recalls that it was 1953 when his wife first showed him a draft of *Yargo.* "She had discovered Ray Bradbury, and the manuscript she showed me was a kind of science fiction love story. Her model for the male protagonist was Yul Brynner, who had just skyrocketed to fame as the star of *The King and I.* Then, in 1956 she took the manuscript along on a trip to Europe and made some changes. We returned on the *Liberté*, where we met George Chasin who was an agent for MCA. Jackie gave him the manuscript. Chasin sent it to several studios, but it met with little response because interest in science fiction film projects was at a low ebb. Ignored, the manuscript remained with Chasin until November 1977, when accidentally, he came across it while cleaning out a little-used filing cabinet."

Once Susann began writing her books, she never returned to *Yargo*, as far as is known, except for a brief period when she considered using part of the story as the last section of *Once Is Not Enough*. Oscar Dystel, chairman and Chief Executive officer of Bantam Books, recalls this incident: "I was haunted by the familiarity of *Yargo* as I read it. Finally, I remembered a long afternoon years ago when Jackie and I were working at her apartment. She outlined the story of her next novel, which would become *Once Is Not Enough*. But the ending she proposed puzzled me. She wanted to have the heroine lifted into space and onto a distant planet where she would meet her perfect love. I was incredulous at the time. Space fantasy had never been associated with Jackie's style, and it wasn't an element necessary for the story. I encouraged her to leave the heroine alone at the end. Now, having read *Yargo*, I see that the story is strikingly similar to the one she told me that afternoon so many years ago."

Mansfield says, "It's ironic that now, over twenty-five years after she first conceived the story, Jackie's *Yargo* will finally reach its audience. She really would be thrilled."

YARGO

JACQUELINE SUSANN

BANTAM BOOKS · TORONTO · NEW YORK · LONDON

YARGO

A Bantam Book / March 1979

2nd printing

ISBN 0-553-12855-8

Published simultaneously in the United States and Canada

Bantam Books are published by Bantam Books, Inc. Its trademark, consisting of the words "Bantam Books" and the por-
trayal of a bantam, is Registered in U.S. Patent and Trademark
Office and in other countries. Marca Registrada. Bantam
Books, Inc., 666 Fifth Avenue, New York, New York 10019.

PRINTED IN THE UNITED STATES OF AMERICA

CHAPTER 1

So this was a psychiatrist's waiting room.
I looked around.

It looked no different from the dentist's
waiting room. The same few pieces of inex-
pensive modern furniture. A bare coffee table
decorated with an ornate but empty cigarette
box. The past few months' issues of *Time* and
Life. I had read them all at the dentist's
office.

I had spent a lot of time at the dentist's.
A girl wants to be perfect when she's getting
married. You feel you must get all those loose
ends tied up. You know, pay all the back bills
at the department stores and discard all
those useless skirts and shoes you never
really wear but always put away. And then,
finally, the trip to the dentist.

This is the most noble act of all, because
you know your teeth are in perfect condition,
but you rush in for a quick checkup and
cleaning. This is really starting marriage
with a clean slate. Then, as all dentists do, he
finds three small cavities. They could wait;
they aren't the kind of cavities you can feel
with your tongue or a cold glass of water.
These are the kind no one knows you have.

Except the dentist, and even he has to find them with a small searching party of prods and Xrays. Yes, they could wait. But feeling positively virtuous, you have them done. You're determined everything must be right. You're getting married!

I looked at my watch, David's engagement present to me. Five more minutes until the actual appointment. Sometimes I think being overpunctual is as big an evil as being late. It gives you too much time to think; and thinking over a momentous decision is comparable to hearing a funny story. The first time you hear it, you laugh hilariously. The second time you smile in appreciation. The third time you are bored; and the fourth time you begin to wonder if it ever was funny.

I was at the wondering stage now. I had arrived for this appointment early. Maybe this was fate, giving me a chance to change my mind.

I've always been a fatalist. If I forget to turn off a light and run back to make sure (invariably finding everything in order), I console myself that maybe it was meant to be. Maybe those few retraced steps kept me from doing something the fates hadn't scheduled for me. It might even have saved my life. If I'd been on the sidewalk instead, a car might have come up and hit me. A flowerpot could have dropped on my head. Any number of disastrous incidents might have been averted by those retraced steps. You read about it in the papers every day.

All right, get up and leave!

And then what? Then back to another night of chain smoking. Another night of migraine sleeplessness, until I succumbed to a Seconal and a few hours of restless sleep.

The dull throbbing began in the back of my neck. I ran my hands through my hair in an effort to ease the pressure, then stopped abruptly. I had no headache. It was just nerves. This was accomplishing nothing except disorganizing my brand-new Italian hairdo.

I stood up. In fact, I even got as far as crushing my cigarette in the ashtray near the door. I looked in the mirror and saw a strange and calm girl. Well, that proved it.

A bland expression can hide anything. That was one thing I had learned anyway: this almost Oriental impassivity. It hid everything I wanted to hide, until now. Until now, when I was going to drag it out, examine it with Doctor Galens.

I returned my glance to the mirror. I looked fine. Even my Italian haircut was intact. The messier it gets, the more stylish it appears. In fact, I even toyed with running my hands through it once again for good measure; but I changed my mind. After all, I had never met Doctor Galens. It would be more practical at least to start out looking neat. Although psychiatrists weren't supposed to be aware of their patients' appearance, were they? Each case was supposed to be purely clinical. There was a big article about Ava Gardner being analyzed. I had read it somewhere. I'm sure that psychiatrist certainly must have been aware of what Miss Gardner looked like. If he wasn't, then *he* needed a psychiatrist.

Well, I wasn't exactly Ava Gardner but Doctor Galens was going to have quite a reaction once I started to talk. I patted my hair in place. Yes indeed, I certainly must walk in looking sane.

I added some lipstick. I looked quite sane and everydayish. The kind of girl whose life worked on perfect schedule, the kind of girl who walked on every city street—worked in every office, did her own manicures, wore seamless hose, and studied *Vogue* magazine for fashion hints.

I was that kind of girl. Only things had happened and that was the whole trouble. Nothing was like it used to be anymore. I had to see Doctor Galens and tell him everything. I owed it to David. Poor David, being engaged to a misfit like me.

The overmodulated voice of the nurse punctured my nagging thoughts. "Doctor Galens will see Miss Cooper in a few moments."

What were moments? Maybe they were a cross between a second and a minute, kind of like a half minute. But then you couldn't say, "Doctor Galens will see Miss Cooper in a few half minutes." I'd ask Doctor Galens. Psychiatrists are supposed to know everything. Oh sure! That would be a nice opening.

Twenty-five dollars an hour and I walk in and ask what moments mean. Doctor Galens will be most cooperative. He'll just reach for the nearest butterfly net and tell me to continue.

I forced my thoughts to center on Doctor Galens. At least that was an affirmative thought. Doctor Galens would help me. He must! It was odd, this hope I was placing in a man I had never met. In a few minutes— no—moments, I was going to tell him everything. I was going to confide in a total stranger.

I couldn't help but smile inwardly at the devious way I'd gone about discovering Doctor Galens. A few discreet questions to David, an innocent remark to my dentist, another to the family physician. All the questions starting the same way.

"I have a friend who's terribly mixed up. In fact she may ruin her whole life. Do you think a psychiatrist could help her?"

I wonder if I had fooled anyone but David? He never dreamed that this bewildered friend was his confident bride-to-be. I guess everyone uses the same methods, persuading themselves that they're actually getting away with it. It's always for a friend, never yourself. But it was comforting that every line of questioning led straight to Doctor Galens. Everyone had recommended him for my unfortunate friend.

But what if he can't help? Sometimes it takes psychiatrists years to help you work out a solution. I had put this off so long. And now there were only three more days. Three days until David and I . . .

The nurse reappeared. Her radiant smile told me the great moment had arrived. I rose and followed the stiff uniform, wondering suddenly if all nurses had bad feet or did they actually like those big ugly white shoes. I entered the inner office just in time to see the flash of a red hat disappear through a door leading to the hall exit. So that was how it was done. One patient snuck in as another snuck out. Why was there a stigma attached to being analyzed? You went to a dentist if your teeth needed fixing. You went to a doctor if your body needed fixing. Then what's wrong with your head needing a little fixing?

But it wasn't my brain that needed fixing. It was a solution to some very real problems that I required.

But would this man really have the answers? After all, he was only a doctor, not a magician or a God.

I sank almost gratefully into the comfortable leather chair opposite his desk. I crossed my legs and waited. The doctor didn't even glance at me. His entire attention seemed to be centered on the routine task of setting up a portfolio and filling it with paper. Next came the proper desk arrangement of his newly sharpened pencils. Finally he looked up and gave me the barest imitation of a smile. I decided I hated him.

Oh, fine! This was a nice start. Here it was going to cost me twenty-five dollars and I hated him. I could buy two pairs of shoes for twenty-five dollars. Maybe even a pretty nice sport dress. Perhaps if I suddenly jumped up and said I was feeling fine and that the whole thing was a big mistake, maybe I could still get out of it. Or, if worse came to worse, settle for twelve-fifty. That would be more than fair.

Now this was childish reasoning, I told myself. I am here, sitting in a chair across from Doctor Galens and he is going to help me. I was grateful for the chair. Why, if he had even glanced at the couch, I'd have murdered him. I looked around quickly to see if there was a couch. There was, but it didn't look very comfortable.

The nurse wrote my name on a card. I murmured my address and phone number. The only noise was the scratching of her pen against the paper. She handed the card to Doctor Galens, who studied it as if it was the Bill of Rights. He nodded and the nurse left the room. Then I made a complete inspection of everything in the room; everything except Doctor Galens.

For a few seconds there was nothing but silence. The kind of silence that causes a clock to tick louder and the floor to squeak at a footstep from a distant room.

Doctor Galens told me to begin.

And suddenly I didn't know how to start.

"Why don't you just start by talking," he suggested gently.

"Yes, but about what? Do you want me to tell you all about myself or just plunge in where the trouble began?"

"Miss Cooper," his eyes were impersonal yet filled with a desire to be helpful. "I see from my appointment book that you have not come to me for analysis but rather for some psychotherapy to clear a specific problem."

I nodded. "Yes, I told that to your nurse when I made the appointment. You see, I have so little time."

He sighed. "That is always the cry. So little time! Well, let us try. Sometimes we can help bridge an emotional hurdle but it is necessary for us to know something about you."

"There's so little about me, myself, that could interest you. That is, as a person; but regarding the problem, the thing that has happened to me . . . You see, nothing ever really happened in my life before then."

He glanced at his desk clock. "You are my last patient for the afternoon, so if you run over, we won't clock ourselves. Why don't you just start at the beginning."

The beginning. I took a few seconds to consider this. Where was the beginning? I decided I'd start at my beginning. The very beginning.

CHAPTER 2

David.

That was my beginning. Nothing important had ever happened before that. My childhood stretched behind me as a maze of unspectacular, uneventful, but not unhappy years. A summer at camp and a season at dramatic school were the sole highlights. Oh, yes, and winning the beauty contest at Atlantic City!

It hadn't been a real contest. Not the kind where judges take your measurements. Nothing like that. This was just one the hotel ran. And I had won. I had a real satin banner and a cup to attest this fact. So even if my mother does claim I am nice looking but not outstanding, I did win a beauty contest!

I understand about my mother. I have no complexes there. Grandma was a genuine dyed-in-the-wool Quaker, and even though Mother never actually followed her stern teachings, she was still not exactly what one might call wildly liberal. Mother believes it is her duty to break down false vanity and make one rely on one's true merits, namely, one's mind and creative ability. God help those who weren't blessed with these sterling qualities. Mother had no time for them.

But since I was her daughter she had to have time for me, even if I wasn't endowed. She seemed confident that I was brilliant. I wasn't making full use of all my capabilities, that was all.

As a girl who will go to any lengths to avoid an argument or any kind of unpleasantness, I suppose I took to retreating into a typical adolescent dream world when I was young. It was easier that way. I'd hand my mother my report card, and as she ranted and raved about my poor history marks, I'd dream I was Vivien Leigh attending a gala premiere with Clark Gable. You'd be surprised how well it worked. Then, when she had finished, I'd become Janet Cooper again, and partake of the pleasures of a very real piece of chocolate cake and a glass of milk. But often, even when I was quite content, I dreamed of becoming a big movie star. It was the only thing that really seemed to matter.

I guess I was sixteen when I gave up this fanciful dream. I didn't really give it up. I was ridiculed out of it, and not just by my mother. By my friends as well. No one ever really became a movie actress. Not from my hometown anyway. I used to argue that, after all, movie actresses had to come from somewhere. They had to be ordinary people once upon a time. But I met with mass opposition. Anyone who thought about becoming a movie actress after sixteen was slightly unbalanced.

Before sixteen, you could wish to be anything. It was something every girl went through. Just as all little boys want to be firemen or cowboys.

So, upon graduating from high school, I also graduated from my secret daydreams and faced the reality of business school and the mysteries of shorthand and typing.

Life was pretty much routine after that. A pleasant routine, but nothing more. A secretarial job—minus the handsome and romantic "young boss" that I had seen in so many movies. My boss was a sleek young woman who wore basic black dresses, a string of good pearls, and a fake beauty spot high upon her cheek.

The only bonus the job offered was two-hour luncheons, because the sleek young boss shared two-hour luncheons with a handsome but married advertising executive in a hideaway restaurant on a small side street.

These hideaway luncheons were the main topic of discussion among my cohorts and myself. I really enjoyed these sessions. Especially on Friday because there was always the weekend to be anticipated and discussed. I'd participate in all the discussions, give advice, share the agonies of several broken hearts, offer wisdom of the onlooker, yet remain just that. An onlooker, never an active participant.

It was almost as if I was marking time waiting and watching for some unknown yet certain appointment.

And then I met David.

David hadn't come prancing along on the proverbial white horse, but he had a shiny Oldsmobile and met a great many of the prince's requirements. To make things even better, he was a lawyer with a fine reputation and was even making a livable wage.

Our admiration was instantaneous and mutual and I thought I was going to die with excitement the day he presented me with the small but perfect diamond. He told me it was completely paid for; he could have gotten me one twice the size for the same price, but the color was off. This was blue white even in the sunlight, he explained, and that was very important.

"That's the way I want our life to be, honey girl," he had told me. "As flawless and as perfect as this stone. Nothing ostentatious —just quiet, in good taste, and perfect."

I had snuggled up to him and smiled my agreement. I longed for him to call me "darling" instead of "honey girl" and to say "I love you" in a romantic way, instead of proving it with actions. But I had no real complaint. It was a beautiful sentiment and the diamond wasn't really too small. Besides, I intended to build the whole thing up with a diamond wedding band. This I would break to David in small easy stages and I hope to God he didn't have some broken-down gold one that his great grandmother had worn across the prairie.

So I had said good-bye to the office, to my

luncheon companions, to the sleek young boss who looked bored but envious, and set about to do all the things that young brides-to-be are supposed to do.

By summer the apartment had been selected, my wedding dress hung in the closet, and nothing remained but to wait—wait six long impossible weeks until September.

The waiting was hardest when David was away. He was forced to take many quick trips for his firm. I felt sorry for him, for no matter the nature of the assignment, his trips always entailed visits to places like Pottsville, Pennsylvania, or Columbus, Ohio. I was so bored when he was gone that toward the end, I was all for accompanying him. And none of this would have happened—what am I saying—it couldn't have happened, if only he had taken me along to Chicago.

Yes, the Chicago trip caused all the trouble. Well, it was the start of it anyway. He had just returned from Norristown, Pennsylvania. No sooner had he unpacked his bag when Mr. Finley, the senior partner, phoned and told him about the Chicago deal.

We had a date that night. I had met him at the train and we had gone right to his flat to leave his bags. It was a hot night and I was wearing an old print dress. That was all I had to wear lately since everything new had to be saved for my trousseau. I told my mother this was all very fine providing I didn't lose him in the meantime. I even voiced these opinions to David that night, apologizing for my dowdy outfit. "Oh, that's all right, honey girl," he said, as he hung up his wrinkled suit. "I never really notice what you wear anyway. It's the girl I'm marrying, not the outfits."

Reassuring, but totally unromantic. David was good—almost too good for someone as flighty and everydayish as myself. I sat there watching his damp white shirt outline the ample muscles of his back and shoulders. It was unbearably hot that night; there wasn't a breath of air in the room. Boxes were piled on each other and end tables looked strangely empty. David was waiting too, eager to relinquish his bachelor apartment, eager to move to our bright and shiny new home.

Then the phone rang.

Chicago right away! The following morning to be exact. And this wasn't just a short hop either. This was for ten days. I listened as he talked and made notes. I couldn't imagine how this exciting assignment had fallen to him. He was strictly a Pottsville man. The senior partners took the glamorous trips. One of the senior partners was on the Coast, and Mr. Finley had a case coming before the books in the morning, so, David had been selected.

I began my campaign the second he hung up. What were we waiting for? This was it! We could elope and use Chicago as a honeymoon. Why wait until September? The end of July was just as good for a wedding.

David refused. The wedding date was set. His Aunt Evelyn from California who had been like a mother to him was coming in for the event. His roommate from Dartmouth was going to be best man. Oh, no, honey girl, everything was planned for September.

I was really let down that night. There wasn't a festive moment about the entire evening, just David's perpetual enthusiasm concerning the proposed trip which was now working on all cylinders.

It wasn't the trip itself, he explained. It was the confidence his firm was bestowing upon him in awarding him this assignment. It was a good evening for David. But for me it was just a hot sticky evening ending with a flat beer at the open-air gardens down the street.

I saw him off the next day and begged to go along right down to the minute he got on the train. By now, I was even willing to come along in single bliss. What could be wrong with that? Just two good friends taking a trip together. It was done every day, and I had never been to Chicago. Marshall Fields was supposed to be such a heavenly store, and then there was the Pump Room and the Chez Paree. But, of course, David wouldn't hear of it. How would it look, he wanted to know. Mr. Finley wouldn't like it. Why, Mrs. Finley never went on business trips with Mr. Finley, and they had been married for sixteen years.

He was quite tender as he kissed me good-bye. He said he'd write every day, and, of course, I promised to do the same. He promised me that after we were married we'd go to all kinds of places together, and then he was gone. I stood there and watched the train pull out, that wonderful train that was heading for Marshall Fields and the Chez Paree.

I was so dreary around the house the following day that my mother suggested I take a little vacation on my own. We could go to Boston together and visit Aunt Isabel.

A vacation certainly might help. But Aunt Isabel's was definitely not the solution, and it was pointless to join any of my girl friends at the resorts they were visiting. They were still "hunting." I already had David.

But meanwhile, I had no place to go; no place to go and ten idle days on my hands.

Then suddenly I thought of Avalon.

I had gone to camp there as a child. It was a small seashore resort and I remembered my stay there as the most perfect summer of my life. I stood up to my mother's objections, agreed that it might be a silly sentimental whim; but I wanted to go—alone! Every girl has a right to spend some time alone with her memories.

I suppose the humidity was on my side. My mother suddenly didn't come up with her usual energy as we battled the point, and I won. And off I went to Avolon, my memories, and the sand dunes.

As always, my mother was right. Avalon

itself greeted me coldly and without affection. Like all trips into the past, it was a complete disappointment.

The camp had vanished, and with it, all the excitement the town had ever known. Now Avalon stood as a desolate little fishing village, and fishing was the whole sustenance of a threadbare township rather than a sport.

Even the Avalon inn was gone. A few charred boards and broken windows told of some three-alarm fire the natives barely remembered, and only a few blocks of uneven boardwalk remained. The natives spoke in monotones of the small but violent hurricane that had demolished the local pier and most of the boardwalk. Even the sand dunes seemed to have grown more barren and austere. Grass grew wildly along their peaks and the ocean was cold and uninviting.

I walked along the boardwalk during the day and combed the town for a familiar face or building. I found nothing but a few over-priced antiques that might have dwelled in my new home. I wondered who would buy them since the entire town appeared about ready to be put up for auction at any second. No, I found nothing in Avalon to nourish my sentimental memories. At the end of the week I gave up and prepared to return home.

But I had decided that I'd never admit Avalon had failed me. Oh, no! I'd come home glowing with stories about the wonderful climate, the picturesque scenery, the quaint people. I'd make it sound wonderful. Not *too* wonderful, because David might suggest going there on our honeymoon. In fact, I suddenly decided not to mention Avalon to anyone, except my mother. I could never let her say, "I told you so!"

Funny about my mother. I love her, more than anyone, except David, of course, but we really never see eye to eye on anything. Except David. We agreed on him immediately. When I had first suggested to Mother that maybe David and I might be in love—or —had Mother suggested to me that David and I might be in love? Well, what difference did it make? I was going to marry David and thank goodness Mother approved.

But it bothered me. Had my mother gently planted the idea of marrying David in my mind? Was David entirely my selection? Oh, of course, he was! And besides, what did it matter if she did? That's what mothers are for, aren't they? To help you make the wisest choice. Mother was just too honest and good —like David. I remember when I had appeared in the lead of the charity play. The whole town had turned out, and the applause I got at the curtain was really deafening. I was a big hit—at least I thought I was— until I saw Mother and David. Mother explained how badly I moved—like a cow, not a countess. David had said, "Just wanting to be an actress doesn't make you one, honey girl. I didn't believe you for one second. You were just my little Janet playing make-believe."

Yes, Mother and David had been right. They were both always right—even about Avalon. But at least I had won. I had come to Avalon alone.

Somehow this thought didn't provoke the delirious joy it should have. I walked the boardwalk alone that last night, skimming from one mood to another. I had learned something. From now on I would stop living in the past, I would live every moment for what it was, for that moment can never be lived again.

My beloved Avalon. The tents that had been pitched on the sand dunes, the wonderful Saturdays at the amusement pier, stuffing yourself with Tootsie Rolls and penny candy, the romantic movies with Lana Turner and Hedy Lamarr, ravishingly beautiful in white fox, like you were going to be when you grew up. Now nothing remained but ghosts. Ghosts and tired fishermen.

I walked through the town that last night, feeling not unlike a ghost myself. I saw myself in the scrawniness of adolescence with my hair limp from the moisture and the wind, camping on the sand dunes.

So it did not surprise me that I found myself cutting off the boardwalk and heading purposefully for the sand dunes, but with no actual purpose in mind. I stood on the highest hill, looking into the sky as if searching for some answer.

We used to lie there at night, six or seven giggling young girls, bundled in blankets, exchanging dreams and confidences. And what confidences! One was going to marry a millionaire and have five servants and a personal maid. One was going to become a famous nurse. Another—we always called her "the idiot"—well, the idiot had no imagination. She just wanted lots of babies. In fact, a husband didn't even figure in with her plans. Just a home and babies. But it was my dream that had been most impressive. My name was going to be in lights on Broadway. Thousands of brilliant people would adore me, and then the most perfect man in the world would battle his way through thousands of other suitors and claim me as his bride.

He was always faceless, this perfect man. Faceless but resplendent in tails, white tie, and faultless elegance. And now he had taken shape at last—as David.

I sat there on the dunes sifting sand through my fingers and envisioned this dream image with David's face. It worked, yes, it worked fine!

I took off my topcoat and spread it on the sand, then stretched out and stared at the sky.

At first my eyes saw just the inky expanse, but gradually the heavens took shape and I located the Big Dipper, and a bright star somebody once told me was Venus. There my knowledge of astronomy abruptly ended.

Suddenly I spotted a shooting star. It dashed across the sky, its bright light ebbing like a dissolving firecracker. My watch was rewarded with two more. I wondered why all the stars did not eventually disappear with so many shooting off into nowhere just like that.

But the night was too peaceful to worry about such practical matters. Instead, I decided nature would take care of itself and busied myself in making intense and romantic wishes on each flashing meteor. After a while, I ran out of wishes. Nothing, not even this, was what it had been.

I stood up and began to brush the sand from my legs when I saw it.

Hanging in the sky like nothing I had ever seen before!

CHAPTER 3

It couldn't be real!

It was not a star and it was too perfectly round and much too large to be the light of a plane. It grew in size with a brilliance that was three times as bright as the moon.

It shot across the sky with the speed of a comet, returned to its original position, and remained almost stationary.

A rush of colliding thoughts flashed through my head. I tried to breathe evenly in spite of the sudden thumping of my heart. I wanted to remain calm and sort the facts from the fiction. Now what had I heard and what had I read? What exactly were they? Or what were they supposed to be? Secret devices our armed forces were working on? Guided missiles? Weather balloons? Ships from another planet? Mass hallucination?

I had read so many things yet had drawn such a sketchy conclusion. Each newspaper had only confused me more. Some denied the reports, some upheld them.

What had the government decided on? Each report I had read had been openly contradicted in another paper the following day. *Look* contradicted *Life*. *Life* contradicted *Time*. *Time* contradicted itself.

I struggled to organize my thoughts. This was no hallucination. And then, with no warning, it disappeared as suddenly as it had come into view.

Now what?

Well, there were proper authorities to whom you reported these occurrences.

Oh, sure! Then you were written off as a crackpot and everyone treated you as if you had been seriously ill.

But I *had* seen it!

And like everyone else who has experienced such a phenomenon, I had been too spellbound to do more than stare in unbelieving wonder. How could I be expected to answer any of the technical questions that might be hurled at me. That is, if I did report the sighting, which of course I would not do, what questions would they ask? How fast did it seem to be traveling? Did it travel from east to west—north to south? Was I sure I had seen it?

Well, one thing for sure, I was going to get off the beach, and fast! Suddenly the beach felt clammy and the bright stars took on a wintery stare, and I experienced an aloneness that was eerie and intense.

I scrambled down the dune, stumbling as the sand spilled into my shoes. My breath came in painful gasps; my face was whipped by the ocean's breeze and my shoes became leaden weights.

Then suddenly it returned! This time it was easily the size of the moon.

I stood very still as if not to disturb it. Of course, this thing—so many miles away—could not possibly see me, but I still wasn't taking any chances. It was almost as if that luminous disc held me in its power.

I suddenly became aware that it had stopped and just hung there, as silent as the moon and equally mystifying. What was it? A shooting star or a plane could not stand in one spot and a moon could not move. I fought off a sudden wave of the panic that always accompanies the unknown. This was ridiculous. Nothing could happen to me. It was up there. I was down here. And besides, I told myself, this is something wonderful to see. All over the world there are records in archives of scientific data on this very subject. At this very second, perhaps, men somewhere are haunting telescopes, hoping for just such a sight. And here it it, bestowing itself on the least appreciative audience it could possibly find.

So I stood there, bathed in the glow of that artificial moonlight. For in that moment, nothing could be heard but the thumping of my own heart which seemed to rise to a crescendo above the ocean's roar.

Then once again it shot across the sky into nowhere.

I knew it would be back, and I would remain to see it again. And what's more, I would report the sighting. No one would ever call me that nice but average Janet Cooper again. I would be somebody now, maybe even get my picture in the paper. Sure I was scared, it would have been easy to run, and maybe it was safer that way, but suddenly I was tired of the complacency of safety.

Yes, I decided, I would definitely wait for it to return, and I would remain calm. I tried to breathe deeply and relax. I must keep all my faculties. I must remember everything. I wished I had paid more attention to astronomy at school—or was it physics I needed now? I wanted to sound intelligent when I was asked those vital statistics that those members of the air force would demand to be told.

I even sat down on the sand and emptied my shoes. Inwardly, I praised myself for the efficiency with which I was handling the entire matter.

I saw myself riding down Main Street in an open car, as cheering crowds threw confetti. No, maybe that was going too far. Well —then I'd give a press conference. Yes, that was it. A press conference with many eager newspapermen swarming about me asking polite questions, which I would answer with a naive intelligence, and they'd snap my picture like mad and murmur with respect dripping from their voices, "Really, Miss Cooper, and you remained so calm. All alone on that dark beach, Miss Cooper . . ."

But suppose they didn't ask those nice questions. Suppose they just dismissed me as another crackpot. I could just see David's face. One week alone in Avalon and she comes up with a story like this!

And my mother! Oh, I know what Mother would say. "Janet always had a vivid imagination. Why, when she was a little girl, many were the times I had to actually spank her to keep her from telling fibs. Janet, haven't you changed? You must remember to tell things exactly as they happen."

Oh, what was the use?

I stood up and started to leave. It returned.

This time it was no ghostly moonlike object. It seemed much closer and almost danced across the sky at an impossible speed. Then it formed a fantastic arc and veered back to my line of vision again.

This was no weather balloon.

It performed several graceful pirouettes, returning each time to its original position above me. No matter how far it careened or how high it climbed, it always returned and remained stationary for a moment, as if to say, "Well, how was that?" I almost felt it expected me to applaud.

As it started out to sea again, I made my way off the beach. Enough was enough. I had lost the desire to be lone audience to this eerie performer. I stumbled along the sand, glancing back every now and then to reassure myself that my visitor was well along its way. I had almost reached the steps that led to the boardwalk, when I knew, without turning around, that it was back.

The steps suddenly seemed miles away and it was directly over me. Oh, God! I pleaded. If only I can make it to the boardwalk!

I began to run, thoroughly frightened and almost blinded by the glare from the disc overhead. I fought to reason away my panic. It was miles overhead. It couldn't possibly see me, I was so small and the beach was so dark.

Suddenly there was another light—a searchlight! The townspeople, of course! That must be it. They too had seen the disc. They were coming to save me!

I turned around and heard a scream! It took me several seconds to realize it was coming from my own throat and that I was powerless to stop. It tore at my lungs and stopped as a strangled wail.

There *was* a light, but it was coming from the ghostly thing above and it was directed at me!

CHAPTER 4

At first I wasn't sure whether the light held me paralyzed or whether I went rigid from sheer terror. I just know I stood there, powerless to move an inch, bathed in that intense light coming from so far away. The boardwalk steps were just a few feet away. The lights of the town so close yet there I stood, rooted by that other light. Everything about me seemed to grow still. Even the waves seemed to have slowed their motion, rippling silently upon the beach.

Then I felt the breeze. Warm and gentle as a lover's caress, it enveloped me.

Even through my fright, it was not an unpleasant sensation, as if I was under the influence of a powerful anesthesia. I felt my body relaxing against my will and I began to sway slightly. I saw the ground falling beneath me, and in one terrible minute I realized the ground was in its proper place, but I was not. I was being lifted by the light and the warm breeze which was now eddying about me like an inverted whirlpool.

Up—up—up—into the ray of light. Up—up—up—and then I must have blacked out.

When I opened my eyes I saw a pale gray

dome-shaped ceiling. Then I remembered the mysterious silver disc and the ray of light. I shut my eyes.

This was no nightmare from which you awakened to find calm reality and familiar surroundings. This was a nightmare from which you awakened to find yourself staring at a gray dome-shaped ceiling.

Keeping my eyes shut tight, I allowed my hand to slowly grope about. Whatever I was resting on was solid, and I had seen a ceiling. That was some consolation. At least I knew I was no longer floating through the air lifted only by light. This gave me the courage to slowly reopen my eyes. For a moment I stared at the gray dome above me as if I could will it away and replace it with the flat white ceiling of my own bedroom. That lovely white ceiling with one of the lights missing from the chandelier.

The ceiling remained gray.

I gathered a little more courage and turned my head. I was in a small room, completely bare except for the small bunk which I occupied. The lighting was soft; the whole room seemed luminous, yet there was no central system that I could see. In fact, the glow was so unearthly that for a split second I actually wondered if I was dead and this was—well—wherever you went afterwards.

I sat up. Oddly enough I felt pretty much intact. For a girl whose flying experience was limited strictly to a ferris wheel ride, I had done pretty well! To have soared through the air like an eagle, on nothing more concrete than a ray of light; that's quite an accomplishment, even for an eagle. I began to feel kind of smug.

Then I saw the window, or porthole, I should say. I must have missed it the first time because it was directly behind me, quite high on the wall. I had to stand on the bunk to look out.

I saw nothing but sky, endless sky. I fell back on the bunk, stupefied. I was actually flying through space!

But to where???? My attention was suddenly switched to the other side of the room. The entire wall was actually opening!

I clutched the sides of the bunk for support. Someone was about to enter. But who? Or what???

Oh, God! I pleaded. If it is something from Mars, don't let it be crawly. I don't care if it has three eyes or two heads, just don't let it look slimy or crawl. I braced myself against the wall and waited.

CHAPTER 5

He looked human. As a matter of fact, I was positive that he was the most attractive human I had ever run into.

However, since I had not exactly just run into him, I felt free to study him with unconcealed interest.

He was extremely tall, well over six feet, and dressed in coveralls not unlike the kind garage mechanics wear.

It was his eyes that held my attention. They were large, emerald green in color, almond in shape, and so beautiful that they appeared almost unnatural. Then I noticed his hair, that is, his lack of hair. He shaved his head! Even without hair, he was still unbelievably handsome, more physically attractive than any movie actor in Hollywood.

He in turn was also inspecting me. Intently, yet as if it was merely the polite thing to do. He lounged against the wall (which had now returned to its original position) and stared.

I stared right back, and, being an extremely practical girl, decided that this was definitely not the time to upbraid him for kidnapping me. No, I should show polite curiosity about the whole thing, demand gently but firmly to be put back where they found me, but, above all, keep it friendly.

Although he had not spoken, I was positive he was not an American. This I gathered from instinct rather than anything obvious in his appearance, except perhaps his eyes. He certainly couldn't be from Mars. He was completely human looking; ravishingly human, in fact.

But since we were going to be friendly about the whole matter (I hoped), I smiled. After all, a smile is supposed to be a universal gesture of peace and goodwill. He must understand that.

He must have. He smiled back.

He was even more appealing with a smile. I felt better. At least for the moment I was safe. After all, you don't lop off someone's head while you are smiling at them. Or do you? Anyway, I hoped not, and no one as beautiful as he could be evil. He was still smiling, baring even white teeth. Wait till I tell the girls in the office about him, I thought. I even began to wonder if he was married. He'd be wonderful for Catherine. She was five feet ten in ballet slippers—well, she could wear spike heels with Mr. Green Eyes here.

My mouth was beginning to twitch and my face felt frozen, but I managed to keep my smile going while I pondered my next move. I had to do something. We just couldn't grin at one another forever. Not that I minded too much. I couldn't think of anyone I'd rather have smile at me, but there was David, and I suddenly remembered I was a long way from home. So I held out my hand.

He didn't understand. He looked at my hand with great interest, and then finding only the usual amount of fingers, he returned his attention to my face and continued to smile.

So, with a bravery that even I didn't quite believe I possessed, I got off the bunk and approached him, reached out, took his hand, shook it, smiling wildly all the while.

This time he got the idea. His smile took on an added voltage and he returned the handshake. Then I returned to the bunk and fell back exhausted. Now what?

I asked him where I was and where we were going.

No answer.

Well, I hadn't really expected him to understand. Now there was no doubt that he wasn't an American.

All right then, what was he? Russians didn't shave their heads, and it's too cold in Russia to run around like that. He could be from the Orient, except for the color of his eyes. Maybe from some part of the Orient we didn't know existed, like those mountains no one explored or some lost tribe.

This didn't add up. I sighed yet suddenly began to marvel at this new found bravery that actually allowed me to catalog my thoughts and rationalize each event. I felt a sudden wave of self-esteem. I was shooting to God knows where with a green-eyed giant staring at me and yet there I sat, thinking things out as calmly as if I was in my own bedroom trying to remember the name of someone I had met at a party. I should be hysterical with panic; instead I felt unusually serene. To ascertain this fact, I lay on the bunk and stretched my arms and legs. My left arm felt stiff, and there was a slight welt on the vein inside my elbow.

My self-esteem dissolved. I could no longer take credit for this calm. They had given me some kind of a sedative. I couldn't brag about my fearlessness. But to whom? My mother? David? It was a sure bet that this flight wasn't going to terminate in my own backyard.

I might never see David or my mother again. Where was I going? And why me? I decided I'd better get right to the point and see the one in charge before the sedation wore off and I fainted from fright. Now who would be in charge? It was obvious Green Eyes was just sent in to kind of look me over. Besides, someone had to be driving this contraption.

This called for a slight tour of inspection. I was entitled to this, wasn't I? I stood up and started for the section of the wall that had previously opened. Green Eyes sprang to action and gently but firmly led me back to the bunk.

I gathered I was not entitled to a tour of inspection.

I flopped down on the bunk and turned my back on Green Eyes. This ought to get to him. Russian or Oriental, a woman's back in any language means anger. It obviously did, when I turned around Green Eyes was gone.

I was sorry. I missed him, even if he wasn't the talkative type. It had been kind of nice having him around; he was so good to look at.

A strange sense of well-being surged through me. I was sure it was not entirely the effects of the needle. After all, you sensed danger, didn't you, and at that moment I felt completely at peace with the world. The swift movement and evenness of the flight added to my new sense of security. I did nothing to fight my growing drowsiness. I fell into a dreamless sleep. I felt a tiny stabbing in my arm and slowly returned to consciousness, just in time to see Green Eyes inserting a large needle into the vein of my arm. I tried to struggle but it was useless. Straps across my chest, legs, and arms were now holding me to the bunk.

Green Eyes withdrew the needle and smiled. If this was meant to reassure me it was a wasted gesture. He returned to his post against the wall and continued to grin. I bravely tried to smile, but I'm afraid it just resembled a nervous tic.

Gone was my beautiful sense of calm and well-being. It was all I could do to breathe against the sudden panic that I now felt.

Suddenly the craft lurched and I was positive we had crashed. For the moment I was thankful for the straps. In panic, I turned to Green Eyes for reassurance. If he experienced even the slightest tremor, there was no sign of it in his unruffled appearance.

Another terrific lurch rocked the ship. Green Eyes didn't bat an eyelash. Then once again the wall began to slide open and two men entered.

I actually felt my mouth drop wide open in surprise and admiration. They were also dressed in coveralls, shaved their heads, and had green eyes. They were every bit as regal and handsome as Green Eyes the First.

They nodded to Green Eyes the First, who obviously accepted this as some order. He crossed the room and released my straps. I sat up, never taking my eyes from the new arrivals.

In turn, they crossed to me, bowed low, shook hands, and smiled.

Well, I felt a little better. Evidently, Green Eyes the First had told Green Eyes the Second and Third that this was my strange custom and at least they wanted to make me feel at home. This seemed like a pretty good omen.

They exchanged a few words with one another. Up until that moment, I hadn't heard Green Eyes come up with so much as a gurgle, but now he was chatting away with his buddies animatedly. I listened carefully.

Not only was it not English but it sounded like nothing I had ever heard before.

It could have been an Oriental language, after all, not all Orientals spoke Chinese or Japanese, did they? Let's see—there was Javanese, Siamese, Balinese—Oh, Lord! Why didn't I pay more attention to geography at school? The unpleasant vision of a fat, middle-aged history teacher called Miss Massinger rushed to me. I had hated Miss Massinger, but right now I'd have adored having her as a traveling companion. Better still, I'd like Miss Massinger to be here in my place.

My captors interrupted these pleasant thoughts by gesturing that I was to rise and follow them. We went through the open wall and down a long spiral staircase. We passed through a small room that housed a lot of clocklike gadgets and what appeared to be a large television screen. We came upon a large room with the same kind of instruments only on a grander scale. This obviously was the master control room. Another handsome, green-eyed giant emerged from the pilot's seat, nodded to me, smiled, and joined our procession.

We came to another small stairway. The pilot pressed a button and another wall opened, but this time the bright glare of daylight entered the craft, disclosing a small ramp that led to the ground.

CHAPTER 6

I walked down the ramp, flanked by my strange escorts. Daylight stung my eyes, but it was with real relief that I set my foot on the solid ground of a magnificent landing field. I took a deep breath and was pleasantly surprised to find it was just common ordinary air, no more or less exhilarating than the air I had been breathing for twenty-one years. I turned and appraised the craft that had carried me to this destination.

So there were no such things as flying saucers!

Maybe not, but that thing behind me wasn't exactly square. It was shaped like a mushroom, with a square-portholed chamber nestled in the top. The saucer part appeared to be a good thousand feet in diameter and was composed of three sections. Even now, settled on the ground, the different sections were still whirling slowly, each in opposite directions. Clockwise and counterclockwise, like the gasping motion of a dying propeller.

Our ship was not the sole occupant of this airfield. There were "saucers" everywhere. Small ones, medium ones, and some five times as large as the one on which I had traveled.

My procession led me across the field. It was a beautiful day; the sun was shining and the sky was an innocent clear blue. It was too placid looking to be the haven of strange disc-shaped objects that sent down kidnapping rays of light.

We walked about a hundred feet and halted before a huge waiting crowd. My captors hesitated a moment, then faced them. After a split second, during which time thousands of green eyes studied me, an immense cheer filled the air, and it continued for a full minute accompanied by deafening applause. It was most flattering and gratifying, and I was tempted to take a polite bow, but my innate modesty argued that this demonstration might be for the aviators who had accomplished the mission, rather than for the trophy.

Aside from the unusual nature of the ships banked at the airport, I found no landmarks to give me any clues to my whereabouts. Even the assembled crowd composed of thousands of men offered no enlightenment. They were from the identical pattern of the handsome giants on the ship; all with those strange emerald green eyes set against dark skin and high cheekbones. And every one of them shaved his head.

They were men who looked like warriors or hunters. There was something almost tribal about them.

However, their dress differed violently from the drab coveralls of the aviators. The vividness of the colors was almost theatrical in effect. They were Oriental in style: silken waists, silk pants that ended below the knee, and flat gold-laced sandals. The colors were bizarre and exciting. In fact, there was a complete air of pageantry about the entire spectacle.

The restraint this strange audience practiced surprised me. There were no ropes holding them at bay, no authorities pleading, "Stay in line." They stared at me intently yet remained at a respectful distance. The only thing that held them back seemed to be their own superior sense of good taste.

As if to add further proof to this observation, they suddenly parted at no given command to allow one of their group to come through.

There was nothing to distinguish him from the onlookers, although his manner conveyed that he had some specific and important task to perform.

This special man came to me, bowed low, and smiled, then led us through the crowd, which once again politely parted to create a passageway.

We proceeded through the airport until we reach a gate which swung open; we walked through to a driveway and stopped before a low, cigar-shaped object, about twelve feet in length, with six small wheels. The moment I realized this object was meant to be a conveyance, I faced the reality that I was in another world.

CHAPTER 7

They motioned me to board the car, and, having no other choice, I obliged. Only part of the entourage followed. Green Eyes the First, who seemed destined to stick with me, and Green Eyes the Greeter; the others remained at the airfield.

I settled back in the car only to leap forward as the ground shot out from under me with a suddenness that made my ears fill and my lungs collapse.

This extraordinary speed did not diminish, and made it impossible to see any of the countryside. All I caught was a kaleidoscope of green and brown. Every so often another car swished by in the opposite direction, but instead of the fatal collision which seemed inevitable, the opposing car would veer off to the side. After about a half dozen of these almost stuntlike exhibitions, I began to realize that it was literally impossible for one car to hit another. It was almost as if some magnetic force was working in reverse, shoving them away from each other.

As my nerves adjusted to the pace, I was able to see brief flashes of the road on which we traveled, which appeared to be composed of steel or some metal resembling steel. I turned to the man at my side, Green Eyes the Greeter, and motioned to the view outside.

"What is the name of this place?"

He immediately answered, "Yargo."

A full minute must have passed before I felt the delayed reaction of shocked surprise. I had been prepared to gesticulate several times, even draw pictures, but he had understood me immediately. Not my exact words, of that I was sure, but the questioning expression on my face.

Now I knew he was intelligent and came from a highly civilized race. It took a lot of perception to arrive at this conclusion. Any country or world that came up with a little flying machine that could snatch people off the earth was not exactly in the Stone Age. Here was a group of people floating all over the universe to their hearts' content, while our most learned scientists were still theorizing about our prospects of ever reaching the moon.

I tried to figure out which planet Yargo could be. I had heard the theory that if there was any intelligent life around us it would most likely exist on Mars or Venus, yet their atmospheric conditions differed from our own, so that life on these planets would most likely take on vastly different forms from that which we think of as human. At least that's what the scientists said, but the atmosphere on Yargo seemed exactly like our own, and I would even challenge Doctor Einstein if he dared to term one of these green-eyed gods anything other than human. We should only have such humans floating around on earth.

We rode in silence for about five minutes, then with no warning whatever, the car came to an abrupt halt. The door slid open instantly and I was motioned to alight. We trooped up a metal driveway. My heels beat a clicking rhythm on its surface. It was not steel, I decided. It was more like aluminum, but as strong as steel. It wasn't slippery and seemed to make walking much easier.

It was a short driveway, ending in front of a large dome-shaped building. I stood before it in open-mouthed wonder. Looking at it, one almost heard the crashing music of a new symphony, envisioned a modern ballet, or an abstract painting. At the same time, the appearance of a knight in armor would not have seemed the least out of place.

I had no time for fear. I was suddenly alive with excitement and an eagerness for adventure that far exceeded any emotion I had ever known. Who cared what happened to me once I entered that building? Maybe I would never come out of this alive, but at least I wasn't sitting around on a sand dune dreaming of shooting stars. I was on one, and it was happening to me!

Flanked by my escorts, I entered a large marble hall, and passed through it into a beautiful salon. My escorts bowed low and departed, and I was alone.

Now what?

I could make a run for it. But where would I run? I was a long way from home.

No, the only thing to do was wait. I gingerly walked around the room and finally settled myself on a comfortable-looking settee.

I don't know what or whom I was waiting for, but I was sure that eventually something would happen.

It did.

CHAPTER 8

I was admiring the view. One entire wall of the room was glass and through it I stared at a snow-capped mountain that was almost too picturesque to be real. The snow on its peaks seemed pink until I discovered that it was the glass that was tinted. Its soft tones even made the sky appear rose-colored but I knew the sky outside was definitely a bright clear blue.

The remaining walls were bare except for small perforations. Soundproof, I decided. They obviously had television too, for there was a nice-sized screen in one of the walls. I couldn't help wonder who was the equivalent of "Uncle Miltie" around here, but my imagination just wouldn't extend to the picture of some green-eyed Yargonian capering around doing time steps and pulling gags.

After carefully examining the room several times, I returned my attention to the mountain. It was quite distant and must be very high, I decided, probably higher than anything we had on Earth. There was a slight mist of clouds covering its highest peak.

Maybe I was on the moon!

After all, the moon had mountains, didn't

it? And no one had ever seen its other side. Then these people would be Lunarians or Lunatics. I immediately changed my train of thought to something more reassuring.

These people were extremely intelligent and peace loving . . . I whirled around. The wall was beginning to slide apart.

I stood up, prepared to greet another green-eyed giant, but this time my surprise was so great, I dropped on the couch, absolutely speechless.

Through the open wall entered the most beautiful woman I had ever seen in my life.

She was dressed exactly like the Yargonian men. The same brilliant colors, knee pants, gold sandals, and silken waist. Her eyes were also emerald color and slightly oblique. But she had hair—masses of it—ebony black, and pulled back with a severity that would have been unflattering on most women. It was caught up high in Grecian style by a jeweled clasp which allowed it to flow down her back to her hips. Her skin was white and absolutely flawless. Her nose was straight, and her mouth full and exquisitely formed. I grudgingly conceded, after downright rude scrutiny, that all this beauty was without aid of any cosmetic.

My admiration was lifted to awe when she addressed me in perfect though slightly stilted English.

"My name is Sanau. I bid you welcome to our planet."

"You speak English." Not a brilliant observation but it was all I could manage.

She nodded. "I do not speak it as well as I should like, but my comprehension is most accurate."

"Just tell me why I'm here, and what are they going to do with me?"

She smiled with almost maddening serenity. "You are sure to be hungry. I have arranged for a meal."

She turned and touched the wall. It parted and two women entered with a rolling banquet table. These women were equally as beautiful as Sanau and dressed in identical fashion. They set the table before me, bowed, and departed.

Sanau appraised the table and its contents. Apparently it satisfied her. She announced, "There is a small pellet. You will consume this prior to your meal."

Then she smiled and left the room, the wall closing after her.

I was hungry and the food looked good. There was some kind of meat, an odd-looking green salad, a cold broth, and a muffin. It was the cutlery that made my eyes bulge. The blade of the knife and the prongs of the fork looked like they were made of solid diamond. I held them to the light and compared them to the tiny stone on my left hand. They were diamonds all right. And the blade on the knife had to be well over a hundred karats. One hundred karats of unbroken diamond!

I took the pellet and began the meal. The water had a strong taste, like our water but, well, heavier. The broth was excellent. The meat disappeared. The salad followed. I flirted with the idea of leaving something. I *could* leave the muffin. I bit into it. So I was a pig! Well, what of it? I hadn't asked to be invited to dinner; the whole thing was entirely their idea. Defiantly, I not only ate the muffin, but used it to mop up the leftover gravy on my plate.

Just as I was stuffing the last crumb into my mouth, the wall opened and Sanau and her handmaidens returned. I got the uncomfortable feeling that they had been watching me throughout my meal. The table was whisked away, the handmaidens departed, and Sanau sat down and stared at me in an appraising manner. I stared right back, yet her gaze seemed void of any curiosity.

We sat this way for a moment, measuring one another like two strange animals, outwardly casual but inwardly tensed, waiting for the other to spring.

My reflexes broke first. In a voice almost cracked with nerves, I asked what they intended to do with me.

She merely lifted a beautiful brow that seemed to signify complete disinterest.

"Why was I brought here in the first place?" Her supercilious manner was beginning to really irritate me.

Again the lifted brow.

This time my voice rose a full octave. "I demand an answer. What are they going to do with me? What do they want of me?"

I don't know whether she answered because of my tone or merely to avoid what might be an unpleasant scene, but as she spoke, I found myself wondering how anyone so physically lovely could lack so completely in warmth and emotion.

"We cannot decide what is to be done with you," she told me, "until we have decided what is to be done about the most unfortunate error."

"What error?"

"You."

"Me?" I tried to keep the color from flooding my face.

Me? An error? By their standards? Or was their entire trip an error? Maybe they had just been cruising around with that big searchlight. Like fishing . . . and I had got caught in the net. Well, they could always throw me back. It'd be all right with me. I had had enough of adventure. I wanted to go home.

"When will they make this big decision?"

"At the next meeting of the council."

"When will the council meet?"

"As soon as His Almighty Grace the Yargo will permit." Her face was still serene and motionless.

"Who is the Yargo?" I wasn't quite so serene. This sounded like it could take years.

"The Yargo!" Sanau's eyes sparkled, and her face achieved an almost exalted expression.

In fact, her look of exhilaration became so intense that I began to feel she was going into some kind of a trance. I repeated my question.

"Is he your king or something?"

"He is everything. He is almighty." Now her expression was beyond rapture. It was beyond anything I had ever seen. Her beauty had increased, and she looked heavenward as if she had suddenly beheld a vision of the Lord. There was reverence and awe in her voice. She acted like one possessed by something almost holy.

I decided that maybe there was something going on between this Yargo and Sanau. I tried a new attack.

"Who was the man who greeted me at the airport and brought me here?"

"You were escorted by Leader Seado and Pilot Hakwa." Sanau's expression had resumed its original serenity.

"Is the Yargo a leader?"

"He is supreme!" Again the look of rapture.

"Supreme like what?"

"Supreme. Almighty."

"But he's human? I mean . . . you can see him?"

"One is indeed fortunate to be allowed to gaze upon him, to even converse with him at times. He is human in form but he is almighty."

I decided there definitely was something going on between the Yargo and Sanau.

"Since you seem to speak English so well around here, then why didn't the leader or the pilot speak to me?"

"My people do not speak your language."

"But you do."

Her smile was self-deprecatory. "That is merely my particular talent. I master every language that we come upon."

"Does the Yargo speak English?"

Sanau's expression implied that not only did he speak it . . . he had invented it, but being an extremely polite young woman, she answered in the same awed tone that seemed to be reserved solely for subject matter pertaining to the Yargo.

"The Yargo speaks the language of every planet, including the tongue of every country on your planet, and also the words of the animals and insects."

"The animals! Do animals and insects talk around here?" I was ready to believe practically anything at this point.

"Animals and insects communicate with one another everywhere, on all planets. The Yargo is the only human who can understand them."

"Well, *your* English is wonderful." The way things stood, I figured flattery would do no harm.

It was wasted on Sanau. Her expression

never changed. "As I have stated, language is a particular study with me. But to master it, I must apply myself. But to the Yargo ... this talent comes as natural as breathing. I cannot fathom the animals, the insects, or birdlife. At present I have just mastered the language of the planet you call Mars."

So there were people on Mars! To cover my mounting confusion I asked another question.

"Have you ever visited Earth? Has anyone from your planet landed in our world?"

She shook her head. "No. But we have studied your customs on our monitors from our spaceships and have intercepted many of your news broadcasts. We know a great deal about you."

"And I'm an error." I smiled apologetically.

Her reply came straight to the point.

"We have already contacted Mars to tell them of the error."

So Mars was in on this too. I leaned forward. "Look, Sanau, I don't deny that all of this is vitally interesting. Any scientist on Earth would give his life to learn these facts. I'm interested, too. But I could relax and enjoy this new knowledge that is suddenly opening to me if I had some little hint as to my future. Like how soon I'll be sent back. I will be sent back, won't I?"

"You would be most interested in the people of Mars. They are of superior intellect compared to the inhabitants of your planet."

I began to lose interest in these new

wonders of nature. Right now all my concern was concentrated on the future of one lonely inhabitant from the planet Earth. I was fully aware that Sanau had deliberately avoided answering my question, so I repeated it bluntly. "Am I going back to Earth?"

"That is not for me to answer. At this very moment our leaders are contacting the ruler of Mars. As I have stated, he must be consulted about this matter."

"Why does he have to be consulted?"

"Because it was at his suggestion that you were contacted."

"*Me*???!!!"

Sanau stood up. "I have said too much already."

"Don't go!" I jumped up and grabbed her by the arm. Her swift movement to break my grasp displayed a real revulsion at my touch.

I felt it instantly, and spoke quickly. I had to detain her; there was still so much I wanted to know.

"Please stay a little longer. You haven't even told me where I am. Is your planet what we call Venus or Jupiter . . ?"

"No. You have not named us. We are in another solar system entirely. You have located our sun and your scientists claim that we are approximately seven light years away."

Her tone conveyed that our scientists were certainly laboring under a grave misapprehension. But I wanted to make sure for myself.

"I haven't been traveling for seven years, have I?"

"According to your time we have spent fifteen hours in flight. We travel a thousand times faster than light."

"But that's impossible. Professor Einstein and every great scientist claims no one can travel faster than light."

Sanau smiled tolerantly. "Professor Einstein is the most brilliant man on your planet. But your planet is very young. Fifty years ago, the people of your planet did not actually realize such a thing as commercial air travel. What would the Professor Einstein of fifty years prior have answered had he been told that within fifty years the barrier of sound would be broken?"

I couldn't argue this logic. And I doubted if Professor Einstein would either.

"But you have made progress," she continued generously. "We have been watching you for over three hundred years."

"You mean the saucers have been floating over us since then?"

She smiled. "I suppose our spaceships do resemble your saucers." Once again she started for the panel on the wall. She turned as if to say good night. Then, obviously remembering some last-minute instructions, she paused.

"You must rest. You have good reason to feel weary. Press that button and the divan will become a sleeping couch. The bathroom is completely fitted for your needs. If for some reason you feel compelled to call on me, press that button and my image will appear on the television screen. We can communicate with one another in that manner."

She touched the wall gently and it parted, although I swear I could see no button, hinge, or buzzer.

"What about the Yargo?" I asked hurriedly. "When will I see him?"

"It is extremely doubtful that you will ever see him. You are far too inconsequential to absorb even a moment of his time. All matters regarding you can easily be settled by the leaders. However, by tomorrow, our plans for you should be well formulated."

I was too stunned by this insult to even attempt an answer. I just stood there dumbly and watched her leave. The wall closed after her and I was alone.

Only then did I unleash my anger. I stormed about the room. Superior race indeed! I couldn't remember ever having been more blatantly insulted, and in such an exquisitely polite manner, too! Nothing hypocritical or obtuse in her delivery. Straight to the point, and what made it even more baffling and infuriating was the calm way in which she stated these snubs. Merely as if she was saying, "Oh, it's a very nice day outside." Well, maybe to a Yargonian her line of chatter wouldn't be termed impolite. Maybe they just termed it "speaking the truth," or maybe she really didn't mean it to come out as brutally frank as it had sounded;

but I was sure she had meant it. She had shown her distaste for me in every gesture. Her lack of emotion merely heightened the effect.

Pacing the room helped me to relieve some of my anger. I felt nothing but the burning mortification I had received at the hands of this woman. "Too unimportant to see His Highness!" "An error!" At that moment I actually wanted to do someone physical damage. I pressed the button and watched the divan miraculously turn into a comfortable bed. I walked into the bathroom and brushed my teeth.

And then I actually got into bed and went to sleep.

What else was there to do?

CHAPTER 9

To add to an already fantastic chain of events, I slept well! I slept so well that Sanau had to wake me.

I sensed a slight impatience in her manner as I dawdled over breakfast. Ordinarily, I would have bolted down my food, as I am at heart a considerate person, but remembering her attitude the previous evening, I took elaborate pains to finish every morsel.

When I could drag it out no longer because every crumb was gone, I turned to her expectantly.

She took command immediately.

"If you are quite done," she said, "we shall proceed immediately."

"Proceed where?" as I rose obediently.

"We go to meet the leaders."

After a quick bath, and a quicker toilette, since I hadn't any makeup to apply, I was ready. I would have felt more confident with at least a dash of lipstick, but after staring at myself critically in the mirror, I had to admit that I didn't look too bad. In fact, I looked better than I had ever looked in my life. I decided there must be something in the food and air; my lips were actually a healthy red and my eyes glistened.

To add to my new sense of vanity, Sanau offered me a brand-new outfit to wear. A real Yargonian getup, identical to her own attire. She apologized for this fact.

"I am sorry I cannot offer you clothing more suited to your taste. At this moment, your dress from Earth is in the midst of repair. It was somewhat ravaged from the trip."

I dismissed her apology as I scrambled into the outfit. I felt like I was going to a costume ball, and I must confess that in the midst of the confusion that had suddenly overtaken my future, my only thought at that second was, "Oh, if David could only see me now!"

"Did the leaders ask to meet me?" I was feeling quite friendly.

"No one has asked to meet you. However, a meeting had to be called to decide as to your future."

"There's no big problem that I can see. Just send me home the way you got me. It's really very simple."

In answer, she merely pressed the panel and beckoned for me to follow.

We left the building and climbed into the same cigar-shaped car. The ride was uneventful; the same whirl of scenery; the same unbelievable pace.

"What do the leaders do?" I asked as I swallowed hard to clear my ears.

"They govern different sections of our planet."

"Oh—like presidents of different countries." In answer to her nod, I also nodded. I was both pleased and impressed. After all, my only previous contact with a public official was the twenty-inch television screen in my living room. Now suddenly I was going to sit around and discuss my future with all kinds of governors and presidents. I grew expansive with pride and turned to Sanau quite chummily.

"Do you work for one of the leaders?"

"I am a leader."

I should have expected something like that. No wonder she was so overbearing.

"What part of the planet do you rule?"

"No one rules this planet . . . we lead in governing different parts."

"What part do you govern?" If nothing else, I am persistent.

"I am cultural leader of the entire planet."

She really was top brass! My tone was genuinely humble when I said, "I'm really impressed that I've been placed in your care. And it's really very nice, all the trouble you're taking with me. I want to thank you."

"There was no choice," she answered in the same even voice. "Aside from the Yargo himself, I am the only person on our planet who speaks your language."

Fortunately, the car came to a halt, because I was just about to say something equally impolite.

I followed her into the building determined
not to say another word. I trod behind her in
sullen silence until my curiosity forced me to
chance another question.

"Do you elect your leaders the way we do
ours?"

She nodded. "In much the same way, save
for the exploitation and personal undermin-
ing that seems to accompany most of your
elections."

I decided they had been watching us more
closely than I had suspected.

"But how does the best man win if you
don't have campaigns?"

"For the sole reason that he *is* the best
man."

We entered a large foyer that shimmered
with crystal ornaments and chandeliers. I
suspected that they might be diamonds rather
than glass. I stopped to admire the glittering
appointments of the room, but Sanau continued the conversation, apparently oblivious
to the beauty about us.

"The public, our public, recognizes the best
man by way of his past accomplishments and
not by the false promises or slander that your
politicians seem wont to stand upon."

We boarded a small elevator that whisked
us to the huge anteroom of an auditorium.
Here we paused, presumably to be announced.
We sat on a small mosaic bench; the presentation would happen momentarily. I wet my
lips and tried to emulate Sanau's fantastic
poise. This was going to be an important

afternoon for me; I had to make a good impression. To dispel my stage fright, I began to chatter aimlessly about the beauty of the building, my admiration for the Yargonian attire, their great strides in science. Perhaps Sanau sensed this gregarious mood was just an outlet for nervous emotion, for she ignored me completely. Only when I mentioned the Yargo did she betray that she was even listening.

"Do the people elect the Yargo?" I asked.

I waited for the exalted look. It came.

"Yes, the Yargo is elected. But not in the same manner as the leaders and the Senate. He is elected in the minds and hearts of the people."

Well, that was a nice simple little answer. But I never got the chance to go into it, for suddenly a green-eyed giant appeared, gurgled a few Yargonian phrases to Sanau, and we were off.

We entered a tremendous auditorium. The assemblage that greeted us inside the hall was rigid and formal. This was really the works all right. All the big shots had turned out except, I guess, Mr. Almighty himself.

I looked around. The scene reminded me of the newsreels of UN meetings. Tier upon tier of men and women lined the huge auditorium. I felt very small and insignificant standing before them until I reminded myself that this whole wingding had been called just because of me. I was the star attraction for probably the first and last time in my life, so I stood very straight, aping Sanau's perfect posture.

One of the leaders in the front tier rose and signaled for attention. He addressed his remarks to Sanau in his native tongue. She answered him, then addressed the conclave. There was no microphone, no public address system. She spoke into a small gold box, resembling a small portable radio, which she wore on the belt of her pants. Her tone was completely conversational. If I hadn't been standing at her side, I couldn't have heard a word—not that I understood even a syllable.

It was obvious that the audience of dignitaries heard her. They sat with a look of rapt attention and I noticed they also wore the same gold boxes attached to their belts. It seemed to work like a telephone.

I stood as rigid as I could, trying not to appear as awkward as I felt. Thousands of green eyes pierced me with the intensity of a radar beam, but I stood my ground, praying they would not rattle me. Somehow I almost felt that the whole world—my world, the Earth—was depending on me to make good. Like it was saying, "Show them, Janet— show them what kind of people come from our planet. You've got to show them. Make them respect us—and make us proud of you!"

But how? Make a speech? Smile? Faint? The last would be easy and probably just what they'd expect. Oh, why did they have to pick me? With all the people that were floating around on Earth with nothing special to do, they had to hook me. It was kind of a shame—for Earth that is. Now, if they had snagged Marilyn Monroe, that would have given them something to think about. They'd probably make immediate plans to take over our entire planet thinking she was a typical sample of the average American girl. I'll bet even Mr. God Almighty himself would have come out to take a look.

I wondered if I'd have to make a speech. I turned my attention to Sanau. She was still yapping away in the little gold box.

She finally stopped speaking just as I had begun to shift from one foot to another to ease the tension of standing in one spot for so long. I cleared my throat expectantly, ready to make a stab at some kind of opening address.

Instead she motioned me to a table with two chairs that faced the audience.

"We shall sit here," she stated.

"I feel almost like I'm in court, on trial," I whispered.

"You are," she answered simply.

This woman had the most depressing effect upon me. I slumped into the chair.

"I am to translate the proceedings for you. It is to be decided what is to be done with you."

"Haven't they decided yet?"

Sanau's glance not only told me it hadn't, but it also told me that if it was left up to her I wouldn't be long for any world. But all she said was, "I will translate as each leader speaks. At this moment, Leader Hallah is bidding the assemblage to come to order."

I gave Leader Hallah my undivided attention. He spoke quietly into his little gold box. Although he stood but ten or twelve feet from me, I could barely hear his voice, but all the men and women in the tiers adjusted their boxes and some even began taking notes.

Sanau began to speak—quietly and intensely.

"Ladies and gentlemen, leaders, members of the Senate, and state chairmen. Never before has the council been called upon to settle a problem as delicate as the one that lies before us. Extreme caution must be used in the final decision, and above all, we must remember that the creature before us is a human, and must be dealt with accordingly and justly."

"Oh, he's wonderful, Sanau . . ." I began.

"Don't interrupt," she hissed. "Do not stop me once to ask a question or I shall miss what is being said."

I sat back obediently. Sanau continued.

"Members of the council, as you know, this female is from the planet that calls itself Earth. We have all been informed of the serious error that was made." There was much of the nodding and murmuring that signifies mass agreement. I sat quietly and tried not to look too pained.

"As you know, one of our spaceships set forth to perform a delicate mission that had to operate with split-second timing. Every calculation was precise, checked and proven before it was attempted, yet, certain factors had to be left to chance and luck. Today is indeed a sad day. Instead of rejoicing in the advancement of our accomplishment, we are faced instead with the fruit of our misadventure. It is indeed a shocking disappointment."

Once again the speech was halted and everyone seemed to be of the mutual opinion that it was indeed a shocking disappointment, while the fruit of their misadventure tried to look unconcerned.

"I cannot forget the great day when Spaceship Areala embarked for the mission. We all entered into the rejoicing and good wishes that went with the aviators on their travels. We even declared a twenty-four-hour holiday. Then even greater jubilation was ours, on the wonderful day that word was flashed to us that the magnetic ray worked in practice as well as in theory. True, it had been tested here. It lifted a Yargonian through space, but it was still conjecture as to whether it would lift an Earth human. That much had to be left to luck." He paused to sip some water.

He was a real public speaker, I decided. My ears had become accustomed to the acoustics of the room and I could hear him now. Although his language was foreign, I

noted that he had the same sonorous drawl
as any public figure on Earth, the same wordy
eloquence.

"Everything went according to schedule.
Spaceship Areala took off, sighted Earth, and
proceeded to the beachhead. It had been
agreed that either Professor Einstein or
Doctor Blount was the Earth being to contact. Both men were educated in astrophysics
and had the capability to comprehend the
problem we would relate. Either man was
held in enough esteem on his planet to have
his opinion respected and acted on by his
people. We decided on Doctor Blount merely
because it was agreed that he might make the
trip with more ease than Professor Einstein,
who according to Earth's standards, is very
advanced in age. Through our monitored
broadcasts, much of Doctor Blount's life and
living habits were known. We learned that
he took vacations at a beach in a place called
Massachusetts, and that he was given to
taking long solitary walks along the beach
at night. At the urgent bidding of the planet
Mars, we were to bring Doctor Blount to our
planet and relay the dangers that were
threatening not only Earth, but his entire
solar system. Such a man as Doctor Blount
would comprehend, be returned to Earth, and
his world might listen to him. Just as Spaceship Areala was about to leave space and enter into the atmosphere that encircles Earth,
she detected an approaching meteor shower.
This necessitated a sudden shift off course

and a ten-minute delay until the shower had expended itself. You all know the rest. The final error is conceded by the pilots themselves. They have already grounded themselves for ten years; this is their own decision, so we cannot overrule it. It was only enthusiasm that caused this final error, the eagerness that sprung them into immediate action rather than a calm stability. But, my good friends, it is only through such accidents that we have learned to banish emotion. When one acts on emotion rather than mental reasoning, there can be no success. Yet there is something to say on the pilots' behalf. Our only real emotion comes from the accomplishment of work well done. We can all see the reason and excuse for the pilots' eagerness and overanxiety: the change in their course due to an unforeseen obstacle such as the meteor shower, their jubilation in finding what they felt was the proper beachhead, the solitary human walking on the beach. These facts coupled with the emotion caused them to act in haste; therefore, the error, and before you, the undesired fruit of such an error."

He paused and looked to his audience for sympathy, and they reacted on cue with solemn nods.

"Now the question put to us," he continued, "is what to do with this female?"

For a moment there was nothing but deathly silence. I felt the back of my knees go weak and the perspiration come to my brow. Why didn't someone say something? Or were they all thinking the same horrible thought I was thinking. Kill her! It would be so simple. Who would ever know?

Suddenly one of the leaders in the second tier signaled for attention. From where I sat I could just about see his lips moving. Sanau bent close to her voice box. I waited tensely for her to translate.

"Honorable Leader Hallah and members of the council. I offer this obvious suggestion. Could not, in some simple way, the dangers be explained to this female? Oh, in the most basic and primary form. Then—could not this female, weak substitute that she is—could not she relay the message to her world or to Doctor Blount?"

I nodded so hard my teeth rattled and punctuated it with a brilliant smile at the leader who had made this gratifying suggestion. What a nice man! Why, with a little more hair and different color eyes and less cheekbone, he'd look like my father. I beamed at him as he sat down.

A leader named Corla demanded to be heard and, once again, Sanau translated.

"Ah, Leader Murtah, do not think this plan was not given some consideration. It was even brought to the Almighty One's attention. The Great Yargo himself said . . ."

Sanau stopped abruptly for, at the mere mention of this magical name, the entire audience rose, shouted a few words that ended with Yargo, went into some sort of chant that resembled a prayer, then fell to their knees and remained prostrate on the ground. And Sanau—the elegant, dignified Sanau— lay face down, flat on the floor.

I stood there staring at them. At first I thought maybe His Highness had entered; but no, we were alone. Just Sanau and myself and the several thousand leaders and senators. There they were, flat on the floor— thrown into a self-imposed trance just at the mere mention of his name.

I didn't know quite what to do. Should I get down on the floor with them? After all, I was on trial, in a way. Maybe this gesture would signify great respect; they might decide to send me home after all, with one of those nice knives as a souvenir.

Just as I was nosing around, looking for a nice comfortable spot on the floor, they all rose. Well, I had missed my chance, but maybe all was not lost. His name might crop up in the conversation again—and I'd be the first one down!

As everyone was settled, Leader Corla resumed his speech.

"Ah, my good friends, His Almighty Grace weighed this problem immediately, then discarded it. Who, on the planet called Earth, would take heed or advice from this female? Even the revered Doctor Blount might have experienced some difficulty in receiving a credulous reaction. Think what a debacle this female would cause if she returned with such a story."

I longed to strangle this man.

"But what *is* to be done?" he continued. "Sending her back to Earth with no message is also dangerous and foolhardy. The tales she would relate, if she was given even a slight amount of credence by her people, would cause panic and disruption amongst them. We must not forget their mass hysteria but a short decade ago when a radio actor, in fun, announced an invasion from Mars. No, the people of the planet Earth are not ready to see or accept visitors from another planet. They are a distrustful and suspicious people. If they believed there were spaceships watching them, it would cause them to become aggressive. This we can see from the constant wars that rage between their own countries. Until the planet Earth rids itself of these shortcomings, they will never see real progress as a people. Such knowledge from the mouth of this inept girl would merely cause them to redouble their efforts with atomic weapons and tests, and that is just what Mars, and we ourselves, do not want to happen."

Another leader rose, signifying he wished the floor. Leader Corla graciously withdrew. The new leader agreed that sending me back to Earth was impossible. In fact, he thought no more valuable time should even be wasted in this useless proposition, that we should get right to the real problem, mainly, what was to be done with me? I could see it really was a problem—that is—if you were looking at it from their side, which, of course, I was not.

Leader Corla jumped up again.

"It is indeed imperative that some action must be taken. She cannot return to Earth. That has been agreed unanimously and, as you know, allowing her to remain on this planet has also been outlawed."

I wondered who had done that. I found out right away.

"As you know, after a brief council meeting last night with the Almighty One, we took polls throughout the planet on such a suggestion. We stated our error, and asked should she be allowed to take up residence in our world. This morning the votes came in. There was only one vote that signified she should remain. Every other vote was in the negative."

"What snobbish people," I stated, but Sanau quickly shut me up with a very severe look.

"We all knew it would be impossible to keep her here, yet in our efforts to be completely fair, we allowed the people of the planet to decide themselves. And we were right, although I must admit that we did not expect such a landslide vote in the negative." He paused to allow himself a brief sigh.

"It is a sad state. The inhabitants of Earth are thirty thousand years behind us in civilization. Even a learned man such as Doctor Blount would not be welcome here as a permanent resident, and you can easily see that this female in question is a very inferior sample of Earth's species at best. It is in our hands to decide exactly what is to be done here and now."

A new leader leaped to his feet with a magnificent suggestion. According to Sanau's translation, his proposition was to brainwash and return me to Earth. This was immediately vetoed. With a complete brainwash, it sometimes took a Yargonian ten to fifteen years to reorganize his thinking. Since my brain could in no way compare to theirs in strength, such a procedure might easily kill me.

Several leaders were all for it. If it worked, everyone would be happy—including me. If I did succumb, it would have been unintentional on their part, so everyone would still be happy, except maybe me.

This caused a twenty-minute debate, during which time Leader Corla had to rap for order many times and poor Sanau found herself almost stuttering in the confusion of trying to relay each message in its proper order.

Finally, Leader Corla took the floor again. By now, I had worked up a full-fledged hate for him.

"Ladies and gentlemen, I can see that it is utterly impossible for the assembly to come to any final decision at this moment. I had almost anticipated this reaction; however, I did want you all to have a chance to view the subject on hand. Several of you have made worthwhile suggestions, others are less workable. However, I suggest that I have another meeting with His Almighty Grace, and place all suggestions before him. Let him make the choice and we shall abide by his decision entirely. Is it agreed?"

Well, even in Yargonian language, I could understand a vote of agreement. It was also apparent that everyone thought this a great idea. Sanau stood up. The cabinet began to file out. No one even glanced in my direction or waved good-bye. I looked hopefully at the nice leader who had suggested I return to Earth with the world-shattering news, whatever it was, but even he did not glance my way.

Sanau took my arm and led me back to the cigar-shaped car once more. I was unbearably depressed. I was not going home. I would never see David again.

Somehow I held back my tears. I wasn't going to let Sanau see me fall apart; it would probably be just what she expected. But what was going to happen to me? It was a cinch I wasn't going to hang around her very long. So I was an inferior sample! Well, they might be very superior beings but they certainly had inferior manners. And this Yargo —was he just like the others? What would be his decision? Somehow I just couldn't actually grasp the enormity of the entire situation. It was almost as if I was on the outside, watching myself play a role in some imaginary plot. I knew this could not be happening to me. It was like having a nightmare that you knew was only a nightmare, yet you were forced to suffer along with it, powerless to wake up. It was time to wake up as the dream went on, growing, expanding, becoming swollen with unknown dangers.

Our car came to a sudden halt. I was surprised to find quite a crowd assembled in front of our building. Evidently word had gotten around about the inferior specimen who was visiting the planet. Well, of course, they had all voted against me, every last green-eyed one of them! I turned, suppressing a wild impulse to stick out my tongue at the whole superior mob. That might have been just what they'd have expected. So I satisfied myself with a glare, drew myself to my full height, and walked through them with what I hoped would pass as great dignity.

They stared at me with polite yet real curiosity. Though I scarcely looked their way I saw enough of them to sense that something seemed strangely amiss about the entire assemblage.

Children! Yes, that was it. So far I had not seen one child on the entire planet. I turned and quickly scanned the crowd. Not one child. Were they born full-sized? They all seemed so alike in height and appearance. As if they came off the assembly line. The men stood close to six foot three or four. The women were tall, about five foot six or seven, all slender and supple as dancers. They all looked like Sanau, though, if I remained for a time, they would gain in differing characteristics. I had to admit that Sanau was slightly more magnificent than the others. In appearance, I doubt if any woman in all history could compare to her for sheer physical perfection. Though in charm and personality, she was a total zero, and I'm absolutely certain she shared the same feeling about me.

She deposited me without ceremony in the chamber I was now beginning to regard as home. She bowed a cool farewell.

"Until the decision has been reached, I trust you will be quite comfortable in these quarters. Your meals will be brought to you at the proper time. I trust the waiting will not prove too tedious."

"Just a moment!" I whirled upon her as she started from the room. "You mean I just sit, locked in this room?"

She nodded, completely unconcerned.

"I'm not going to run away anywhere. I have no idea what will happen to me when the Yargo and his cabinet make the decision, but until then, couldn't I at least enjoy my freedom?"

"I am most sorry." She didn't sound sorry at all. "We do not imprison people. However, until a decision is made, you must remain here in seclusion."

"That's not very fair, is it? Dragging someone away from their home and friends, then locking them up in a room because you, the great superior race, can't come to a decision."

Sanau nodded. "I can make no argument against this excellent logic. I can only share your hope that the decision will be agreeable to you and will arrive with haste."

"If I'm not going home nothing will be favorable."

Once again she merely pressed the panel and left the room. I stood there and watched the wall close behind her.

For a moment I stood motionless, then my outrage spurred me to action. I rushed to the wall and pressed the panel just as she had done. Nothing happened. I banged and hammered at it but the wall remained a wall, as impenetrable and obstinate as if never in its life had it slid apart and become a door. I was trapped, and suddenly my nightmare was real.

I looked around the room like a caged animal. The sun had gone behind the mountain but its pink shadow still stained the sky. I reexamined the room, but there was nothing—no books, no radio, and, as for the television screen, if I turned that on all I would get would be Sanau!

There was nothing to do, and I was not sleepy. Dinner would probably arrive soon but I wasn't hungry. I was homesick and really scared for the first time in my whole life. I was just an inconsequential girl from

Earth pitted against this vast Yargonian world, at the mercy of their unsympathetic decision. To them, I was just an inferior specimen from an inferior planet.

But I was also human, with human emotions. Not just a "female" but a real woman who couldn't be cut off from her world and the people she loved just like that. And, being a woman with frayed emotions, I did what any sensible woman would do; I flopped on the couch and sobbed.

CHAPTER 10

I awoke of my own accord the following morning. It looked to be a fine summer day. The sun was shining, the sky was bright. Somewhere on Earth the sun was also shining from a bright sky, and a girl was waking to face another day. Maybe she even yawned and thought, "What should I do today? A movie? Lunch with the girls?"

I stretched and let out a heavy sigh. Don't people realize how lucky they really are? Why can't we enjoy something when we have it? The things we take for granted: the privilege of waking in our own bed, having breakfast with our own family, the freedom to walk down our own street and greet our friends and neighbors. Even people who work and scrimp and save and punch a time clock, they're lucky, too. They're working and scrimping and saving in a world that belongs to them. They can make any kind of a life for themselves they choose. If they are unhappy they have only themselves to blame. Just as I have myself to blame. If I had only realized these things; if I hadn't gone off to Avalon to search for dreams and dwell in the past, this never would have happened. Now,

I would never be allowed to enjoy all the wonderful things that I once took for granted.

I buried my face in the pillow and tried to force my mind into a blank but my chest began to swell with the ache of memories of the things I had left behind. I might have gone into another fit of hysterical weeping if the two handmaidens hadn't suddenly appeared with my breakfast.

They wore the ever-present smile and took great pains with my service.

I studied them carefully. They seemed to like me. I couldn't help but wonder if they had voted against me in the election. It had been a complete landslide rejection. Of course they had! The supercilious little snobs!

Unconsciously, I stiffened in my attitude toward them. I was about to motion both them and the breakfast away when a perverse thought attracted me. Maybe it upset them; two self-righteous Yargonians forced to serve the inferior specimen. I bit into my muffin and felt better. I hoped they hated their jobs. I hoped they hated serving me. Maybe it would upset them so much they'd have a nervous breakdown. I wondered if they had psychiatrists on Yargo.

Probably not. They didn't need any help on Yargo. Yargo. So the planet was named after him, too. Maybe it had been in his family for years. Yargo—sounded like something you might use to fry fish—Yargo!

There was a sudden commotion. I stopped eating and looked on the floor. There they both were—Oh, Lord, I probably said the name aloud! I studied them in a lordly manner. They were in some kind of a trance, all right. The same look of ecstacy, the same pagan chant I had witnessed the previous day. I returned my interest to the muffin. They'd get up in due time, as soon as they were finished with whatever they were doing.

They did, and looked quite refreshed, too, as if the entire thing had been so soul-lifting that it had purged all their sins. That gave me an idea. Maybe I should pray, too—not to him, but to God, my God.

When I was alone, I did just that, but not without the conscience of self-rebuke, the guilty admission that one only turns to prayer when the chips are down. At first, I searched for a dignified prayer to fit the occasion, but I found my greatest feeling of release when I dismissed all protocol and prayed with the unabashed simplicity of an adolescent.

I felt much better. In fact, if it hadn't been for the deadly monotony of the day, I would have felt almost cheerful. The only thing that relieved the stretch of endless waiting was the regular appearance of the handmaidens at mealtimes. There was no sign of Sanau.

Not that I actually missed her. Besides, there was the knowledge that I could summon her on the television screen. That was a thought. Maybe she could tell me what was going on. I crossed the room, then stopped. No, I wouldn't call her. This inferior specimen would give them a little display of an Earth person's fortitude. No matter how lonely or unendurable the wait became I would hold my ground until she came to me.

Keeping that vow was the hardest thing I ever did. I sat alone three whole days and nights, without a book, magazine, or person to speak with.

On the morning of the fourth day, I was ready to admit defeat and call, scream, or beg Sanau for some word. I no longer cared whether or not these people admired my strength of character. I was now haunted with the obsession that, perhaps, the decision had been made, and this was it. Keep me here, feed me, and let me die of natural causes, loneliness, or madness.

Then, with no warning, Sanau made her appearance. She offered no explanation for my long stretch of confinement. She motioned that I follow, indicating we had some definite place to go.

I didn't speak until we were in the car, hurtling down the shiny road.

"Sanau . . ." I stopped because my voice had cracked. After all, I hadn't used it in three days.

I tried again, this time with better results. "Sanau, have they decided?"

"Just about."

"What are they going to do?"

She gazed directly ahead. "You may be sent to the planet Mars."

Mars! I was to be sent to—

"Mars!!!"

I guess I shouted the word Mars! Now, Janet, keep your head. Don't shout, don't get hysterical, keep your wits about you, you'll need them. Keep calm. But Mars, Mars!!!

It could be worse. It wasn't exactly a trip to Coney Island, but it was a planet in our own solar system. Maybe the people of Mars would be more sympathetic. Maybe I could persuade them to send me back to Earth. It would be just a short hop in comparison.

"Won't I die of the cold on Mars?"

My question seemed to startle Sanau, who obviously had her own share of thinking to do.

"We have discussed the climatic problems of Mars. You see, our planet is in the exact position that your Earth occupies in relation to your sun. Therefore, our atmospheric conditions are practically identical—except for the added purity of our air. Also, our sun is far superior to your sun."

It figured. But I also knew this was no time to start a debate on the merits of Earth versus Yargo.

"Mars is further from your sun than Earth," she continued. "However, an underground dwelling with atmospheric conditions identical to that of Earth could be prepared for you."

"You mean I'd spend my entire life underground!"

"In due time a mask would be made for you, I presume, to enable you the freedom of the planet. Perhaps, as time passes, you may adjust to the climate and thinness of the oxygen. All these things will be discussed at great length. I promise there will be complete preparation, if you go to Mars."

If I go to Mars. She had said if . . .

"Sanau," I kept my voice down, "What do you mean, *if* I go to Mars?"

"Because Mars may not accept you."

Suddenly all my reserve snapped.

"And suppose I don't accept Mars." My voice shook with rage. "Look, I didn't ask to be brought here. I was kidnapped, taken from my home and family, and you all sit around and act as if I crashed a very exclusive party. I think I should be given some rights."

"I am most sure the entire situation causes us all discomfort."

"It may cause you discomfort, but it's practically ended my life!"

In answer, she turned her attention to the maze of scenery that flashed by. After a moment she added, "We have spent three days discussing this situation. Leader Corla and I thought of Mars, since it was at the suggestion of Mars that you were brought here."

"And what did the Yargo suggest be done with me?"

She didn't answer immediately. I wondered why she didn't fall on her face when I mentioned his name, and asked why.

"When one person alone hears the Almighty's name, it is merely the custom to chant a silent admiration ritual. But if two or more people are together at the time of the mention, then the kneeling ritual and full admiration chant is performed."

That explained the behavior of the handmaidens, and the entire assemblage in court. It also explained that Sanau did not consider me a person. When she was with me, she considered herself alone.

Then she told me of the Yargo's decision, which immediately dropped him to the cellar of my esteem. It seems that this sympathetic soul wanted to send me off in a spaceship. Not a spaceship going somewhere, just to drift about.

Our car halted before another remarkable-looking building, but I was too stunned by the Yargo's suggestion to do more than barely notice it. I quickened my pace to follow Sanau's long easy stride.

"But if I was just drifting in outer space, what would happen to me? Wouldn't I just drift until I eventually crashed into something?"

"You could never crash in outer space," she answered easily. "Once you have passed the pull of gravity of a planet, the motors are cut off and the ship would automatically assume the position of a satellite moving around the world on its own orbit."

"And what would *I* do? Just rot away inside this ship?"

"Not at all. The ship would be equipped with books of every possible nature and there would be every means of self-education. I personally would attend to the translations. There would be enough food to last several years. The ship itself would be rocket-propelled. At the end of a certain period, a piloted ship would contact your ship and you would be supplied with further articles of food and literature. In this way, you could spend the rest of your life in complete peace and ease, entirely free to revel in the luxury of self-improvement and the expansion of your mind."

"For how long?"

"Forever."

I almost tripped as I stepped into a small elevator. As I leaned back against the wall for support, I dismissed all hope that this mighty ruler might intervene on my behalf. What kind of a heart was housed in this supreme being? Did his superior strength also encompass superior frigidity and superior dismissal of another human's fate? This new blow lessened the fear of my place of banishment, for whatever perils Mars might hold, they could never equal the fear that shot through me when I thought of the loneliness of eternal space.

As we left the elevator, I clutched Sanau's arm and pleaded for her support.

"Whatever happens," I begged, "don't let them send me off to space. Please, Sanau, please!"

In answer she merely pulled away from my grasp and stood at a safe distance, as if to preclude any future physical entreaties on my part, as she spoke.

The lack of compassion in her voice was almost unbelievable in contrast with the genuine sympathy of her statement.

"I sensed you would feel so, and explained this to the Yargo. You see, to one on our planet, to spend one's life in ease and study is a dream fulfilled, for in so doing, one may come upon a bit of knowledge that could be passed on for the benefit of future generations. But, if you were to study ten lifetimes, there would be nothing you could contribute to our civilization and the joy of mere self-improvement would mean nothing to you. At first His Excellency could not comprehend this. Although he has been informed that you come from a backward planet, he cannot quite visualize the extreme limits of your intelligence or capabilities. I must admit that I went to great lengths to explain the futility of his kind offer and, in the end, he conceded to send you to Mars—if—Mars accepts you."

She turned and walked down the corridor. I had no choice but to follow.

This time we entered a large observatory and even though I'd never set foot in one, there was no mistaking the function of this room. A tremendous telescope pointed through the open roof to the skies and alongside it was a full-sized television screen.

Across the room stood two other telescopes of equal size, their gleaming eyes shooting heavenward.

On still another side of the room there were row after row of benches, not unlike those used at the circus and ball parks. There sat about fifty or sixty of the leaders. I spotted Leader Corla and a few other familiar faces from the previous day. This jury on the final decision of my fate was an intimate gathering.

Once again the session was called to order through the little gold voice boxes and once again Sanau assumed the role of interpreter.

"We are going to reach Mars through television telescope," she informed me.

"You mean we'll actually be able to see the people on Mars?" I asked.

She nodded. "And what is more important, they will be able to see you."

Leader Corla rose. He motioned to Sanau, who took me by the arm and placed me before a square box that resembled an Xray machine.

"Stand before the box," she ordered. "They have already contacted the ruler of Mars. He and his council wish to inspect you."

I did as ordered and hoped my appearance pleased the leader of Mars to a greater degree than it obviously did the Yargonians. The lights went off and I stood alone in complete blackness. The situation at hand seemed more unreal than the previous unbelievable experiences. That someone on a planet in another solar system was able to study me, to see me. Suddenly a strange purple light emanated from the box behind me. In a reflex action, I started to move away.

"Stand where you are," Sanau ordered. "They are watching you."

I stood there and tried to force a smile. At least that is what it was intended to be, but my lips trembled violently, and one side of my mouth suddenly decided to go numb. I tried again—this was no time for my nerves to fail me. Suddenly I felt I had to go to Mars. Compared to Yargo, it was actually close to Earth, and once there, anything—anything might happen. And anything was preferable to floating through space.

While I forced a feeble leer, the purple light dissolved and simultaneously the lights of the observatory switched on.

Leader Corla immediately took the floor. I decided I thoroughly despised him. He directed some inquiry to Sanau, who answered him tersely. He walked to the television screen, adjusted a small microphone, attached some earphones, and rapped for order.

"We are about to receive an answer," Sanau whispered.

I listened intently. Even the leaders seemed to share my anticipation. Leader Corla began talking to Mars. I can't exactly say he was talking; he was using numbers—rather like equations in algebra with much X equals A and Y minus X.

I nudged Sanau. What was this gibberish about?

Well, it was all about me. She explained that only the divine Yargo could actually speak the language of all other planets. Therefore, they contacted Mars through universal language. Entire messages could be relayed numerically. Of course, if it was anything important, the Yargo himself did the actual speaking. Not only could he understand the language, he could rattle it off like a native.

I didn't miss the slight behind Sanau's seemingly innocuous statement. She didn't have to blast headlines for me to realize I was an unwanted object that could be disposed of in a few numbers and fractions, too subhuman for any undue consideration.

I asked Sanau if she understood the numerals. Of course she did.

She explained that Leader Corla was giving a full report of my mental ability. Naturally this statement did nothing to lift my hopes.

It seemed to take forever. First Leader Corla would intone some fractions, then cock his head attentively at the earphones and write down some answers.

Well, it couldn't be going too badly, I decided. I must have passed the physical inspection if they were so intent on the

contents of my brain. I wondered what they'd
be like. Would they resemble the Yargonians?
Maybe they'd be a little less superior. They
might even grow to like me. I might find
some friends. Anyone would be preferable to
the snobbery of Sanau. It might not be too
bad after all. I might be given a royal welcome, come to be sort of the visiting celebrity;
then, in time, I might charm them into
returning me to Earth.

This thought inspired me to greater
heights. What an ovation I'd get from my
Earth. Janet Cooper—girl from three worlds.
Yargo, Mars, and Earth. And, perhaps, I
could tell them how to contact Mars—through
numbers. Doctor Blount or Professor Einstein would know, and I'd be the girl who
had paved the way for the first interplanetary
communication system on Earth. I'd go down
in history, like Marconi. Teachers like Miss
Massinger would be forced to teach their
students about me. They'd study my life like
Joan of Arc's or Queen Elizabeth's.

Suddenly Leader Corla switched off the
microphone and removed his earphones. Even
Sanau leaned forward expectantly. Everyone
was tensed, except me. I was still floating on
Cloud Number Seven signing autographs and
posing for cigarette testimonials.

I sensed the air of concentration around
me and snapped back to the present.

Leader Corla spoke into his voice box.
Sanau didn't even take the time to translate
for me. She was too intent on listening.

Leader Corla finished and sat down. The room was filled with a pregnant silence. Sanau turned to me.

"The leader of Mars has rejected you!"

The sentence hit me like ice water right between the eyes. Somehow I had never thought of rejection. This had been the big "open sesame." I was too bewildered to attempt a reply. I turned to Sanau but no words could find their way from my throat to my lips.

She put her hand on my shoulder. Her green eyes narrowed into catlike slits, yet she spoke in an almost gentle tone.

"I am sorry. There lies no alternative except the spaceship."

I tried to answer. Instead the effort only caused me to sink to the floor. I knew I was going to faint, and although I would have welcomed even this temporary release from reality, something made me fight against submission.

I put my hands over my face and pressed my head as if sheer physical force would cram this ugly decision away from my mind. I had been rejected. Why couldn't they have liked me? All my life I've wanted to be liked, but I never got it until I met David. My mother was forced to accept me for what I was; even at school I had no intimate friends. And now the pattern had shaped; I was alone —forever. I felt the tears come to my eyes. They slipped through my fingers and I sobbed softly.

Sanau tapped my shoulder, signaling I should rise. Already the meeting showed signs of disbanding: leaders were standing in small groups discussing the situation with one another; an undertone of foreign chatter permeated the room.

I stood up and wiped my eyes.

"Are you all right?" Sanau asked. She looked at me intently, and her look suddenly changed to complete amazement.

"Your eyes," she pointed. "What is the matter with your eyes?"

My eyes! For a moment I was frightened. I put my hand to them. Aside from the tears that still dropped down my cheeks, they seemed intact.

"Water is falling from your eyes," Sanau insisted with actual alarm in her voice.

If the situation hadn't been so tragic, I might have laughed, for it was obvious Sanau had never seen tears.

"I'm all right," I explained. "I was crying, that's all."

"Crying?" She stared at me as if I was a rare laboratory specimen. "Crying?" she repeated. Then a look of eagerness replaced her incredulous stare.

"Crying. But, of course. Tears! You mean they still perform such a rite on Earth?"

I didn't answer.

"We have read about tears," she explained in a voice vibrant with excitement. "About old and extinct civilizations that expressed sadness, anger, and even happiness through small waterfalls spilling from the eyes. It's in the archives of our own records. They state that such oddities occurred on our planet some ten thousand years back. I, myself, thought it was only folklore. Oh, do turn about, the leaders must witness this rare phenomenon."

Before I could voice my objections, she had whirled me around to face the departing assemblage. A few words immediately brought the entire group to my side. They crowded around me, displaying none of the previous restraint extended during my past appearances. I could not help but be aware of the comical aspects of the situation. All my attempts at strength and intestinal fortitude had failed to arouse a gleam in any green Yargonian orb, yet this one helpless weakness I had displayed had suddenly garnered their complete attention and interest.

No one is ever exactly proud to display tears, except maybe the heroine of *Way Down East* or *Camille*, but I could not help but feel some kind of pride in this rare emotion I was exhibiting to some fifty eager-eyed Yargonians. At least I was finally capable of doing something they could not. And to add further accomplishments to my dying ego, I did what any sensible girl would do under similar circumstances; I deprived them of their new-found pleasure. I stopped crying. In fact, with new courage, I even went a step further. I turned my back on them and crossed the room—with dignity.

Sanau came to me instantly.

"You resent their interest?" she asked with surprise.

I turned on her. "Mars rejects me. I face the alternative that your haloed leader has suggested. I display a normal reaction of fear and unhappiness and am suddenly regarded as a clinical specimen."

"But we have never seen tears."

"No. And you've never heard of compassion either," I retorted. "Or has that word also been dropped by your people generations ago?"

She hesitated a moment. "You wish to go to Mars very much?"

"I want to go home." My voice was beginning to break, but I quickly regained my poise, lest I once again became a "rare occurrence."

"I, myself, will make another plea for you —to Mars," she announced. "The ruler of Mars respects my opinion on a great many matters. I will state that it is my opinion that he should accept you."

"He won't," I answered. "The mere fact that you and your people don't want me alone makes me undesirable."

"I have thought of that. You have a point. Leader Corla presented the facts pertinent to your person. I will state our objections; there is nothing we can learn from you. You represent an evolution which we have long since surpassed. But I will state that for the planet Mars, you will be a most interesting specimen to study."

Before I could voice any objections, she called the meeting to order and presented her decision. Obviously, it was accepted, for they all returned to their seats. Sanau went to the television set and adjusted the earphones. Soon the familiar droning began.

I listened to her swift calculations; I watched her write down numbers, which she would instantly relate, then the pause as she listened, then more numbers, more listening, writing, numbers. It seemed to go on forever.

At last she removed the earphones and clicked off the set. I looked at her; the leaders looked at her.

"All is not lost." Her voice held some confidence. "The ruler of Mars states he will reconsider with his council. We shall receive his answer shortly."

"But you turned off the machine."

"It will take a good ten minutes. Mars is extremely low on certain minerals which supply the power to operate the connection. There is no sense in wasting this power to keep the connection going. At the present they are farming some of these minerals from their moon, but it will take many years before their supply is restored. They will only contact us if they agree to accept you."

There was nothing to do but wait. I tried the power of positive thinking. They would accept me. They had to! What was he like, this ruler of my neighboring planet? Did he have more compassion than the Yargonians? The fact that he had agreed to reconsider proved a certain amount of elasticity, a certain willingness to revoke a decision.

As if reading my thoughts, Sanau whispered, "If you *are* accepted, the ruler himself shall accept you in person."

"In person? You mean he'll come here and get me?"

"Of course not! Mars has no spaceships. We are the only planet in any of the solar systems who has conquered space. If Mars does decide to accept you, we will receive the image of the ruler on our television screen. It takes less power to send through his image than the two-way radio system we have used up till now."

We continued our silent wait, but my thoughts had plunged into hopeless despair. Suddenly it didn't matter if Mars accepted me. They had no spaceships. This simple statement had erased any faint hope that lay in the banishment to Mars. Mars no longer represented a haven from which I could ultimately leave to return to my own Earth. Mars would merely be an exile, slightly preferable to exile in space, but prison enough for me.

I found myself beginning to grow tense as the minutes passed. Funny how we never give up. If I had been given such an alternative to accept, theoretically, I would probably have said that neither would be worth accepting and that it would be futile to go on trying to live. But since this was not a hypothetical situation, since this was all very real and it was happening to me, I found myself waiting with something very like hope for the appearance of the ruler of Mars. Which proves, I suppose, that the average person can take more adversity than he realizes before he throws in the sponge. For I hadn't given up—not by a long shot.

It came to me suddenly that I had been sitting for quite a spell. Shouldn't we have received word by now? I turned to Sanau. She sat by my side, refusing to look my way. I couldn't tell what thoughts she experienced. The set of her shoulders was as erect as ever, her face externally impassive, yet I think she was disappointed. Not disappointment through compassion, but disappointment in her own inability to revoke the decision.

"The time's up, isn't it?" I whispered.

She didn't answer. Just as I was about to repeat the statement, she turned to me.

"It's over now. Ten minutes have passed."

I looked at her. If she felt any personal defeat, her bland expression belied it. The very callousness of her calm brought a final flare of anger from me.

"And don't say you're sorry," I spit out. "I can see you're not."

"I am not sorry. I certainly could not wish you to be willed on the good people of Mars if they themselves do not desire it. They are superior to you in mind and manner; it would no doubt be almost as large a hardship to suffer your presence for the people of Mars as it has been for our people to bear. I know that were the situation reversed, we would not accept you."

I just sat and stared in frank amazement. I couldn't quite digest the cruel message conveyed in her polite tone. No human could speak to another with such a lack of feeling, but she had no feeling and she was proud of it.

She touched my arm, signaling that it was time to leave. Suddenly there was a sharp intake of Yargonian breaths. A bright beam of light began to dance across the screen.

"You're accepted," Sanau said coolly. "In a moment, the likeness of the ruler of Mars will appear."

I wrung my hands with excitement. In a moment I would see him; the kind man who had changed my fate.

"I want to warn you about the ruler of Mars," Sanau began . . .

She never got any further. My stifled scream drowned out her words.

The image of the ruler of Mars filled the screen. My eyes bulged in terror. The ruler of Mars definitely did not look like a Yargonian.

He looked like nothing I had ever seen before!

CHAPTER 11

He was a man. That is, I assume he was a man. He was tall—taller than a Yargonian, yet stooped double. His arms hung to the ground like a gorilla's and he had webbed feet. His skin was encrusted with scales like a reptile's. To accurately describe him is impossible. There was only a semblance of features on his lizardlike face: bleary eyes that flickered like a lizard's, a flat nose, a fish's mouth. He wore a shield of armor.

I buried my face in my hands.

I couldn't remember any horror movies that terrified me more than this monstrous vision. And he had accepted me!

After a moment, this vision disappeared, the lights went up, and a huge cheer echoed throughout the auditorium. The Yargonians were delighted.

I stared at them. What kind of people were they anyway? Was I supposed to revel in joy at the prospect of a lifetime among a race of monsters?

Without a word, Sanau hurried me from the room. Possibly she hoped to avoid any emotional outbreak on my part. She kept up a steady flow of conversation during the ride home and to my chambers.

I barely listened. I did gather, however, that extensive preparations now had to be made. A crew had to be selected, a chaperone for me, probably herself, as I would have to be presented to the ruler. Proper flying conditions must be calculated, the advisability of going in a fleet or in a large mother ship. There must be no slipup anywhere.

I was left completely alone for two full days. At the end of this period, Sanau appeared.

She seemed bursting with official business, despite her perpetual calm, but I could see that she had been hard at work. There were slight gray circles under her lovely eyes; even her shoulders had lost some of their West Point bearing.

"I have not slept in forty-eight hours," she announced, as if I was supposed to cheer her or something.

"I am here to take your measurements. We are making you a climate suit for Mars."

I stood in defiant silence while she measured my shoulders, hips, and waist.

"You will take six pressure suits," she explained as she wrote down the last measurement. "They will protect you against the climate of Mars. The people of Mars have developed their own skin covering to protect themselves, and their fight for survival against their cooling planet and lack of oxygen is so rigorous that they will have little time to attend to unnecessary comforts for you. Therefore, it is important for us to provide such needs."

I remained silent through all of this. There was nothing for me to say, unless it was a fresh outbreak against their cruelty in this banishment and, since it would only fall on deaf ears, I decided it was best to spare myself the effort. I was wise enough to know futility when I met it.

My silence stimulated Sanau. Perhaps I wasn't acting in the hysterical fashion she expected. She hadn't learned to recognize mute and complete desolation.

She became more gregarious than was her custom. "I suppose the appearance of the ruler of Mars seemed startling."

I could only stare in reply to this understatement.

"Keep this in mind," she cautioned. "Under that reptilian body is the soul of a human and in that head is a brain more massive than your Professor Einstein's. You must realize a conventional appearance is not the most important thing in life, my little Earth friend."

"That's all very well for you to say!" I had finally found my voice. "Tell me to go off happily to dwell with this monstrous-looking race while you live happily in comfort, dining with diamond forks and wearing satin pants. Tell me to live on a cold planet with six space suits and little oxygen. It's easy for a great superior person such as you to give me this superior advice, but if you were to answer honestly, could you accept this decision with real happiness?"

"My friend," she spoke seriously, "it would make very little difference to me, or to any Yargonian, if I wore bright silken pants or a pressure suit."

I didn't answer. There was no refuting this statement. If Sanau lacked warmth, emotion, or compassion, she certainly did not lack perception. She sensed that she was far from making her point and, in an effort to guide me, she sat down and began to speak. I knew it was an effort on her part, for she had many duties to attend to, and spending time conversing with me was the least of her pleasures. Her eyes were heavy. Her physical weariness seemed to surge through her entire frame. She spoke low and intensely.

"Have you noticed, my friend, the absence of stores and shops on our planet?"

I said I had noticed nothing except flying scenery.

"We have buildings where wearing attire can be obtained," she went on, "but we do not have shops and stores such as you know them, for as you have seen, everyone on our planet dresses alike."

I hadn't realized this. The panorama of color had been too startling for me to notice the lack of individuality.

"And do you know why this custom was instigated?" Sanau asked.

Naturally, I couldn't even hazard a guess.

"The first step toward self-advancement on this planet came when we abolished what you call the seven deadly sins: pride, covetousness, lust, anger, gluttony, envy, and sloth. For example, to rid our planet of envy, we first had to analyze what caused envy. To make a basic example that even you must perceive, let us say a woman attends a social function and sees another woman attired in a more elaborate outfit. This causes her to receive attention beyond her merits and the less attractively gowned woman immediately feels envy. But, place all women in the same costume and the one with superior intellect gains the plaudits and attention. This causes women to divert their energy to self-improvement rather than personal vanity."

I knew she was explaining all this to fit me for life on Mars and the grim climate suits, but it wasn't going to work. One carefully planned argument couldn't send me off with cries of gratitude.

I told her as much. I also stated that I liked pretty clothes and enjoyed shopping for them.

"Ah, but if your mind was mature, you would have no time for such foolish vanity."

"I don't agree." I crossed the room and stared out at the cold mountain to signify that as far as I was concerned, the discussion was terminated.

"Enjoyment after a time becomes comparable," Sanau said softly.

I kept my back tense and straight.

"When you were a child, how did you divert yourself?" she persisted gently.

I sighed and crossed the room. "Games, I suppose. Tag, roller skates, and all the rest." It all seemed so long ago.

She nodded in agreement. "That is correct. Then, as you matured, you no longer found such games diverting. Other pastimes replaced them."

I grudgingly nodded in assent. I knew she hadn't finished.

"Transfer this thought to centuries of maturity. Dressing one's form is as mildly diverting to a Yargonian female as a game of tag would be to you in your present stage."

I didn't answer, but no answer was needed. Sanau's eyes were sparkling. Her fatigue seemed to have vanished. I was aware that she was no longer speaking for my benefit alone. She was reveling in the development of her people and their accomplishments.

"Real excitement is the comprehension of facts of which you were formerly unaware. A new language is an excellent example. What can replace the thrill of learning a new tongue and, in so doing, unfolding thousands of mysteries of another race and civilization?"

"What about the men of this planet? Are they also free of all vanity?"

Of course they were. Sanau went on to explain that they too were spared the burden of physical competition. Some five hundred years back, the males began shaving their heads when they learned that the man who lost his hair sometimes felt a physical inferiority to his more fortunate brother who was blessed with a full crop of hair. And since feelings of inferiority are contributing factors to envy, lust, and gluttony, they found the complete elimination of hair for all males an excellent solution.

This logic managed to filter through my depression, and I was forced to concede to the wisdom of this plan. Without having to contend with envy and physical attraction, life would be more simple. Perhaps, if I eliminated the seven deadly sins from my personality, I wouldn't even mind a life on Mars.

This thought snapped me back to the grim realization of my hapless future and I suddenly hated this calm woman who sat and told me what I should like and dislike. This couldn't actually be happening to me—Janet Cooper—it couldn't be!

But somehow I'd find a way out. I wasn't going to accept this with calm resignation. There had to be a way!

My mind echoed this chant long after Sanau had gone. I kept repeating it to myself as I watched the sun slip behind the mountain, and I repeated it as I fell asleep. This couldn't happen to me, but I was beginning to feel that it might.

CHAPTER 12

It was still dark, yet Sanau was shaking me. At first I thought I was dreaming, but the gentle but persistent shaking continued. I opened my eyes; the light in the room was dim. I sat up.

"What time is it?"

"It is almost dawn."

Then I became thoroughly aware, filled with thoughts of impending disaster.

They were sending me off to Mars now, in the middle of the night.

But Sanau's rare smile dispelled this fear. "I have magnificent news for you." She was radiant.

"They're going to send me home!" For a moment I also looked radiant.

She shook her head and I sank back on the pillows.

"Today will be the most memorable day in your life," she stated.

My interest became slightly aroused for Sanau was not acting like Sanau. Her hands fluttered and a vein on her temple throbbed visibly. In fact, Sanau was almost behaving like a human being from Earth. A very composed human, by our standards, but I'm sure that in Yargonian circles she would be classed as wildly emotional.

"Tonight at sundown . . ." she stopped abruptly and made an effort to force her voice to its usual pitch of composure.

"Tonight at sundown, you will be presented to His Almighty Highness, the Yargo!"

There! It was out! She looked exalted and stared at me as if she half expected me to spring to my feet in ecstacy. I must admit that I was slightly impressed, or maybe it was more curiosity than anything else. For once, it was I who achieved the bland expression, and I merely asked how it had all come about. She said His Almighty Highness himself had made the request.

"Does it have anything to do with my being sent to Mars?"

She nodded and somewhere an ember of hope grew warm. All was not yet lost, not until I was on Mars.

With rare calm I announced that I would be ready at sundown but for the time being intended to resume my slumber.

"You will not sleep!" she commanded, as she ripped the covers from me. She raised the blinds and the pale early sunlight slithered apologetically into the room.

I had no alternative but to rise, shower, and fully arouse myself. Once again, as I brushed my teeth, I was startled by the seemingly increasing attractiveness my rather plain features had taken on. I stared in the mirror. My nose was always short and fairly presentable, my eyes were blue; the change was almost indefinable. There was a smooth perfection my skin had never known, a luminous quality to my eyes, and a true blood-red color in my lips. Even my cheeks had taken on a faint tinge of color to add the flattery that no artificial rouge could ever equal. No matter how great my antagonism toward these people, I was forced to admit that perhaps there was something to the superiority of their planet. Physically, even I was growing into a better specimen.

The moment breakfast was served Sanau plunged into the details.

"There will be a large banquet this evening. All the leaders will be present."

I attacked my cereal and asked just how and why the Yargo had come to make this fantastic request.

"A full report of your intended journey has been presented to him, as well as your hostility against the planet Mars and its inhabitants. He displayed extreme compassion."

"He did!" My mouth was full so I did not sound as startled as I actually was.

"This should not surprise you, or rather, it would not if you were acquainted with the magnificent and unbelievable powers of His Majesty which fully extend to the most insignificant beings. As I have so often stated, the Yargo is unlike any other mortal. It is most natural for him to have complete compassion for your plight. He is the most compassionate man in this or any world."

"Then how can he even think of sending me off to Mars?"

"Because his feeling extends to the plight of the people on your planet as well. To be truly just, one must do the most good for the most number. What is one life such as yours against an entire civilization?"

I told her it was my life and since it happened to be the only one I had, I was plenty particular about what happened to it.

Well, it seemed the Yargo even understood my feelings about that, or so Sanau led me to believe.

"He is also aware that you have known little but anxiety during your stay on our planet and, therefore, is desirous of receiving you formally before you depart and conveying his apologies."

The bright new ember of hope turned to a cold lump of ash.

Come what may, I was headed for Mars and this big dinner was merely a formality, lest they secretly admit they had acted in a most unsuperior manner. Bring the prisoner in; treat her as an equal for one short evening; feed her well; display the great Yargonian charm and hospitality; even bring out the Great White Father himself, then send her off with your own consciences bright and sparkling. "We did our best, gentlemen, till the end!"

I pushed my chair from the table and walked to the window. All I could see was my own immediate peril. There was no hope anywhere. The quiet room, the calm Sanau, even a bird that resembled a robin seemed to chirp it outside the window. "Give up, girl, this is the end, this is the end."

I unclenched my hands. Maybe I should stop fighting. Maybe I should just relax and accept my fate like a drowning man. They say if you don't struggle, it's actually a peaceful sensation when your lungs fill with water the final time. Just relax, go live with the Martians—the Martians! *No!* I whirled around. If the Yargo was so superior maybe I did have a chance. If I could really make him understand how I felt, convince him that I could return to Earth and remain quiet about all I had seen. I'd fight for my life tonight, but with dignity and brains. I'd show them how inferior an Earth-being was. I'd outwit them and their precious leader, and get back to Earth.

I returned to the table and asked Sanau if I was to attend the dinner as a guest. I wasn't sure. After all, they might expect me to serve it.

"You will be presented at the dinner as an honored guest." Then she summoned the attendants to remove the breakfast table. She ordered me in the tone of a commanding general to sit down and take heed of her every word. I obeyed, wondering what was coming next.

"Now then, there is much I am forced to teach you in the ways of protocol. I doubt if you can absorb all the proper form in one short day, but we shall accomplish what we can. There are some very important facts with which I must acquaint you."

"Like which knife and fork to use?"

She smiled. "We are not concerned with your eating habits, but there are some customs you must adhere to. If nothing else, you must remember the Yargo is untouchable."

I nodded. I hadn't the least intention of touching him.

"You must not extend your hand in greeting. Should you gather enough courage to actually converse with our magnificent leader and enter another plea on your behalf, which I am sure is uppermost in your mind, you must refrain from grasping his arm, as seems to be one of your most annoying customs. Above all, he must not be touched."

"You mean literally?" This was a surprise.

"Literally and absolutely."

"What about his wife?" I've always been the practical type.

"What is a wife?"

I looked at her quickly, expecting some kind of veiled levity beneath this question, but Sanau's open stare convinced me her question was a serious one.

"You mean you don't know what a wife is?" I couldn't keep the pleasure from my voice. Oh, the gloriousness of life for a moment, to actually have to explain something to Sanau! At first she appeared completely ignorant on the subject of wives, so in great detail I explained the meaning and significance of a wife, not neglecting to point out that very often they were the power behind the throne and that I had been on the verge of becoming one when her off-beam spaceship kidnapped me.

She listened with interest mingled with amusement, then gradually her face brightened. Yes, now it came back to her. History, I must understand, was not her best subject, but now that I had gone into it, yes, she did recall that at one time, maybe several thousand years back, the condition called "marriage" had existed in their planet. But, of course, with other evils, it too had long since been abolished.

"But if there is no marriage," I insisted, "what are your moral standards around here? What about children? What about love?"

She seemed about to answer, then abruptly changed her mind.

"There is not time to inform you of the ways of our planet. You will have no cause to need such information, but there is much information you must know about tonight's meeting."

I was insulted and told her so. After all, I had answered her question about a wife. I had gone to great lengths to make it clear. Did she think I was too inferior to understand the domestic life of her great planet?

Her tone was almost gentle when she answered. "Perhaps I have misled you. We do not think of you as inferior. Not in the way you interpret the word. A child is not inferior, it is young, uneducated, and therefore, unwise, inferior. You and your people have thirty thousand years of trial and error before you can even hope to approach our civilization."

"But those leaders said I was an inferior specimen." This still rankled me.

"The leaders saw you as a female with no other purpose in life but to serve your own emotions. Compared to Doctor Blount, you are an inferior specimen. What the leaders failed to grasp at that first meeting is that you are typical of ninety percent of Earth's female population. No, I would say you are a very true specimen."

This explanation helped to restore some of my self-esteem, and gave me the added courage to express some of my innate friendliness. I leaned forward. "Sanau," I said gently, "I really could like you, if you'd let me, and I feel you could like me also. Why should we be hostile? Try and understand me for what I am, just as I'm trying to do with you. Understand me and use your influence with the Yargo. Ask him to send me back to Earth."

"I will do no such thing."

"But why? You're the only one who can help me!"

"Because my opinion, as well as that of the leaders, is that you, with possession of this knowledge, would cause great havoc on your Earth. Your planet would become a

menace to the entire planetary system. I stand
in firm agreement that exile to Mars is the
only solution."

"But I won't even say I've been here. I
swear it! I give you my word!"

"What is your word? We value only proof
and facts. Words, promises, luck; these are
unknown quantities on this planet and many
other planets. With your insatiable ego and
vanity you could never hold still."

"I could," I wailed. "I want to go home!
I'd do anything to go home!"

"I am not concerned with your wants or
hopes or wishes. My only concern is to dismiss
you from this planet as soon as possible. The
strain of wasting so much time with you is
beginning to tell on both myself and my
work."

I stared at her in mute embarrassment and
pain. No one, not even my mother or grandmother in their most deprecating moments,
had ever defined my faults with such stark
finality.

She couldn't hurt me anymore. I put my
next question to her, heedless of the stab the
answer might bring. I didn't matter anymore; now I was merely satisfying my
curiosity.

"Sanau, why do you hate me?"

"I am not capable of hate."

"Then I'll put it this way. Why don't you
like me?"

"Like you? Whatever could I like about
you?"

"But there are things about me that you dislike?"

She smiled. "I neither like nor dislike you. There is nothing actually to dislike in you, yet neither is there anything about you to like or admire. You know very little, yet you express no desire to learn. Instead of looking expectantly toward a new life on a planet inhabited by more intelligent people, you whimper to return to a stagnant place you call home. In view of tonight's meeting with His Highness, you are not enthralled with the opportunity to meet the greatest man in this or any world. You merely look upon it as one more chance to enter a further plea to return to a backward civilization."

"Sanau, if you were stranded on another planet, wouldn't you do everything in your power to get back here?"

"Yes, for we are the most brilliant and most advanced planet in this or any solar system. But if I was given the opportunity to get to a planet that exceeded Yargo, even if the people did not resemble me, if they were peace-loving and willing to accept me, then I would be exhilarated at the opportunity."

I stood up and began to pace the room. There must be one chord I could strike that would put us on a common meeting ground. Somehow I must inspire some human feeling within her. Thus far, the only animation I had witnessed was the change in her expression each time the great Yargo's name had been mentioned, so I tried an illustration that might in some way be comprehensible to her.

"Look, Sanau, suppose for some reason beyond your control you would never be allowed to see the great Yargo again. How would you feel?"

"Never to gaze upon him again? Never to enjoy the advantage of his divine leadership? Life would lose its motivation."

I hadn't expected such a soul-baring answer. This was no time to pry. At least I had her thinking along the right lines.

"Sanau, on Earth, there's someone about whom I also feel this way. His name is David. Now can you understand?"

"David?" She turned the name on her tongue. "David? You have no ruler by that name."

"He's not a ruler; he's just a man. The man I love."

She laughed quite merrily. "Oh, love. Love which develops into your union called marriage." Then her eyes narrowed and the scorn shot from her voice.

"Love! Do you dare call that love? Do you dare defile the sanctity of the great Yargo and compare my devotion toward him to that retarded passion you hold for this mere man? Love! Love is to behold a vision of perfection. That is the Yargo. Other than that, there is no love!"

On this I gave up. I knew the futility of a closed mind. Sanau didn't have opinions, she made statements. Statements of fact. And statements of fact, in this world, were not to be contradicted.

She obviously sensed that I had abandoned the point I had been striving to make, for in a sudden brisk manner she turned the conversation back to the coming events of the evening.

Once again she stressed that I must not touch the Yargo, to which I nodded wearily in agreement.

Point two: I was not to start a conversation unless he addressed me first.

Point three: I was not to touch food until he did. I listened and nodded like an automaton. I was drilled in court etiquette. I must bow low, I must never open a new line of conversation or subject matter, I must not touch him, I must not touch him, I must not touch him. I listened, I nodded, I grew sleepy.

Most of the instructions were fairly simple, but Sanau repeated them over and over as if I was a dumb animal that didn't quite understand and must learn the sound of words to associate it with an action.

Finally, I had taken enough. I jumped up and firmly stated that, simple of mind I might be, I only needed to be told a law of etiquette twice.

Oddly enough, she took my outburst in good grace. She even managed a smile.

"I suppose your nerves are frayed. Even a Yargonian finds himself slightly off balance at the actual prospect of presentation to the Almighty One. There is more I should impart but I can see your condition does not warrant additional absorption. You will do well to rest the remainder of the day." She walked to the wall and pressed the panel.

"I shall return at sundown. You shall be prepared and waiting. Rest your fears; it will be a glorious experience. I only trust you will not be too filled with awe to enjoy it."

On that note she left me. Filled with awe indeed! The only offering this meeting held for me was one last chance to enter a plea to go home. As for the man himself, I hadn't even given him a thought.

Maybe I was inferior as Sanau had said. I felt in no way uplifted at the thought of meeting this fantastic man, and I very much doubted if I could ever rise to the heights of superiority to fall on my face at the mere mention of his name.

I flopped on the bed. It was useless to rant and rage in solitary confinement. No, I would do well to rest and have all my wits about me, for no matter how I dismissed the importance of this man, tonight would be important to me; for after tonight there was tomorrow and tomorrow meant Mars.

I rested a little. I thought and planned and schemed, always winding up in a blind alley. Finally, I grew so tired that after a bit I did doze fitfully, only to awaken and rehash my plans once again. Actually, I had no definite plan. I'd have to meet him first then try my strategy. What would be more practical? Honesty? Charm, or my wits? I just didn't know. After a time I gave up trying to think. But I never gave up hope—those Martians weren't going to get me, not without one whale of a struggle.

CHAPTER 13

Naturally, I was dressed and waiting long before sundown, and when sundown should have arrived, the sun lingered on top of that mountain as if it was glued there. Its descent was so fractional that it reminded me of the hands of a clock. As a child I used to fasten my stare to a clock hoping to catch the hand in its jump from minute to minute. I was never successful, yet somehow it did manage to move. So did the sun, but by the time the last bit of rosy had disappeared, I was as exhausted as if I had literally pushed that great ball of fire behind the mountain with my bare hands.

Sanau appeared just as the sky settled into its gray early-evening glow.

For a moment we appraised each other in silence, as if both in final accord as to the importance of the coming event. She nodded and led me to the waiting car.

Once again came the familiar ride through the city, but it was shorter than usual and this time the car halted before a small drawbridge. We left the car and crossed the bridge by foot with four sentries in attendance. Although the building we approached differed little in architecture from the other imposing structures I had visited, somehow I experienced the feeling of entering a medieval castle. Maybe it was the drawbridge and the sentries, but there was an added feeling of pomp and ceremony in the atmosphere.

Once over the bridge I stopped a moment to survey the grounds. So this was the residence of Mr. God Almighty! Close up it took on the added feeling of a royal residence. In fact, I began to visualize the Yargo as a fat sultanlike man, sitting on a cushion inside, surrounded by a bevy of Yargonian beauties. Huge yellow ground lights flanked this castle and attached to each light a guard stood at attention, forming a human chain of man and light around the building itself.

I leaned close to Sanau and whispered: "If your race is so superior, then why all the guards around the Yargo? I should think your people would certainly be above violence, and especially if they worship him so!"

Sanau explained with frigid politeness that the sentries were merely honor guards. To a Yargonian youth, the highest honor he can attain is to stand allegiance to his leader, to be allowed the proximity of the Yargo.

Drawing herself to her full height, she added, "In schools throughout our planet, this assignment is the award accorded to the most brilliant student."

Were the ground lights to prevent enemy attack?

"They are radar beams," I was told. "Each

beam is in direct contact with a spaceship. In this way the Yargo can communicate directly with any ship off in space."

We entered the building and walked through massive reception halls lined with honor guards. They stood so erect, their bald pates gleaming in the light, their eyes directly in front of them.

I told Sanau they reminded me of the guards in front of Buckingham Palace.

"Is that a dwelling of one of your leaders?" she asked.

"Not ours. England's."

"Is not England part of your planet?"

I nodded in an offhand manner. I was completely immersed in the beauty of the palace. I was sure no king in any land dwelled in such splendor.

But Sanau persisted. "Is not England's leader also one of your leaders?"

"Well, not exactly." I followed Sanau to an ornate mosaic bench. We sat down presumably to await our admittance to the inner chambers.

"What do you mean 'not exactly'? Are you not one world?"

"I guess not. Not at the moment anyway."

I was thankful for the sentry who came to claim Sanau's attention. She stepped aside to discuss some matter, probably me, because he turned to glance at me several times during their conversation. In turn, I sat and tried to appear completely unconcerned, in imitation of one of Sanau's most bland expressions. At the moment I didn't care what was said about me; anything seemed preferable to Sanau's persistent interrogation. No matter what we discussed, even if it was something as impersonal as England or Buckingham Palace, I wound up on the defensive and always seemed to come out second best.

The more I explained, the less attractive Earth appeared to be, or so her questions made it seem. A strong protective instinct welled within me for England as well as America. It was odd. I was the girl who had never been as far from home as Chicago, yet suddenly I had stopped thinking of my world as just American or the city in which I lived. It was my planet, every bit of it, from the darkest jungles of Africa to the iron curtain that veiled Russia, for Russia was part of my planet, closer than the planet Yargo or Mars could ever be. Some of us thought differently, had different policies, but we were all human beings on the same Earth, breathing the same air, warming in the same sun, and looking at the same moon. It was amazing: suddenly I found myself looking at Russia as the black sheep of a large family, rather than the aggressive warring nation that she actually was. At that moment it seemed impossible to think otherwise; how else could you think when you began to encompass other worlds and other universes?

The sentry and Sanau, having apparently settled things to their mutual satisfaction, parted, and she returned to the bench beside me.

"The meeting will take place in a moment. At present the leaders are taking their seats. You remember everything?"

I nodded and smiled slightly. For at that moment Sanau reminded me of a nervous mother who prayed her child would not disgrace her at the school recital.

Her next question was even more in character.

"You are quite sure you remember. What, above all, must you always bear in mind?"

Tonelessly I chanted, "Above all, I am not to touch the Yargo."

She bobbed her head in a quick nervous nod, then settled back with an air of resigned patience, as if she had mentally said, "Well, come what may, I've done my best." But she was far from calm. The telltale pulse on her brow gave her away and, upon closer inspection, I noticed her delicate nostrils quiver slightly. All highly irregular actions for Sanau.

Not that I was completely serene. How on earth *was* I to act before this man? Maybe he'd have two heads. They'd probably think that was fine up here, nothing freakish at all. Just two superior brains instead of one.

Superior world indeed! "Don't touch him! Don't talk to him!" I probably shouldn't even breathe in front of him. Down on Earth people shook hands with the president. Even kings shook hands. We sure could teach them a few things about democracy.

Sanau suddenly arose to greet the man who was approaching us. On closer inspection I noted it was Leader Corla; the one who thought I was such an inferior specimen. But this time he was smiling pleasantly, his handsome face radiating a welcome.

At first I thought this good humor was just for Sanau, but after greeting her, he turned his bright smile on me, and then, just as if we had never met before, he said to me in perfect English, "I bid you welcome to the shrine of His Almighty Highness, the Yargo."

I was all set to bury the hatchet and compliment him on his English, but suddenly he was lying on his face. So was Sanau. For a second I was floored at this new respect. I rather felt he was overdoing things until I realized he had mentioned the Yargo's name in the presence of two people—himself and Sanau.

They both rose after the necessary chant and Sanau turned to me.

"I think it was extremely gracious for Leader Corla to master a welcoming speech in your tongue."

I agreed. I thanked him and said I thought it was very nice, but from the expression on his face I realized his knowledge of my language did not extend beyond the one line he had so painstakingly learned.

"You will follow Leader Corla," Sanau announced.

Willingly, I turned and walked after him but Sanau remained in the reception hall. I half stopped. Wasn't she coming? Then, since Leader Corla was already a good six feet ahead of me, I stumbled after him. There was no time to ask questions, yet somehow it had never entered my mind that this meeting would take place without Sanau. I suppose, without realizing it, I had depended upon her for some kind of support and guidance. Now, some strange kind of loyalty demanded that I do Sanau proud, so I followed Leader Corla down long corridors and up a wide stairway.

It was a staircase fit for a king. Crystal chandeliers threw off soft indirect rays of light. Velvet, soft as fur, covered the steps. Four sentries stood waiting at the top. They joined us and escorted us down a corridor that ended in a blank wall. I was sure it would open, and of course, it did.

It opened on a ballroom that glittered like a movie set. There must have been a thousand individual tables spaced about the floor. These faced a horseshoe-shaped dais that was situated at the far end of the room. My eyes beheld a panorama of color and spectacle that no stage director could hope to equal. The glittering array of Yargonians, the dazzling reflection of the cutlery that sparkled like the diamonds they were, the massive dais to which I was being led.

It was a banquet all right, a banquet to end all banquets. Every Yargonian Leader and subleader was present. Every important personage on the entire planet must have been there.

As I approached I slowly got my bearings and I quickly searched the dais for Him. Well, if he was there, he looked like everyone else. I walked straight, fully aware that every superior Yargonian eye was trained directly on me. I held my head high and felt pretty sure I didn't look too inferior.

Leader Corla led me directly to the center of the dais. There were three empty chairs. He took one, pointed to another that I was to occupy, and that left one empty chair between us, obviously for Him.

I thought of Sanau's warning—"Don't touch him"—and had to smile. The seating arrangement took excellent care of this. On my one side sat a leader; I couldn't remember his name, but he had been at my hearing. On my other side was the empty chair, separated from me by at least three feet, and another three feet separated it on the other side from Leader Corla.

I sat and waited expectantly but nothing happened. Then a horrible thought struck me; maybe he was already here! Maybe he was invisible or maybe he didn't actually exist at all, except in the minds of these people. Maybe he was God—the same God as ours—only maybe these people had pro-

gressed to such a degree that they could
actually speak to him.

I looked at the empty chair and smiled
weakly. I looked around quickly to see if my
action had been noticed; if it had, no one
reacted.

No, I decided, he had to be real. There was
too big an air of expectancy permeating the
room. Even I could sense it. These people
were definitely waiting for someone and it
hadn't been me.

As if to bear out this decision, a sudden
electric tension seemed to grip the room. A
complete silence settled over everyone and
they sat at attention. On the dais around me
I even felt the leaders go rigid as if from an
electric shock, and then, as if a command had
been given, every eye was suddenly riveted
to the side wall.

The tension reached out and swirled me in
its grip. My eyes also shot to the wall. It
began to part slowly, ever so slowly . . .

CHAPTER 14

Sanau had been right. He *was* supreme!

Every Yargonian present, magnificent as he might be, paled into insignificance in comparison with this ruler among men. It was as if viewing a lion standing amidst scrawny cubs.

At first I thought it was his carriage that made him so different. He moved like a panther, with the regal bearing of a lion. Yes! That was it! So majestic, so graceful, so unreal were his movements that he seemed— like a panther—a lion—a true king. His dress was identical to the others, yet his body was disturbingly different; not in stature, but rather in muscular coordination. I felt I could almost see the play of his muscles in perfect rhythm. He reminded me of a statue of a god in bronze, the likes of which an artist sees only in his mind's eye.

He walked slowly, seemingly unaware of the spellbinding effect he created on all who gazed upon him. He reached the dais and raised his hand to signify a greeting. His people rose in a body and stood at attention for a moment, gazing upon him in open admiration and worship.

There was worship in their gaze, as if a group of priests were suddenly to behold a vision of their most holy saint. And, as I watched this spectacle, it came to me that this complete adoration was self-imposed among his people. There was nothing in his manner to demand or signify that he expected it. He was neither pompous nor autocratic. His attitude toward his subjects was that of quiet dignity and genuine regard.

I was fighting for my own equilibrium, and when he turned his gaze toward me, I became so rattled I was unable to meet his eyes. I found it impossible even to return the warm smile he bestowed on me. I was about to say something to cover my nervousness when I fortunately realized it was not proper to speak unless he opened the conversation. This sudden recollection probably saved us both a good deal of embarrassment, for heaven only knows what inanity might have dropped from my lips.

I kept my eyes glued to the floor. I wanted to look at him; I was drawn to him with almost a hypnotic force, yet it was impossible to meet his eyes. His eyes! Yes, that was it. His eyes!

They were not like the others; oblique in shape, yes, but they were a brilliant aquamarine. An aquamarine so startling they looked like two large jewels against his bronze skin. Perhaps he had a hypnotic power. After all, one glance and I had lost all sense of balance.

He motioned me to sit. Somehow I managed to do this with my usual charm and grace which merely sent a glass tumbler filled with water crashing to the floor.

But he never even blinked one of those devastating eyes. He flashed me another lethal smile and said, "May I extend a belated welcome to the planet Yargo."

I said thank you. Not very noteworthy, but at least I managed to speak.

Again he smiled and again I looked away. It would take time to build a resistance to those eyes.

He turned his attention to Leader Corla. This gave me a brief respite to gather my disintegrated thoughts. I was filled with self-loathing. He had welcomed me. He had spoken first, and I had acted with less poise than I had ever shown in my life. I sure was a credit to my race. He had said welcome and I had mumbled thank you. Thank you! Thank you for what??? For snatching me off Earth, humiliating me, and now packing me off to join some subhuman-looking race. Oh, why hadn't I had the gumption to say "Don't welcome me, just send me back where you found me"?

But I hadn't. Brilliant in repartee when I am alone but dim-witted, faltering, and always conforming to the expected when a real situation arises. Even on another planet, I was the same—plain, ordinary Janet Cooper.

But I would change. In my dreams I'm the

bravest heroine of all. In my imagination all these things are within me, and tonight they would come out. I might go to Mars, but at least I'd go with some self-respect.

The next time he spoke to me I'd avoid his eyes, that was all. But his voice was disturbing too.

The first course of food was placed before me. I tried to force it down my throat. I had to eat to prove I was not as stupefied by his presence as I had appeared. With this thought in mind, I managed to get some of it down.

It was during the second course, just as I had despaired that he would ever turn my way again, that he spoke. Before I even looked up, I knew he was going to speak. I could actually feel his gaze.

He said, "I want you to know I am most sympathetic to the situation in which we have placed you. I am completely aware of your feelings."

The real but hidden Janet Cooper shouted mutely, "Then send me home!"

But the lump of flesh that was present merely simpered idiotically and marveled at the perfection of his English and thought, didn't he have marvelous teeth!

He returned his attention to Leader Corla. I had missed my chance and probably for good this time! He had led right with his chin, given me a perfect opening but, no, I had sat there grinning as if he was awarding me a silver star instead of desolate exile. Well, I deserved to go to Mars. I deserved everything that was coming to me, but my luck had definitely changed for once again he favored me with a remark.

"I trust you find our food palatable."

"It's marvelous." I was ready for him this time, determined to keep the conversation going if I had to discuss the price of potatoes. "It must agree with everyone," I plunged on. "I have never seen such beautiful women as the women on your planet." During my statement, those incredible eyes had never left my face and the effect was actually unbearable for my equilibrium. I looked away and tried to breathe naturally.

Then he laughed. I turned quickly, but it was a genuine and innocent laugh. Innocent in intent, but devastating to me. It was difficult enough to keep my bearings when his face was in repose. But when he laughed the effect was spellbinding. I gave up fighting against his abnormal charm. He was not the king of men for naught. There definitely was something super human about him. This man would never have to invade a world; he could walk in and charm it into paralysis.

He allowed his features to regain their composure but let the smile linger in his eyes.

"My dear little Earth friend, our women are beautiful, but I take it you have not studied your own image of late. You are also lovely without the aid of any artifice."

I didn't answer. I couldn't. Even if he had added, "And would you like to go home?" I would have only stared in the same idiotic gaze. He thought I was lovely! Me, Plain Janet Cooper! Plain even by Earth's standards. I was lovely! Among all these superwomen, this fantastic man thought I was lovely.

But when I had finally recouped enough courage to look at him, he had returned his attention to his food and Leader Corla.

I had lost him again. Probably for good this time. Dessert and some wine had been served. For all I knew he could rise at any second and bid me good night. Yet there was nothing I could do. I wasn't to start any conversation unless he began it. But Sanau hadn't said anything about continuing a conversation.

So I said, "Why?"

He turned to me in mild surprise.

I hurried on. "I mean why do I look so much better? I have noticed it myself."

Again that devastating smile, but this time I held my ground and did not lower my glance.

He actually answered my question. "Long ago the women on our planet aided their complexion with powders and oils just as I presume your Earth women do. But that was centuries ago. It is merely a matter of advancement."

That same word again—advancement. Superiority.

"On our planet we've advanced too," I insisted, "experts are inventing new cosmetics and oils all the time to rejuvenate women's appearance."

He nodded thoughtfully. "Yes, but at the same time your planet is also going through the advancement of aggression. First the atom bomb, then the hydrogen bomb. There will be feeble attempts at space conquest with the motive that the country who first succeeds will be first to control the world. Only after these things are attempted and abolished can your scientists turn their full attention to the achievement of life and its real fulfillment."

"But you've conquered space," I insisted. "Why shouldn't we try?"

"Because space cannot be conquered until one has conquered oneself."

"Your Majesty," I said in an earnest tone, "it's true that we are ages behind your planet, but our scientists are trying. We do make bombs but doctors and scientists are working on other things all the time. Our hospitals have progressed, we have miracle drugs . . ."

He interrupted with a wave of his hand, "But these miracle drugs were only discovered out of necessity during your last war. Think of the advancement that might be made on your planet if all the forces that are creating war materials, political graft and corruption, and personal fortunes were no longer needed and were turned toward the advancement of your race. Think of the cures that would be discovered for so many so-called incurable diseases. The prolonging of your life's span, which would permit each individual to remain and create more that is good. You are blessed with many creative minds on your Earth, but all of Earth's man-made energy is divided into so many channels. You know, it is most amusing, especially so, when one of the well-known quotations that echoes from your Earth is, "United we stand ... divided we fall." Your entire Earth is divided in countries, in politics and religion. You would be such easy prey for any aggressive planet."

He dismissed me by addressing someone through his voice box. I couldn't see the one honored with this privilege, but I was left with no doubt in my mind that our conversation was terminated.

I toyed with my wine. It was hopeless. Even he spoke of the inadequacy of my planet, as if I personally was responsible.

I finished my wine to the company of a tremendous clash of cymbals. This was really turning into a court banquet for sure, complete with dancing girls.

For with the advent of the cymbals, we were treated to the gracefully exotic gyrations of six Yargonian beauties. They writhed, twirled, and chanted to some strange melody. I stole a glance at the Yargo and it seemed he was not wildly enthusiastic.

It was during the second dance that he turned to me.

"How does this compare with the dances on Earth?"

"This is much more exciting," I answered with honesty. "They seem to be telling some story behind each step."

He nodded. "They are telling the story of you, our strange little visitor. The girl in the center portrays you."

I was impressed. She was lovely beyond words, yet not as perfect as Sanau. And, breaking all protocol, I announced this fact.

The Yargo obviously returned Sanau's mutual admiration. He seemed pleased at my compliment.

"I am sorry she could not find time to attend this banquet. She is busy at the observatory."

His tone was gentle but the implication didn't escape me. Sanau had been invited, but she had turned it down. Probably has gasped, "Dear Yargo, I see enough of that creature, please spare me tonight."

He spoke again. "Since you obviously seem to admire beauty, I feel it must be a natural trait and desire amongst women on your planet. It seems a pity that you leave so much undone. There is no reason why all your women—and men—can't be perfect physical specimens."

"You mean there's something we could do about it?"

He nodded, and began his explanation while my eyes devoured his unbelievable face. He was oblivious to my stare. I half listened and recklessly allowed my gaze to wander from his eyes to the symmetry of his cheekbones to the straight nose, then back to the wondrous eyes. All the while I was completely aware that I was doing nothing to further my own cause, yet I dawdled in a hypnotic lethargy. At that moment my own immediate fate somehow seemed very unimportant. The only paramount thing was to look at him, to remember every muscle on his face, every expression in his eyes, the sound of his voice. I was drugged by some emotional barbiturate; I knew it and I didn't care.

Somehow I forced myself to absorb the sense of his words, and dragged myself back to consciousness during his final statement.

"The body is like a tree," he was saying. I blinked my eyes in an effort to follow his statement. "It should increase in beauty with age. No Yargonian ever becomes distorted with wrinkles in old age. From birth to death his countenance is unspoiled."

I tried to piece together the words that lingered in my subconscious mind. I had heard them all. He had said something about air, and at that moment I had noticed he had a cleft in his chin. He had spoken about moisture bombs and dehydration bombs when I was taking an inventory of his eyebrows.

It was all beyond my comprehension but I nodded as if in complete agreement.

In summation, he flashed one of those electrifying smiles and said, "And most of all there is the peace of mind and lack of personal aggression that prevails on our planet. However, I am sure you have heard enough. I am also certain that the only real problem that concerns your thoughts is the decision we have been forced to make on your behalf. May I say that I am exceedingly sorry that it could not be more favorable for you personally."

Well, there it was! The opening I had been praying for and he had led, plunged right in and left himself wide open for any plea on my part.

That was it. His innocence was beyond brilliance. A plea on my part would be too obvious now. He had put me on the defensive, but he was not so devious that he had outwitted me. I was not given credit for any great intelligence so I would have to act in the most obvious way. I said simply, "Please send me home."

He looked at me for a moment. There was compassion in his eyes. Compassion, yet I felt my hopes dissolving for with this compassion there was an element strangely missing. Sympathy; yes, that was it. He understood my plight, could sense the urgency of my wish, but he lacked the sympathy to understand the depth of my personal misery. His intelligence was superior enough to allow him to understand the emotion of all creatures; understand, but not feel. I definitely knew at that moment that he was capable of feeling nothing.

Why couldn't this superior man understand unhappiness? Was it because he had never experienced this emotion? A man such as the Yargo would not know what it would be to feel frustration, misery, sadness. He would never know the humiliation of feeling inferior.

For a second he didn't answer. At first I was afraid he was never going to. He fastened his attention on the dancers who were now coming to the end of their recital. He rose and signified he had appreciated their endeavors. They in turn fell flat on their faces to display their gratitude. It seemed an eternity but eventually they bowed off and once again he turned to me.

"I anticipated your request, my little friend. It is with deepest regrets that I must answer that I cannot comply."

I turned away. I didn't want him to see the tears that had come to my eyes lest once again I create a panic.

Perhaps he sensed the emotion I was suffering for he spoke even though I refused to look up.

"Janet—that is your name, Janet," he repeated the word. "Janet, as we mature, we learn certain facts must be accepted. My little friend, for you, this is the beginning of maturity. You cannot return to your Earth. You cannot remain here. Once you accept these facts you will have taken a great step forward."

"How?" I kept my eyes averted but the tears were heavy in my voice. "By accepting defeat?"

"Sometimes defeat is moral victory."

"I can't follow that." Sanau hadn't said anything about starting a discussion, yet somehow I knew she'd be choking with rage if she even thought I'd dare to take exception to any statement this man might make.

"It's not difficult to follow." His charm never wavered. "Once we have willed the mind to accept what we at the moment term defeat, we have already progressed. Only when we have made rationality rule over emotion can we first begin to use the mind to its fullest capacity."

My arguments melted with my hopes, and together they shared a final and dismal death. In complete defeat I turned to him.

"All right. Then tell me how to go about achieving this state."

His glance held genuine respect, and in spite of my own despair, I actually felt pleasure in his approval. This moment of satisfaction was unjustified and I knew it. His nod of approval was the formal signature of my death warrant, and I was in full compliance.

I was caught in the dragnet of his magnetic personality and fighting with the fierceness of a minnow. I should hate this man. He was no different from the others, just endowed with some unholy magnetism; the same Svengali power attributed to dictators like Hitler and Napoleon. Even criminals possessed it to an alarming degree. Harnessed in proper channels it could accomplish miracles, but in the possession of an egomaniac it could destroy—just as I was about to be destroyed. I was going to Mars.

He was speaking of Mars. I forced myself to allow his words to penetrate the confusion of my thoughts.

"I assume you have been informed that the ruler of Mars himself caused our intercession and this unfortunate mistake."

I nodded.

"Has the sincerity behind our desire to aid your planet also been explained to you? This alone prompted our action."

"Is something wrong with our planet?" At this moment I really didn't care.

"No. It is your sun about which we have concern."

Our sun? I had heard one day that it would fall to Earth or something. My interest was slightly aroused.

"What's wrong with our sun?"

"It is a cepheid."

A cepheid. I had no idea what that might be, but from his inflection it sounded like some kind of social disease. I could nod knowingly, and die of old age on Mars wondering what a cepheid was or I could come out and ask. Since I hadn't exactly overpowered them with my dazzling intellect thus far, I asked.

"A cepheid is a pulsing star whose radiation and illumination and consistency may vary and fluctuate on an atomic tide. They enlarge and decrease themselves in size because of the impossible pressures that constantly rage within."

Had he answered me in his native tongue, I could not have understood less.

So I tried a blind stab. "Aren't all suns the same?"

"No, my little friend. A sun is not always a cepheid, yet a cepheid is always a sun."

In spite of my oppressive mood, I laughed. Good old American double-talk coming from His Highness, but there wasn't a flicker of amusement in his jeweled eyes. I asked how many suns in the universe were cepheids. I was sure we couldn't be the only planet so disgraced. Although he hadn't in one word or gesture implied a cepheid was undesirable, I somehow knew it definitely wasn't anything to get up and shout about.

"There are many cepheids," he answered, "but none share the present danger that your sun is facing."

This sounded urgent. For a split second I forgot my own impending disaster.

"The leader of Mars called our attention to this peril seven years ago."

"Is that when you first sent your ships around?" I asked. "Is that when the 'saucer scare' began?"

"No, it is not the first time we sighted and watched your planet. It was the first time we sent ships into such close radius, making them visible to the naked eye. We have been watching your planet for several centuries. But it is your recent atomic blasts that cause us real concern."

Suddenly pieces began to fall together. "Is that why you wanted Doctor Blount or Professor Einstein?"

He nodded and concern erased some of the sheen from his eyes. "I should not burden you with these problems, but since you are unhappy, perhaps you will be more sympathetic if you understand the good intent and urgency that caused us to take such drastic measures, only to have it . . ." He stopped abruptly.

"Only to have it end with a big mistake." I finished for him.

His smile was soft and melancholy as if, now that I finally understood his position, he could begin to sympathize with mine.

"You can see," he reiterated, "far from harming you personally, we were intent on saving your entire solar system."

"But what actual danger is our sun facing? What about the atomic blasts?"

He hesitated. This time it was I who read his thoughts. Was I worth the involved explanation that my question obviously demanded?

He made a sudden decision and suddenly rose.

Everyone else rose and fell to the floor.

I remained seated.

He addressed the prostrate forms in his native tongue. Leader Corla and several other leaders took instant flight.

He turned to me. I was staring in a half-paralyzed trance.

"We shall go to the observatory. I shall personally endeavor to illustrate my words."

I followed two guards out of the ballroom. Everyone was scurrying in some direction. The Yargo had disappeared through a wall.

Outside a car was waiting and I was amazed to find that Sanau was in the waiting car with Leader Corla. Even she had been alerted to the strange turn the dinner party had taken. The Yargo evidently had his own means of transportation.

This observatory was larger than the one in which I had suffered my indictment. The Yargo and several leaders were already present when we arrived. I had been too dazed by the sudden action to even discuss the situation with Sanau and she had come forth with no explanation herself. It had been a swift, silent, unnaturally tense journey.

Apparently everything was in order, awaiting our arrival. Sanau wordlessly motioned me to a telescope. I approached it dumbly and turned to her questioningly.

She peered through, made a slight adjustment then turned the machine over to me.

"Look at the moon, the moon of your own planet."

The brightness of the very white moon

was almost blinding in its glare and I could take it for only a few seconds at a time. I watched it for some time, looking away every so often, but compelled to return each time. So close, yet in another solar system. Nowhere on our Earth did we have telescopes that even remotely approached this kind of power.

That moon shed its silvery light on my Earth. On David, on my mother, my friends. On lovers in some secluded lane, on children who prayed on bended knees by their bedroom windows. It was white and glistening and scarred with those deep crater holes that I had seen in so many illustrations. It looked icy, uninhabitable, and tortured, yet at that moment I felt I'd rather be on that cold planet than on Yargo, because it was *my* moon.

Leader Corla barked something, and Sanau suggested that I go to another telescope and view Mars. I obeyed.

My new home. It was not as bright as the moon, yet it seemed equally desolate. A big ball populated with lizard men who were awaiting their new citizen. A few tears of self-pity blurred my vision.

My next view was a moon of Yargo. This was overwhelmingly bright, but after a time my eyes adjusted to this glare. Now, the Yargo announced, my eyes were ready to view the sun.

This time I was fitted with dark glasses and a new telescope was properly adjusted.

Even with this added precaution, the impossible glare brought tears to my eyes. I shut them, tried again, shut them, and tried once more. After a while I was able to take the light for almost a full minute.

"An atomic explosion will occur on your Earth in a few minutes," the Yargo explained. "When the explosion occurs I will give you a signal. I want you to watch your sun."

I nodded obediently and left the telescope. Sanau motioned me to a bench.

"We have seven minutes," she explained. Then, as an afterthought, "I assume His Grace has told you that your sun is an orange dwarf."

The Yargo nodded and I made no move to correct him. Orange dwarf? He had said nothing of the sort. Merely that it was a cepheid. This new title sounded even more ominous. All these peculiar titles hurled at our poor little sun. I couldn't help but think of all the misguided souls on our Earth who at this moment were possibly lying on beaches absorbing its rays, completely unaware of the miserable sun they had inherited.

"We can only hope it does not become a novae," she added.

Sanau could tell from my expression that I was completely bewildered. So, as she adjusted telescopes and consulted charts, she attempted an explanation. It was as if she understood that the Yargo hadn't even begun to fathom the limitation of my mental ability.

"Novas, the most electrifying phenomena of the universe, are stars that suddenly break their bounds. The stars that are most apt to do this are cepheids. And among cepheids, there is one type that is most likely to explode; that is the orange dwarf."

That was us! Then a new and horrible thought occurred to me. Our sun! Maybe this was the little explosion we were all sitting around waiting for. I immediately put this fear into words.

No, it wasn't going to explode. Not for the time being. We were waiting for a minor explosion. The testing of the newest hydrogen bomb.

"How do you know such a bomb is being tested on Earth?" I wanted to know.

"Our spaceships have notified us."

That was nice. A lot of privacy we had! I thought of the great lengths we went to in keeping these secrets from foreign agents and the people of our own country, while up here, these people calmly sat around watching our every move, knowing to the exact second about a bomb that was going to explode on Earth.

I turned to the Yargo. "But our sun; it will explode eventually?" I was thinking of my mother and David.

"We cannot tell when a star will explode." There was sympathy in his voice as if he wished he could prevent this eventuality.

"However, we can recognize certain danger signals long before a cepheid becomes a prenovae."

"Are we a prenovae?"

"No. But there is a definite disturbance in your sun and if this disturbance is continually aggravated, who can foresee the outcome?"

Sanau touched my shoulder and motioned me to take my post before the telescope. I assumed the zero hour was approaching. "It is these disturbances the Yargo wishes you to witness," she explained. Then she spoke to Leader Corla in her own tongue. He in turn looked at the watch on his wrist, barked a few orders, and adjusted his own telescope.

I looked through the machine before me. Our sun seemed in excellent condition.

"Close your eyes," the Yargo suggested. "There is no need to strain them. We shall count off the final seconds. Open your eyes at the count of one."

I stood before my telescope with my eyes shut. The others took their stations. The Yargo folded his arms with an air of bored resignation. He had witnessed this show too many times.

For a moment there was nothing but the silence of waiting. Then Sanau began to count.

"Ten ... nine ... eight ..."

I stood rigid with my eyelids glued together, ready to spring at the count of one.

"Four ... three ... two ...

"One!"

I opened my eyes! I almost expected to hear the explosion, to see the great mushroom of destruction form, but nothing greeted me other than the silent blinding brightness of the sun, and then I saw it! It wasn't much at first, just a little dark speck, like a flaw in a brilliant diamond. Then suddenly, this speck shot out a small mountain of flame as if the sun itself had hurled a piece of itself into space. It shot back with the same velocity in which it had been sent forth and then there was nothing, just the blinding brightness and the small dark spot.

Now my eyes saw nothing but that black tumor. It was like a bottomless whirlpool, evil and foreboding.

Sanau walked over and clicked off my telescope.

"Did you see it?" she asked quietly.

"I saw something. What was it?" I turned to the Yargo.

"You call them sunspots," he answered.

"You mean scientists on our Earth can see them?"

"Not exactly, for you have no telescope that begins to approach an instrument such as this. It is impossible to actually get an honest view of the sun from your Earth, the ultraviolet rays would blind one. We have managed a filter lens . . ." He paused, sensing an explanation on this new subject would merely be a useless delay.

He continued. "A sunspot, such as you term

them, indicates inner turmoil comparable to a volcano within a volcano, and each atomic blast that occurs on your Earth causes larger and more violent spots."

"But I've heard of sunspots," I insisted, "I'm sure our scientists are aware of them."

He nodded. "Aware of them, yes, but recognizing the extent of the danger, no. They are not in agreement that sunspots can cause a cepheid to become a prenovae; justifiably so, since they have not the apparatus to receive an accurate view. However, Doctor Blount and a few other men in astrophysics have theorized on this possibility, but the government that controls your military power cannot discard what it considers vital defense measures, just on the theory of some few scientists. Unless it was a proven fact, no nation would relent on its manufacturing and testing of defenses, and since your planet is divided into so many nations and governments, each nation still competing with the other for control of power, it could easily become merely a political issue to ride one party into power. Nothing could be done unless this became a universal agreement. It is an overwhelming obstacle." He shook his great head in sadness.

Unfortunately, his words were true. We wouldn't stop testing bombs unless we were sure other countries did the same. No, as far as I could see, the sun was doomed.

"What actually happens when the sun explodes?" I asked with an almost morbid curiosity. "Does it just suddenly crash or is there a warning?"

"It is not quite as dramatic a spectacle as you might envision." he explained, "yet it is a fabulous phenomenon to watch . . . for inhabitants of another solar system."

"It must look like a huge Roman candle. A Roman candle with people inside."

"When a cepheid explodes," he explained slowly and with great patience, "it turns into a gigantic fireball. In a short time it changes from an unimportant little star into one of the phenomena of the sky. Long before the final explosion occurred, all life would end. Oceans would evaporate and turn to scarred deserts. The earth would crack and sear, all living things would perish. Then the temperature would rise and flame would envelop your entire planet, vaporizing it entirely. This intense heat would expand to the orbit of several surrounding planets, especially Mars, and, although Mars might escape complete annihilation, all life on it would be destroyed."

I sucked in my breath. No wonder Mars was so concerned!

"The planet Mars is aware of this danger," he continued as if following my line of thought, "but lacking spaceships, they had no means to communicate this peril to your planet. This left them no alternative but to contact us. We were merely acting as a friendly agent in the matter. Your novae would, in no way, affect our solar system."

"But what happens to the sun after the explosion?" I wanted to know. "Does it keep going, burning everything it contacts?"

"Indeed not. After a time, as all fires must, this one would burn itself out, but not before it had destroyed your entire solar system. Even planets as remote as Uranus and Neptune would be affected, for all planets and satellites need the sun to revolve themselves about. Without this pivot, they would become planets without a course. Some would break apart and become asteroids; some might even join remote edges of other solar systems, but the solar system which you know today would cease to exist."

"What happens to the sun itself? Does it turn to ash?"

"It becomes what is known as a white dwarf. It shrinks into about half its size, becoming fantastically heavy with a density that would make one square inch of matter weigh over a ton. It would give off very little light."

"Do you think there's a chance that our scientists will learn all these things before it's too late?"

"They already know most of the things about which I speak. It is merely the peril of the atomic blasts of which they remain unaware, and the true picture of what they refer to as 'sunspots.' They prophesy these events to occur billions of years from now. But there is no need for it to ever occur. Your sun—cepheid that it is—may never become a novae if handled with care. Conversely, with new and intense aggravation, it could even occur during your lifetime."

For a moment I couldn't speak. It was an impossible situation. Here I was, knowing all these salient facts, but I could do nothing to help the fate of my planet. At that moment, all selfish thoughts ceased to exist. It didn't matter what became of me if all life such as I knew it was in peril of complete destruction. Earth had to be warned; the people had to know.

I leaped to action, literally. I grabbed Sanau.

"I must warn my people . . ." I turned from her inanimate face to the Yargo.

"Please let me go back, let me tell them." I felt Sanau's restraining hands tensed to become bands of steel lest I take one step closer to the Yargo.

I stood my ground but my eyes searched his eyes frantically for a sign of agreement, a flicker of understanding. I saw two hard, glittering, extraordinary jewels, jewels so flawless, they reflected only the light of beauty and not the glimmer of human compassion.

I turned away. I didn't even need to listen to his answer; it came exactly as I anticipated, kindly and sympathetic in tone but hopeless in context.

"My child, had we been so fortunate as to secure Doctor Blount, our findings might have been presented in a scientific manner to your people from Doctor Blount as if they were his own evaluations. He might have convinced your people through his power and the respect in which you hold him. In that way, we could be completely withheld from the picture. That was our original intent. Doctor Blount would have been wise enough to have agreed. He too would have understood that your people are not ready to accept the theory of other worlds and other races without the fear of invasion or greed to become the invaders themselves. Oh, no. Not for several thousands of years will your people be ready for such knowledge. Perhaps then, if they have not destroyed themselves and their planet, they will be one nation."

"I understand your logic and your reasoning," I pleaded, "but I also know the people of my world. I know how they think and feel in every nation, because underneath, we laugh, cry, and hope for the same things. We're alike, more alike than you or I could possibly be. That's why I can speak for my people. I can say with certainty if they knew their planet faced destruction, maybe this knowledge would bring about a unification that might have taken thousands of years to occur."

"And who is to tell them and lead them. You?"

I couldn't answer. Who was to tell them and lead them. Me? Janet Cooper? Janet Cooper, ex-secretary? David's fiancée? He was right. It was a hopeless thought.

As if suddenly realizing the amount of valuable time he had bestowed on such an insignificant being, he was almost abrupt in his departure.

His final advice came in short, terse sentences.

"I trust you now understand the fears that beset the good people of Mars and that this common bond will help you find peace and contentment in this new world. Good night and good-bye. I wish you a safe journey."

He bowed and was gone before I could nod a dazed acceptance. The three leaders followed a safe distance from his heels, and Sanau escorted me to the waiting car.

The great evening had come and gone.

CHAPTER 15

The sky was bleak and gray on the morning they came for me. Even the glistening mountain seemed shrouded in murky mist. I would have supposed that "perfect flying conditions" should have prevailed, but on this, my personal D day, the weather was as dismal as my spirit.

We were a grim little party that set off for the airport. Sanau, Leader Corla, Leader Kleeba, two aviators, and myself. We sat silently as the car swished through the now familiar scenery for the last time. It was as if we shared a pact in a wordless agreement as to the enormity of the journey before us. Sanau stared straight ahead, and every inch of her tense body seemed to shout, "Look, I don't like the idea of this little jaunt any more than you do; I too am forced to go along."

But at least she was coming back.

Even the airport was gray and cold. There was no sun to dance on the surface of the great silver mushroom that was already whirling around its tremendous circular rims, warming itself for flight, almost displaying an impatience to be off. Everything was gray. The sky, the ship, even the dark material of the space suits we all wore were as fittingly dreary as the atmosphere.

No brass band to see me off, not even one lone curious spectator. The airport was empty except for a few mechanics who went about methodically checking the ship. The trembling climb up the staircase, the one desperate moment that I turned and took a long last look at Yargo, the superior and unfriendly planet that was casting me off, and then the spaceship itself.

I was strapped into position on the small cot, accepted the takeoff needle without question, and we were off.

I'm not sure how long I slept under the sedation of the needle. Sanau was reading when I awoke. Leader Corla and Leader Kleeba were working on some official-looking papers. It was a homey scene, homey and serene. It gave the impression of the club car on a train heading for some familiar destination.

Sanau cast me the barest of nods when I opened my eyes. It was not a friendly nod, or even meant for reassurance. It merely stated that she noted I was alive and acknowledged it.

I lay on the bunk for a long time. I tried to assemble my thoughts but they refused to shape into any coherent form. Until the actual takeoff time, I had still nurtured the secret hope that something would happen on the final moment to prevent this catastrophe. Yet, here I was on my way!

I lay there in a suspended state, fully aware of this self-created anesthesia. I didn't want to think, for underlying all my grief was the deeper pain that by one flick of his magnificent eyes this entire tragedy could have been averted and that he had neither the desire nor compassion to prevent it.

Despair in itself is a torturous emotion, but despair inflicted by someone held in reverence is unbearable. No matter how I evaded the thought, I knew without a doubt that I, like every last Yargonian, was now completely dominated in heart and mind by this unbelievable ruler. I was completely enmeshed in his spellbinding power and my fear of banishment to Mars was completely overshadowed by the pain of leaving this man. Never to see him again; how was it that Sanau had put it? Never to be allowed to see his vision, to admire his leadership; life would not be worth living.

It is natural, I suppose, that my thoughts veered to David. What an infinitesimal thing was this emotion that I had considered was my love for him! David, who quaked at an order from Mr. Finley. David, who called me honey girl and looked all square and clean and self-righteous in his seersucker suit. But David wouldn't do this to me; he would have protected me. This thought brought fresh waves of despair and righteous anger against my new idol.

I leapt from the bunk and took refuge at one of the portholes. There I stared into endless space as if hoping to escape from the thoughts that dogged me. Space, nothing but limitless space high above the gray atmosphere. I watched a long black ship zoom by. It resembled a big black cigar, its portholes barking ugly fire. I had read a few reports about these ships too, along with the "saucers"; probably reconnaissance ships marking our speed and returning to Yargo with notes on our progress.

Without turning from the window, I called back and asked Sanau the real mission of the cigar-shaped ships.

"What cigar-shaped ships?" she asked.

"The long, burning, cigar-shaped ships. Several of our pilots have seen them too. They're smaller than this ship. But from what I read in the newspaper reports back home, they go at a remarkable speed."

She obviously translated this statement to the leaders, for they both looked up, then she smiled at me in a disparaging way.

"Yes, we have heard of these reports from your Earth. On the last broadcast we monitored there was a sighting reported of three such objects. There are no cigar-shaped ships. Any pilot on your Earth stating he has seen such a ship is merely looking for publicity and attention."

I didn't answer, for it was obvious to me

that for some reason Sanau was bent on keeping these ships her own affair. Perhaps it was some secret weapon they were working on. Maybe Mars knew nothing about this ship and she saw no reason for me to arrive armed with any extracurricular knowledge.

I forgot about the other ships until after dinner. It had been a fine meal although I had little stomach for it. Throughout the meal Sanau had constantly consulted charts. Mars, acording to all calculations, should be sighted in about twelve hours. No one had ever made this trip before and they were elated at the progress of the trip. Not even one meteor shower! Everyone seemed to be enjoying the journey, except me.

I had gotten up from dinner to give my place to one of the copilots when the subject of the cigar-shaped ships returned to my mind. Several times during dinner I had noticed their lights flaring past our porthole. Since I was the only one who sat with a view of the porthole, the others were probably not aware of my sightings. But the last one seemed too close for comfort.

With extreme nonchalance, I said, "Does our ship have tail lights or something?"

Sanau shook her head. She was too preoccupied with the charts to give me an oral answer.

"Well, maybe we better hang out a lantern or something," I told her, "because that cigar-shaped ship that doesn't exist almost bumped into us."

I was totally unprepared for the look that came to her eyes. It was disbelief mixed with real anxiety, and, as that look transmitted itself to me, I felt a real stab of fear. Sanau hadn't been covering up. She had been telling the truth.

She quickly jabbered something to Leader Corla and Kleeba, who both looked as if they had been kicked in the stomach. Then she turned to me, made a great effort to regain her poise, and asked me to be extremely explicit. Just exactly what had I seen?

I gave her a graphic picture. I also reminded her of my earlier sighting. She relayed this to the leaders. The aviator leaped up, his mouth filled with food, and bolted for the control room. In one second flat the other pilot appeared. From his worried expression I knew he had heard my story. Sanau related it again. He shook his head, an anxious look clouding his emerald eyes. His whole body seemed to sag as he returned to the control room.

I was thoroughly frightened now. Leader Corla was arguing with Leader Kleeba and Sanau was peering from the porthole, her worried eyes frantically searching the black space.

She turned from the porthole, her voice ringing like a bell above the dissension of the two leaders. She stated a firm command to them both, then turned to me as if I had been on their side of the argument and reasserted. "We cannot turn back. We must go on."

Now everyone was on edge. "If it's not your ship, whose ship is it?" I demanded.

Sanau shook her head. "We have traveled in outer space for thousands of years and have sighted no other ships. To the best of our knowledge, no planet in any solar system had thus far mastered space travel. I do not state that there does not exist space travel in some solar system millions of light years away. But such travel would have to be confined to solar systems within their own orbit. No member of their crew could live long enough to make such a journey."

She paused as if to organize her thoughts. When she did speak, it was with a precision that came from thinking aloud, rather than actual conversation.

"If there are such spacecraft as you have sighted, then they can only come from our solar system, your solar system, or a solar system six light years away. Our navigators have completely explored that system. Lenea, their most advanced planet, is about three thousand years behind your Earth in civilization, and, as for our own solar system, only two planets have progressed to the stage to receive our communications, let alone set out in space."

"Then where do they come from?"

Again she shook her head. "I cannot fathom. Mars, Neptune, Jupiter, and Pluto all support a type of life. Mars is the most advanced..."

"What about Venus?"

"It is doubtful, although not impossible." She paused once again. Then, as if making a final decision, "No, it could not be Venus. Venus is the only planet in your solar system we know very little about. It is completely covered with dense cloud formations. The few times our pilots have tried to break through, the density of the clouds and heaviness of the atmosphere made any systematic exploration impossible. There is no way to study Venus unless you came into her actual pull of gravity, close enough to land. This is always hazardous, and since the chances of Venus having any life, let alone intelligent life, are extremely remote due to the atmospheric pressure, we have not risked further exploration."

"But you still can't discount Venus," I insisted.

"I think we can. A planet so immersed in fog and cloud formations would find the study of other star systems an insurmountable obstacle. Therefore, if there is any life on Venus, it is safe to say they believe they are the only life and planet in existence. If they have a moon, we cannot see it, and I am also sure that very little sun filters through. On such a dismal planet, life would not progress and, if it did, it would not have progressed to the state of space travel. To my mind, its fight for survival would retard any actual growth in civilization. Oh, no, at best it would be a struggling, retarded race."

It went on for over an hour. Sanau forcing her mind to race through every avenue of solution, returning each time to the same blind alley. On and on she went, using my questions to drive her thoughts to explore every possible loophole. But it was always the same. They couldn't exist. But they did. Every now and then the leaders threw in a few words and I'd lose the whole conversation as Sanau returned to her native tongue.

Everyone was thoroughly alarmed. We searched for a reappearance of the mysterious craft, but it was almost as if our thoughts had telegraphed themselves to the ominous strangers. There was nothing but space and stars million of miles away.

No one slept. It seemed an eternity until the cold unwelcome world of Mars was sighted. At first glance it looked like the moon. I saw dim markings of mountains and some green and brown patches. It was strange and wonderful to see this lonely ball in the sky and to know that soon it would grow into a world.

We were just preparing to enter the atmosphere of Mars when all hell broke loose. There is no other way to describe it. It started with one of the pilots breaking into our compartment. He had seen it! I couldn't understand his words, but I just had to glance in the direction to which he was wildly pointing and I knew.

I knew, and I saw! It was off to the left some fifty feet away and it was definitely interested in us. It was banking around like a killer shark, playing with us as if we were a large helpless whale. It definitely didn't look friendly.

The pilot spurted question after question. Sanau remained firm and shook her head. Leader Corla argued her decision. She restated it more firmly, then, for my benefit, she explained the stand she was taking. She felt there was no need to fire on it. Thus far it had shown no belligerency toward us. Any type of life that had the intelligence to create such a craft must have the intelligence to avoid aggression.

I hoped she was right. I wanted to agree with her, but it seemed so odd that we had sighted these ships from our Earth, yet her people, who constantly cruised the sky, had never seen them. I put this to her and awaited an explanation.

"It must have desired not to be sighted by us," was her only reply.

Leader Corla offered another opinion. Again Sanau disagreed but without as much authority. I looked at her questioningly. In these moments of common peril, she had ceased to regard me as an inferior being. We were together against a common and unknown threat and for the moment she treated me as an equal. And why not? She could die as easily as I.

She explained that Leader Corla felt it was

definitely hostile. I turned to the taciturn leader. He had lost some of his olive color. Even his bald pate looked pale.

"Why does he say this?" I was fighting against hysteria.

"He states," Sanau explained, "that the reason we have never sighted such a craft is due to the fact that prior to this, we have never traveled alone. On our voyages, there has always been a mother ship, and the flotilla never numbers less than twelve. This is the first time a lone ship has set forth on such a journey. The day on which you were spotted, a mother ship was stationed right beyond the atmosphere of Earth, and eleven sister ships stood by waiting for any sign of danger. Now that we are alone, this strange ship dares to allow itself to be seen."

As much as I hated to, I had to go along with Leader Corla's reasoning. Why was the ship showing itself at such close range? Even the Martians must be able to see it. I told this to Sanau and for once I had come up with an appropriate suggestion.

She sprang into action. "Of course! Why didn't I think of it? We must radio Mars and ask them their findings."

She dashed into the control room. Obviously the leaders did not set much hope in this solution. They sat enveloped in a hopeless gloom. I remained with them and alternated between hope and despair. When Sanau returned, the expression on her face did nothing to add to my sense of well-being.

She spoke to the leaders, who immediately rose and entered the pilots' chambers. Then she turned to me.

"It is some kind of enemy attack. Mars is almost in a state of panic. They have been watching for our arrival since dawn. Three hours ago they noticed the first of these ships. Naturally, they thought they were some kind of advance craft of our own, so they sent up flares. Immediately a death ray of some sort was emitted from the ship. Six Martians were killed instantly and a crater the size of a small mountain was burned in the ground. All of Mars is completely under cover, but seven volunteer groups have been waiting for our signal. They have been afraid to send any to us for fear they might be interpreted, but they warn us not to land."

But what were we to do? The killer shark was not alone now, he was accompanied by six other beasts. They surrounded our ship, but so far they did not attack.

"They probably know we could demolish several of their own ships before they could obliterate us," Sanau grimly observed.

No one answered. We could hold out several days before our fuel ran low, but they obviously could outwait us, returning to some mother ship for refueling in shifts.

We held our ground, remaining motionless in space, all the while using our precious fuel. They too waited.

Some decision had to be made. Everyone had suggestions. And everyone's suggestions were heard and fully explored—including my own. Still no one actually came up with any solution.

Radioing Yargo for help was impossible. It was even impossible to reach Mars by radio now. The cordon of enemy ships encircling our own blocked any chance of radio messages getting through. We all paced the cabin, growing more tense as hours passed and still no attack came.

The glaring portholes of the tiger pack surrounding us looked like a chain of bonfires. Our only chance, Leader Corla insisted, was in a surprise takeoff.

The prime decision to make was our destination. We had two alternatives: to return to Yargo or make a stab at landing on Mars. If we did escape the net of ships, they no doubt would take off after us. And, as Sanau pointed out, they would doubtlessly split into two groups—one following the direction of Yargo, the other Mars.

It was her opinion that we select an entirely new destination, head for it, then radio Yargo for help. This point was mutually agreed upon, save for the direction itself. Where could we land? Leader Kleeba suggested a moon on Yargo, but since that was in the direction of Yargo, it was immediately vetoed. And then, quite naturally, it was I who came up with the suggestion:

"Let's land on Earth."

It was a daring idea and to my delight it was not dismissed as completely unfeasible.

Sanau transmitted it to the leaders immediately. Then came the arguments pro and con. We were in no position to attempt a secret landing on Earth as our flight had to be swift and immediate. And, what if Earth should fire on us?

I took a firm stand against this possibility. Newspapers had reiterated time and time again that aviators had been given orders to follow all unidentified aircraft, but never under any circumstances to fire upon them. This statement I followed up with a lengthy discourse on the desirability of landing on Earth. From the way I raved, you might think Earth was just sitting around with bated breath, waiting for us to appear. But I did explain in all truthfulness that there were people, important people, who did not scoff at the possibility of spacecraft, and that once we did go into the atmosphere of Earth, we could contact them by radio and I would speak to them personally.

Sanau was sure Earth would think this was a sneak attack. Leader Corla stated they might think it was merely an invasion from one of their own hostile nations, and added to all these arguments was the haphazard manner in which we would have to land. There was no time to prepare extensive navigation maps; we merely had to find an open landing site and drop. We could have no assurance that we would pick up an English-speaking nation, let alone America. But to me, even Africa was a comforting

destination. From the North Pole to the wilds
of Australia: any place so long as it was on
Earth.

Because no one actually had a countersug-
gestion, they finally agreed on Earth. I was
absolutely wild with joy. I tried to hold my
ecstacy in bounds as I could still read doubts
in the eyes of Sanau, Leader Corla, and
Kleeba. But what other alternative faced
them except to take me home as a hero and
begrudgingly accept my world's hospitality.
I was so elated I wanted to blow kisses to
those ugly black shark planes that had driven
us to this radical move.

The pilots were called in and told of the
plan. Maps were hurriedly brought forth.
According to their calculations, we could
make Earth in five hours, barring no unforeseen obstacles. Yet we were all painfully
aware that the entire success of the plan depended solely on a surprise escape. We would
make our move on the hour, which would
come in exactly ten minutes.

The pilots returned to the control room.
Those final minutes of waiting were tense
and silent. I prayed sporadically. So much
depended on the success of the trip that I
was at a loss to put the prayers into words,
and I merely sat in quiet meditation, comforted in the knowledge that the powers
above were well aware of my wishes, and
this was a time when no actual words of
prayer were needed. Sanau was silent too.
Possibly she was thinking of the mighty

Yargo and the possibilities of not seeing him
again. Or, even if all went well, the possibility of his displeasure in the plan of action
we had been forced to take. After all, this
trip to Earth was against the wishes of the
entire planet. He had been firm in the decision to keep me from returning, so how
would he feel about Sanau and the leaders
also dropping down for a visit? I, too, must
face the eventuality of never seeing him
again, unless, perhaps, he relented and came
to Earth for a visit to thank us for the hospitality. Maybe.

"*Now!*" Sanau's voice hissed through the
cabin.

I felt our ship shoot forward. We made
our move. Up . . . up . . . up . . . It was our
only hope. Higher and higher into the atmosphere. My ears began to ring; my chest felt
as if my ribs were crushing my heart. In the
mutual panic everyone shared, they had forgotten to give me the pressure needle. Blackness closed in and I felt I was going blind,
my breath came in short jerky gasps . . . and
then we leveled off.

We were safe! The lights of the encircled
enemy craft hadn't moved. They were far
below, content in the thought that their big
fish was still safe in their net. We shot away
with our fullest speed until those threatening
lights became mere pinpoints below us.

Then suddenly they noticed our absence!
Even from our distance we could see them

scramble like a bunch of angry animals unable to believe they had lost their prey.

They broke into two factions, one heading in the direction of Mars, the other toward Yargo. Sanau had been right! We were safe! Safe! And on our way to Earth!!!!

CHAPTER 16

It was some hours later we spotted Earth. Oh, God! My beautiful lonely-looking little Earth. It looked just like Mars or any other ball of gray and green rolling around in space. Poor little Earth, so important unto itself and so unaware of its true insignificance in the scheme of the heavens. It reminded me of a spoiled little child, revolving so proudly on its invisible axis; a child that thinks the whole world and people in it are created just for him.

"I think we had better wait for Earth's dawn before we chance a landing," Sanau suggested.

I didn't want to wait a second. I couldn't bear to wait. It was so near.

I insisted on immediate landing.

"No, my friend," she replied, "strange people and strange things seem less frightening in the bright light of day. We must hover about and let your people see our craft. Let one of your planes come up and contact us. Let us even try for a peaceful descent under their guidance, for above all, we must neither surprise nor frighten your people."

I was forced to admit the logic of her

decision, yet I still argued against it. The point in favor of an immediate landing was the ever-present threat of the shark ships. As long as these marauders lurked anywhere at all in the heavens, I could not feel safe. But Sanau was determined in her plan and the leaders and pilots were in full agreement. So there was nothing to do but wait.

Dawn was slowly making its first appearance on Earth. Silver and gold streaked out through the black night, disbanding clouds and darkness below us. We began our deliberate approach to the atmosphere. We had ten thousand miles to cover, ten thousand miles before we would become a mere pinpoint of light to the inhabitants of my world. And yet through the telescopic lenses of the portholes in our cabins (made so to perceive any approaching meteor from miles off) Earth looked very close to us.

I clung to the porthole, and my happiness swelled in proportion to the growth of the now enlarging ball of land I called home. It grew larger and larger until we were almost inside the atmosphere. It would be a matter of minutes, then I'd be breathing my air, basking in my sun, that now cast a silver reflection on our ship. My sun, my world!

Then we all stopped breathing. I screamed!

For there, looming in our path, was the shark ship! Large and black, its ugly portholes leering at us, ridiculing our feeble attempt at escape.

After that it all happened too fast. I know

we shot up like a rocket. Then as my ribs crushed my heart and my lungs tore at my sides for air, I blacked out.

Sanau brought me around. I came into consciousness with a cry. We had lost! Leader Corla and Leader Kleeba were intense and frantic in their discussion with one of the pilots. It was obvious we were headed toward no destination. The quick flight had been an involuntary action of the pilot's own initiative. Now he had come to seek explicit instructions.

There were no instructions to be given. It was gone. My wonderful little Earth. I stood at the porthole and watched it dissolve in the distance. It had been so near; I broke into hysterical sobs.

Sanau sprang to my side. "Janet, you must get hold of yourself. We are all in mortal danger; only calm and unemotional thinking can save us all."

I made an honest effort at composure, for there had been genuine sympathy in Sanau's voice. She had included my welfare in with the others and she had addressed me by my Christian name. In short, Sanau was treating me as an equal for the first time.

As if to add further proof to our new relationship, she added, "We must all think without fear. Including you. After all"—she paused and admitted with a wry smile, "to land in the dark on your Earth was your suggestion. Perhaps we might all be safe at this moment if we had agreed. So dry your tears. We must all remain calm and help one another."

We were gaining altitude but so was our pursuer. The ship was right at our heels and was undoubtedly radioing its teammates. We were outdistancing it slightly, but without a definite destination, there was no definite escape.

This time it was Leader Kleeba who made the suggestion that was accepted by all.

Venus!

Venus. It was our only haven. Venus, a remote and, as far as we knew, unoccupied planet. It offered us a chance to nestle in its cloud banks and await a new opportunity to once again elude the enemy.

This time, Sanau promised, we'd dispense with strategy and land directly, in the black of night.

I stopped sniveling and began to feel better. All was not completely lost. Venus was only six hours away. We must not give the shark the slightest inkling of our plan. So began the game of cat and mouse.

We'd rise and so would the shark, which was now accompanied by half of its fleet. We'd shift to the left in the direction of Venus, the sharks would follow. Then we'd gain altitude and move to the right a bit to create the impression that we had no definite objective in mind. Again the same shift. Higher, then to the left again, then to the right a fraction, yet all the time we were nearing Venus.

Finally we made it: the soft, billowy, dense cloud banks of Venus. We dove into them. Not a thing was visible. Night was around us, and to add to our success, not a light from the enemy craft appeared.

They seemed to fear the cloud banks. Sanau decided they probably had not charted Venus.

Now once again we must wait, then circle Venus and come out from the opposite side.

What were their plans? None of us could attempt a guess. There was no doubt that they were hostile; their attack on Mars proved this, as did the deliberate circling of our ship. Yet they had tried in no way to signal us or make any contact, and thus far they hadn't opened fire.

Sanau once again stated that she felt it was their desire to take us without losing any of their craft, and their only solution was to trap us in space until we ran out of food. Then they could safely approach us and guide us to some destination, wherever it might be.

Then what? Did they want us, or our ship? If this happens, Sanau vowed, we would never allow them to take us. We'd zoom it into the atmosphere and self-destruction.

This was a noble thought but it offered me little comfort. Not with that wonderful ball of Earth just six hours away. But for the moment we were safe. I still had hope. I kept it close to me during that hour that we hid in the cloud banks of Venus.

Then Leader Corla gave the pilots the go-ahead signal. We burrowed into the heart of the cloud banks, then circled the unseen planet beneath and came out on the other side of Venus. Now came the slow and silent maneuver back, back to the waiting lights of the sharks. They were there, holding their vigil. But there was a good opening, a blind spot we could slip through.

I was just about to hold my breath and pray we slip through their net when suddenly, for no apparent reason, we swerved off our course and returned to the cloud banks. There we dug deep and halted. Sanau and the leaders sprang to the pilot's cabin while I sat stiff with alarm and waited for the new developments.

They were new and disastrous. Sanau returned with a hunted look in her lovely eyes.

We were low on fuel. The leaders clumped back with the same air of defeat stamped on their faces. There wasn't a chance of making Earth. We faced a six-hour flight, barring obstacles, and we had enough fuel to last three hours at the most.

For once I made no suggestions. I demanded how they dared come on this trip so shorthanded.

Sanau explained they had come fully prepared: prepared with more than enough fuel to reach Mars and return to Yargo. Their tanks carried enough for a two-day flight, and, as an added precaution, they carried extra fuel that would keep them in the air for two days more. However, we had been in the air for close to three days. We had used half our supply reaching Mars, detoured for Earth, played hide-and-seek to Venus. Even a superior ship such as this was not bottomless in its fuel capacity.

There was no choice. The tanks must be reloaded from the emergency supply. The engines had to be rechecked after a refueling and this could not be done in midair.

There was no alternative but to chance a landing on Venus. Sanau tried to assuage my panic by stating that all in all it might be a fairly simple procedure. We could land on Venus, refill the tanks, and take off immediately.

To land on an almost uncharted planet was no easy task. It would doubtlessly be covered with forests and marshland, whose base might be quicksand; the ship might sink into the ground and never rise. There might also be no clear patch of land. The pilots had to leave the ship to refuel. We had masks fitted for the atmosphere of Mars, but would they hold good on Venus?

"If it resembles Curasiz on our solar system," Sanau was saying, "it will be a steaming tropic. Curasiz is situated ten thousand miles closer to our planet than Venus is to your Earth, but their distance from the sun is alike, and that determines climatic conditions. Curasiz is swampland inhabited by large insects and snakes. We have come into its atmosphere but it is too evil looking to attempt a landing. There would be no gain in disturbing that planet for what we could find on it to benefit life on Yargo."

I listened fitfully as we sank lower and lower into the clouds. Then with an unexpected burst the ceiling opened and there was Venus. Sanau had been right. We could see nothing but jungles, masses of vegetation like movies about Africa. I wouldn't have been the least surprised to find Tarzan flying through the treetops.

We circled for an hour. On closer inspection there were several clearings. We decided on one and so began our descent. We had chosen an island with a small mountain on its edge and some clusters of trees in the center. Otherwise it was quite barren. I held my breath as we dropped lower and lower. The pilots then tested the atmosphere. No oxygen masks were even needed. We were surprised with our luck, and Sanau declared it was almost incredible. The temperature was 130, even in the black of night, but our pressure suits would take care of that. Built to hold out the cold of Mars, they would protect us from the heat of Venus as well.

Sanau's apprehension was completely dispelled, replaced by a genuine feeling of exhilaration of the explorer who has found a new and livable planet for her beloved Yargo.

Her jubilation was so great I began to think she was secretly elated that the unfortunate incident had occurred. She was still the same Sanau, the Sanau to whom nothing exceeded the importance of a new bit of knowledge.

The landing was quite smooth. Everyone got out of the ship. The pilots immediately set about refueling. Leader Corla picked some of the strange vegetation and scooped some of the strange stream water into a bottle. Sanau and I stretched and sniffed the air and listened to the strange noises of Venus.

Everything might have been all right if it hadn't been for Sanau's insatiable thirst for knowledge.

If Venus had oxygen and could support vegetation and insects, she reasoned, then why not intelligent life of some sort? Suddenly she was insistent on a short trip of exploration.

I was relieved when Leader Kleeba and Corla immediately opposed this suggestion, but Sanau was adamant. It was inconceivable to land on a strange and habitable planet and return with such sparse knowledge: a shrub and some stream water. She intended to take a look around.

In spite of my antipathy to her suggestion, I appreciated her desire and anticipation to explore this strange planet. She, with all her superior knowledge, had actually never strayed from Yargo. In fact, with one exception, everyone's personal experience was limited to one planet, and this one exception (who had never even been to Chicago in a

Pullman car) was now blithely setting her dainty foot on a third planet.

So with a burst of compassion that I was to live to regret, I offered to accompany her —with reservations.

"I'm afraid of the forest," I warned her, "but we can wade across this little stream and climb the hill. At least on top of the hill we'd get a fairly good view."

She rewarded me with a look of real gratitude and together we started forth. As the stream was shallow with no toads or fish in evidence we waded right in, shoes and all. We walked about the distance of a city block to the foot of the hill. It was a small hill, not more than thirty feet high, with a plateau on the other side (or so we figured) and then a mile off, the large green-covered mountain.

It was an easy hill to mount. Convenient rocks lent themselves as steps and the ground was neither soft nor slippery. We reached the top in no time. To our surprise there was no barren plateau on the opposite side. Instead, we beheld a magnificent lake. A dark, cool, blue lake with the ghost of a small moon's reflection shimmering in its center. It was perfect enough to seem unreal. We both stretched out on our stomachs and lost ourselves in the beauty and strangeness all around. Far off there was the distant sound of birds and all around us were the Venusian equivalent of crickets. My eyes were now well accustomed to the darkness of the night.

Once in a while the moon broke through the clouds and shimmered the trees with silver.

It was during one of these occurrences that I thought I noticed something on the lake, something that moved. I nudged Sanau and pointed in its direction but at that moment the moon chose to slip into the clouds again. We waited a few moments, my eyes glued to the spot. When the moon reappeared, I found I had been right; it was still there.

Sanau also saw it this time. It was about the size of a man and appeared to be floating on top of the lake. In the darkness, even with the help of the moon, we couldn't discern if it were a floating log, a small boat, or a bit of foliage.

It was too dangerous to attempt to slip down the side of the hill and approach it. While Sanau held vigil, I scrambled down our side of the hill to get Leader Corla and the binoculars. How could I transmit this idea to him in other than sign language, I had no idea, but Sanau had been insistent that one of us remain to hold the thing in sight. Since I had no intention of remaining on top of that hill alone, I chose to be the courier.

I made it down in no time, slopped across the stream, and reached Leader Corla. I pantomimed my message. An anxious look came to his eyes; he thought something had happened to Sanau. He started for the hill. In desperation I pulled him back and tried to make sign pictures of binoculars. One of the pilots interrupted us. I gathered from his expression the ship was ready. This was enough for me. Sanau's sightseeing excursion had come to an end. We could die in peaceful old age always wondering just what was on the lake of Venus, and I would never suffer a pang of regret.

I dismissed the idea of the binoculars and set out to bring her back. Once again we were about to head for home and this time I was sure we'd make it.

I hurried across the stream. Already the circles of our ship were slowly rotating, warming up for the journey ahead. Exhilaration hurried my steps. I had just reached the foot of the hill when I heard a scream, a scream filled with horror and death.

It was Sanau!

CHAPTER 17

I stood rooted to the spot. For a moment there was such silence that even the crickets seemed still. Then everyone immediately scrambled to action. Leader Corla, Kleeba, and one of the pilots were instantly at my side. With hitherto unthought-of bravery, I actually ran ahead and led them to the top of the hill. There was no sign of Sanau, nor was there any sign of the dark floating object on the water below.

We lay on our stomachs and searched the bottom of the hill. Perhaps she had lost her balance and fallen. We knew this was not true, yet we clung to this thought as we crept down the other side of the hill. We searched relentlessly, relentless in action but without hope, for each of us in our hearts knew something far more horrible than a sudden fall had overtaken Sanau.

The hill yielded no sign of her. We stood there desolately with no course of action to take. To comb the entire planet would take months, years. We couldn't leave without her, yet we couldn't remain indefinitely. We started our return to the top of the hill, where once again I lay on my stomach and searched out over the lake. It was clear, beautiful, and innocent looking. The leaders followed my example. Perhaps they felt in some strange way I was trying to tell them what had happened. Their magnificent eyes dug mutely into mine, as if beseeching me for the answer.

I stared dumbly at the water. How could I explain what we had seen? It had looked so innocent, so serene. It seemed impossible to believe that anything dangerous lurked out there.

Suddenly there was another blood-curdling yell!

This time it wasn't Sanau. I jumped up in time to see a giant bumblebee, a bumblebee larger than a man drop down on Leader Corla like a dive bomber, swoop him up in its claws, and fly off. My reflexes made me turn and rush down the hill, I looked over my shoulder to see the pilot disappear in the same fashion. Just as a petrified scream was fighting through my numb throat, I felt two strong hairy arms grasp me by the waist and lift me into the air.

I can't remember each detail. It was a fear so terrible that it numbed my senses. Those wiry arms, strong as steel, encircling my waist. The repugnant feeling of its furry throat against the nape of my neck. The sickening sound of its ghastly buzz, almost as loud as the motor of a plane; the wind created by its great wings fanning the night, and me in its grip like a small animal in the arms of an eagle.

I screamed. I screamed until I could no longer wrench a sound from my raw and gasping throat. In the end, I merely fought to breathe, to breathe and stay alive. And then, this monster circled down to a clearing that resembled a small village, a village populated with beehives, beehives as large as any city apartment house.

The buzzing was almost deafening. The entire community had turned out! Thousands and thousands of these creatures, some close to twenty feet in height.

I was taken inside a hive. It was clean and bare and comfortably cool. The monster deposited me almost gently on the floor and there, huddled in a corner, was Sanau. She was as petrified as I, but thus far unharmed.

When the monster took off, I crawled beside Sanau and clung to her. She made no effort to push me away. Fear causes strange friendships and, at that moment, we were united as we had never been before, in common terror against this giant peril.

Sanau was first to gain her equilibrium. Her first concern was the safety of the other members of our party.

"They're all captured?" she asked.

I nodded dismally. "Everyone except the other pilot, who was standing guard over the ship. He must have seen what was happening and probably ran for cover."

Sanau was tortured with worry over the welfare of Leader Corla, Kleeba, and the pilot. She held the fact that they were not cast with us to be an ominous sign.

Although we were neither bound nor gagged, we both recognized the futility of any attempt to escape. Outside of the hive lurked the malignant shadow of one of the monsters.

Sanau immediately began to speculate on the prospects for our future. She held out little hope for survival. In fact, she seemed to take a macabre pleasure in prophesying the various means by which we might meet our end.

"They do resemble bees, as you say," she mused, "yet, on the other hand, they might be of the giant spider family. I doubt if their intelligence exceeds the lust of a clever animal in search of food. We are no doubt being stored away for just such a purpose."

I expressed some doubt that they were merely carnivorous, as the creature had been too careful in its handling of me. A giant insect, hunting solely for prey, might have taken a few nibbles right away to test if I was appetizing fare. There had been several times in flight that my head might have been bashed against the rocks, or I could easily have been scraped against treetops. The bee had intentionally maneuvered to keep me clear of any obstacles, and though its arms were like bands of steel, it had taken special care not to crush me. Though none of these realizations lessened my panic, they did lead me to believe these creatures had some scheme regarding us, rather than mere nutritional purposes. Besides, anything so immense in size had to be equipped with a brain. Whereupon Sanau immediately pointed to the enormous bodies of prehistoric monsters compared to their tiny brains.

We sat exchanging theories pro and con for almost an hour before one of the frightening things reappeared. It crawled in on all fours, its beady eyes the size of apples, its slimy antennae almost three feet high. Then it stood upright and made chittering noises as if it actually was trying to tell us something.

"It has sense," I whispered to Sanau. "Try and communicate with it!"

"Oh, if only His Almighty Grace was here—he can understand the language of insects."

"Sanau, try! For God's sake!"

She did try. She tried with numerals, but no sign of comprehension appeared in those glassy eyes. She uttered strange sounds with even less rewarding results. Finally she gave up and sank to the ground, weak with sheer horror from the appearance of the thing. I too found it impossible to look at it without experiencing a sense of complete revulsion.

Then, without warning, it approached and extended a hairy arm toward me. I screamed and crouched in a far corner. It continued its approach slowly, like a cat stalking a mouse. I retreated until my back pressed painfully against the wall. Sanau was huddled close beside me, the superior woman no less frightened than the inferior one. Just as it reached for me, she proved her right to her claim by throwing herself in front of me as a shield; with one swift movement, we were both grasped in the creature's arms and taken from the hive.

There were thousands of them waiting outside. They were everywhere; some standing upright, nibbling at the leaves on the trees; others lying on the ground. Their wings glistened in the moonlight, and their ebony bodies shone like metal. Another monster approached and took Sanau; the original demon held me firm in its clasp. Almost as if a signal had been given, there was a mass takeoff.

We soared into the air, my captor leading the group. The sky was black with them. I shuddered. If this was the population of Venus, it was well that this evil planet was hidden by the impenetrable clouds. I hoped Earth or no other planet ever stumbled across this swampland.

We flew quite low, just barely skimming the treetops. The creature cradled me almost as a mother would a child, and I had to admit those ghastly glaring eyes looked at me with something that resembled admiration.

We came to a huge clearing and with one glance my fears multiplied to insurmountable panic, for right before my eyes, banked in neat rows on the ground, were hundreds of the cigar-shaped craft that had pursued us. These were the creatures that manned them!

We were settled gently in the center of the clearing. To our relief Leader Corla, Leader Kleeba, and the pilot were also present; but they had not been treated with the same consideration. The three men were tied to trees by a gummy substance. Leader Corla had a huge gash on his brow, and Leader Kleeba's space suit was almost in shreds. The pilot, half-mad with fright, seemed otherwise unharmed. I wondered if the leaders' disheveled appearance came from an attempt to battle their captors or if the wounds had been intentionally inflicted. Sanau and I were led to the center of the clearing and held gently but firmly by two of the monsters. She forced a semblance of a smile to urge the leaders to renew their courage. We stood while the monsters apparently settled themselves. It was obvious that we were waiting for someone or something.

"Probably their leader," Sanau whispered.

She was right once again. Suddenly the sky blackened and a new swarm approached; but in the center flew a monstrous queen bee, so evil and grotesque she could only have been in a madman's nightmare.

She must have been twenty-five feet in height. Her head was three times the size of my own and her wingspread was easily twenty feet across. She landed with an easy grace then turned and appraised Sanau and myself. Then, with deliberation, she lumbered to the trees which held the leaders and the pilot captive. For a moment she stood motionless; her unearthly eyes piercing them. Her next action was so swift and violent that it happened before my brain could record its meaning.

Twice she crawled laboriously up and down in front of the men, then pulled herself to an upright position and faced Leader Corla. For a second I thought she was trying to make contact with him. So did he, poor soul, for he inclined his handsome head expectantly. She came closer and then, with no warning, a spearlike tongue three feet in length shot from her mouth and stung him through the throat. Sanau moaned. It seemed like buckets of blood poured from his neck as he screamed in agony. It took him ten fully conscious minutes to die. I kept my eyes to the ground, gritting my teeth, but ended up retching painfully. I heard Sanau muttering some prayer. I knew it was a prayer because I heard the name Yargo chanted softly.

Leader Kleeba and the pilot were brave men. They knew they were next, and were prepared for their fate. They faced the queen without flinching, waiting for their horrible end.

But the queen obviously intended to extend no more of her royal energy toward these captives. She turned and crawled away. Then, standing upright, she nodded to the throng and flew off. Half the crowd followed.

We remained, staring at Leader Corla's lifeless and bloody form, now slumped against the tree. Leader Kleeba and the pilot gazed somewhere far off: I am sure they were envisioning the Yargo and their beloved planet to give them fortitude.

As if to prove my deepest fears, six of the monsters came from the ranks and faced the remaining two men. This was the firing squad. The queen's intent was now obvious; she had merely picked Leader Corla at random to show what she wished done with them. It was up to her men to finish the job.

For some reason, we were to be spared, at least for a time. Suddenly Sanau and I were lifted in flight, but not soon enough to escape hearing the agonized yells of Leader Kleeba and the pilot.

CHAPTER 18

Sanau and I remained alone and unmolested for twenty-four hours. The creatures appeared only to bring us food. It tasted like honey, but it was in solid form. We nibbled at it silently, both carefully avoiding the subject of our dismal futures. There was just one faint hope to which we both clung: the missing pilot.

Somehow they had not yet discovered our ship. But what could one lone pilot do against such an army? Even if he attempted to escape with the ship, he would soon be overtaken by their vast fleet.

No, it was just a matter of time before they captured him and sent him to his end in the manner of the others. While I persisted in searching every avenue of escape, Sanau was completely reconciled to the futility of any such action.

It was her opinion that the monsters were merely keeping us alive until their queen decided what outrageous form of death we should suffer for her amusement.

As the complete hopelessness of our fate crystallized in my mind, I suggested in all sincerity that we take our own lives. No matter how we bungled it, it would certainly be easier than anything the queen would dole out.

Sanau turned a deaf ear to this suggestion. She seemed immersed in clucking her lips and making odd sounds. Just as I was beginning to fear she had lost her mind from fright, the realization hit me that she was trying to reproduce the sounds she had heard the creature make, and was doing her best to try and interpret them. I had to hand it to her. I was either talking cowboy-and-Indian methods of escape or giving in to suicide, but this woman was fighting with her brain and wits to the very end.

She kept at it hour after hour. Every so often she'd scratch some numbers on the ground with a twig and try to work out her findings mathematically. The hive felt almost as if it was air-conditioned, and there was some kind of indirect lighting. I felt my limbs relax and I guess I actually fell asleep, for the next thing I knew Sanau was tugging at me.

"Janet! I've got it! I've actually got it!"

I became alert instantly. Her eyes were sparkling. She actually seemed overjoyed.

"It works!"

I stared at the hieroglyphics on the earth— numbers, circles, fractions, and strange signs. She quickly erased the marks with her feet and smoothed the ground.

I stared unbelievingly. "You mean you actually understand their language?"

She nodded with quiet excitement. I looked

at her with real envy for in that moment everything was forgotten for Sanau: our imminent danger, the creatures themselves, everything had been obliterated by the ecstacy of her accomplishment.

She had worked it out thoroughly, down to the last vowel and consonant. She tried to explain these findings to me. Of course, I couldn't follow a syllable.

She jumped to her feet in impatience.

"I'll summon one of them immediately," she said jubilantly. "I'll speak to it in its own tongue."

I almost broke an ankle in my frantic effort to grab her before she reached the entrance where the massive shadow of a guard lurked. I reached her in time.

"Don't be an idiot," I whispered, "it's our one advantage. We understand them, but they don't understand us. As long as they have no idea of our knowledge, they'll make no effort to conceal anything from us in conversation."

She hesitated for a moment, not absolutely convinced. Sanau, the superwoman, was without trickery or guile; but it was I who suddenly sprang to battle with the tactics of a street fighter, the alley cat that I was.

I rushed on. "Sanau, what do you want to do? Go out and converse with the queen? Display your knowledge and accomplishment and get killed like Leader Corla and the others? These creatures aren't Yargonians, you know. Have you forgotten what's already happened?"

The last statement snapped her around to my way of thinking. She returned to the far end of the cave and sat down. Some of the glow had faded from her eyes.

"I suppose you are right. Even if death did follow," she added with a sigh, "it would be wonderful to actually converse with a member of the insect kingdom. Oh, if only the Yargo could know of this accomplishment!"

I fully understood her wish. I too would have liked this almighty man to know I hadn't been a complete dud on this trip. After all, some of my suggestions hadn't been entirely without merit.

I sank to the ground beside her in weary silence. This was no time to dream of kudos. This was a time to force my brain to work on every cylinder.

In every adventure story I had ever read, heroines always fought through to the bitter end, made incredible escapes, and came through victorious. They never just sat back and awaited inevitable doom, but for once, my too-active imagination refused to function.

We sat for hours, neither one of us offering a pregnant thought. Twice we were visited by two of the things and fed the same honey-like mixture. Sanau listened intently to the weird buzzing sounds. The moment they were gone she turned to me in open amazement.

"They're actually worried about our health!"

"Our health?"

She nodded. "Or so I gathered from their conversation. One said, 'Do you think they can exist on this food?' and the other answered, 'I think their bodies require the meat of living animals.' Then the other replied, 'Perhaps some bird flesh. We must try. The queen would put us to death instantly if anything happened to them.' "

Neither of us could fathom this strange turn of events. Of course Sanau was all for going directly to the queen and having a talk. Once again, I had to point most graphically to the fate of the men to deter this impulse.

I was not in the least optimistic. Somehow this new concern for our welfare spoke of new dangers to follow. Even when the creatures returned with some small plucked birds I still feared the worst. I almost had to clamp my hand over Sanau's mouth to keep her from asking that they be cleaned and cooked. I insisted that we continue eating the honey, rather than give away our one secret weapon. She sighed with disappointment but conceded my point. We both pushed away the birds and forced down the honey. It was beginning to taste sickening and I was also beginning to have a wild craving for water. In no way did Sanau's enlightening news about the queen's sudden interest in our welfare give me reason to hope. I was positive she was merely saving us for some jubilee celebration. I weighed the possibility of starving myself to death.

We passed a restless night. When the creatures brought us more honey in the morning, we were both weak with the need for water. I kept warning Sanau that no matter how thirsty we became, she must in no way signal for it in their own tongue.

Finally, I did concede that we should try and show them that we were thirsty using some kind of sign language.

We pushed the honey away. They stood for a moment, nonplussed at this sudden refusal. Sanau diligently made signs of scooping water from a brook, but I had to turn away and leave the communicating to her. The sight of these ugly insects made me physically ill.

Sanau kept making signs but took time to whisper that they were holding a worried consultation.

She took my hand and made a motion toward the door. They obediently allowed us to pass. We walked outside; it was unbearably hot. They followed. We entered the woods. There was no stream in sight but we ploughed on, pushing our way through weeds and bushes of the dense forest, and right behind us came the crunch of our ghastly captors.

We found a stream. It looked muddy, yellow, and unappetizing.

"Maybe it's polluted," I warned.

Sanau leaned down and drank deeply. "I only hope it is," she said fervently.

I fell to my knees and scooped some in my hands. I drank a great deal. I tasted the grit of sand but didn't care. Sanau was right. This would be the easiest way. I washed my face, my neck, even ran some through my hair.

We made our way back. Sanau said the monsters were not in the least surprised. They had merely commented on their own stupidity in not offering us water, and were proud that they had been liberal enough to allow us to demonstrate our need. They were anxious to report this new finding to the queen.

"Oh, they're intelligent," she agreed, "but to what degree, I cannot tell. A cannibalistic native of your planet has intelligence. A good horse has intelligence . . ."

"So has a criminal," I added morosely.

We settled back to wait for another endless day to pass. I shut my eyes but sleep refused to come. When I opened them I noticed Sanau was staring off into space with an almost wistful expression. I felt close to her; it was hard to remember how intensely I had disliked her on her own planet.

"What are you thinking of?" I asked.

I was aware when I asked the question that I never would have dared such impertinence back on Yargo; but we had nothing else to do but talk.

She answered: "I was thinking of His Almighty Highness."

That was all. If I allowed myself to think, many things would come to my mind. David, my mother, my home, and yes, His Highness as well. Was there no one else Sanau had any regard for?

Curious, I asked, "Have you any children, Sanau?"

"I have twenty-seven that were acceptable."

My head jerked forward. She had said twenty-seven in the same tone I would have said, "Oh, two or three."

When I got my voice back to its normal pitch I asked, "What do you mean 'acceptable'?"

She didn't answer immediately. I could sense that her first reaction was to ignore the trend the conversation had taken. Then, perhaps she too realized the wisdom of conversation instead of the monotony of our own morbid thoughts, for, after a long period of silence, she said, "My dear Janet, we do not bear children on Yargo in the same manner in which you reproduce on your planet. The actual act of conception is the same, but from there on all similarity ends."

"How on earth have you improved on that? I thought this was one action that has been going on since the beginning of time."

"In a way, we have not gone ahead. In fact, it is much more simple."

"Now Sanau, don't tell me you lay eggs?"

She smiled. "It could be comparable. On our planet when a woman knows she has conceived, she takes a 'reproduction pellet' after four months pass. Then, six days to the hour after taking the pellet, she expels an 'egg.' The reproduction pellet has formed a hermetically sealed disc about the fetus, stronger than steel and softer than flesh. It is comparable to the mother's womb and is supplied with an environment to sustain the fetus for forty-eight hours. The mother immediately takes the disc to the nearest 'bank' and states the exact time she has given birth. The disc is then labeled with the mother's name . . ."

"Not the father's?"

"It is the mother's product. The father is unimportant."

She stretched herself on the ground and closed her eyes, thus signifying the conversation had ended.

But my curiosity drove me on.

"But Sanau, you still haven't explained what you mean by 'acceptable.' "

She answered drowsily, her voice a monotone.

"To have a perfect race, there must be equality. Therefore, when a cell is taken to the 'bank,' it is first studied for imperfections, then for sex determination. If it is female and there is an overabundance of females at the bank, it is destroyed."

"Even if it is perfect?" I was horrified.

She nodded. "The same rule applies if there is an overabundance of males. There is no discrimination toward sex. However, if the cell is perfect, and the quota is open, then the cell is acceptable. It is then placed in an incubation bank where it is given all it ordinarily would extract from the mother's body. In this way the fetus thrives and the mother in turn is spared the parasitic encumbrance."

"Then what happens? I mean, when the baby is ripe, or, well, born. Do they return it to the mother again?"

Sanau shook her head. "The mother rarely sees the child again."

"Never sees her child? But Sanau, why? How can she bear it?"

"Because she is a Yargonian, a creature of the perfect race. An unemotional race."

I argued this point hotly. "A race cannot be perfect unless it has emotions. Strong emotions."

She sat up against the wall. Some of the spirit had returned to her eyes. After all, she was discussing her beloved planet. Venus, the monsters, and even my presence were temporarily erased.

"An emotional people cannot be perfect." Her voice was low and vibrant. "You have wars. Tell me, what are the causes of wars? Emotional disturbance, the desire for wealth and power, or gluttony. This desire causes a leader to rouse his people over some cause that he creates. It might be religion. Think of your history. The first wars on your planet were religious wars; the Crusades, your last World War was caused by hatred for a religious sect. Remember, my friend, there can never be a war unless the people are stirred emotionally.

"Eliminate lust and greed and the leaders

themselves will have no desire to become dictators. When true power comes only with knowledge, there will be no strife. What can money buy if wealth is judged solely by the power of one's mind? If an entire civilization thinks along these lines, the entire idea of war and petty riches becomes completely infantile. You can create one leader, one language, and one universal desire to perfect one's planet and remain, above all, the superior planet in any solar system."

"All right, Sanau." I interrupted her oration. "I'll go along with your reasoning for the elimination of war. Maybe you have got that licked with unemotional logic, but I think it's a good emotion to raise and bear your child and love and live with a husband. It makes for a fuller life."

"Any emotions, even 'good' emotions prevent rationalization. To abolish an evil you must be absolute. Until all possessiveness of one human toward another is erased, the thirst for power abolished, none of the former can be accomplished."

It was getting dark outside. Another fearful day was passing and there was still tomorrow. Perhaps the same thought came to Sanau, for she forced herself to return to the subject at hand, as if in its discussion she could erase the present.

"Marriage is emotional," she went on, "that is why the state of marriage was abolished. It retards a race. Consider yourself, what do most women desire from marriage? There are many and varied reasons, I'll admit. One, and the most altruistic, is to recreate a human form in their image. The reproduction of their own ego."

"Well, what's wrong with that?" I demanded.

"Merely consider the evils it must bring. Children are at best a great responsibility. Men support this responsibility, are expected to remain with one mate all their lives or risk the disrespect of society by abolishing this union. Now, my friend, how can anyone grow to full maturity if he must spend his entire adult life with one mate? The human system screams for variety. No one person can exist solely on the love and devotion of one other person, yet your laws of society demand this; when your people are forced to break these laws secretly or otherwise, they pay society with their emotion-laden consciences. If there is no escape, the tortured people grow frustrated and seek release in some abnormal outlet. In this fashion all sorts of complexes and neuroses are formed."

"But what about the children of your planet?" I insisted. "How are they raised? How can they be normal, never knowing a mother's care or love? Are they kept at the 'bank' until they're adults?"

"They are raised with perfect maternal care."

"But you stated the mothers rarely see their children."

"I said maternal care, not mother's care.

There is a great difference. How many mothers on your own planet are essentially maternal individuals?"

"Everyone has a maternal instinct," I averred hotly.

"Instinct, yes, but how many mothers actually enjoy domesticity?"

I thought about this before answering. Unfortunately, I could see what she was driving at. I knew too many girls newly married who looked back to the days at the office as carefree and happy days. Girls who complained of the endless drudgery of raising their young and running a home. In fact, at that moment I could not actually think of one married friend who actually enjoyed wheeling a baby carriage or cooking up a brew of Pablum. Now and then there was an isolated case of some hardy type who tossed one newborn into a carriage and a three-year-old onto the jump seat and merrily went her way, completely unruffled by such strenuous activities, but I had to admit that these lone individualists were looked upon as peculiar rather than noble by most of their associates. Each new thought served to strengthen Sanau's argument. To most modern women, raising children was a necessity and an obligation rather than a looked-for pleasure, even when the child was loved. I wanted a child. I had assured David that I wanted two or three, but I couldn't honestly admit that I'd revel in early rising and predawn feedings. Perhaps a great love for the child added to the burden, for with it went a conscience that mumbled it was not right to dislike these tasks.

On Yargo all this was changed. Sanau went on to explain that hundreds and hundreds of years ago a study had been made on this subject and the results proved that only twenty percent of all females actually enjoyed raising and caring for children. Of this twenty percent, eight percent were either barren or without children for some reason or another.

The twenty percent who actually enjoyed this task were given positions in the 'bank.' There they tended the fetus from its primary acceptance. In this way perfect babies grew into happy, contented children, who were spared the anxiety of fretful mothers who were constantly overworked, overtired, and overemotional about their welfare.

"This idea in its most elementary form is just beginning to take hold of the minds of your people. Some of your psychiatrists have stumbled upon the theory that love and tender care is the basis for a normal, well-balanced child. Love without hysteria, without emotion. You are just beginning to learn that there is no such thing as insanity, unless a child is born with a physically damaged brain. There is no such thing as a bad child; emotional disturbances create evil. They must be arrested as quickly as one would attend to a malignant growth. To go one step further, if emotion was banished, no child would be emotionally disturbed."

"But what about mother love?" I persisted. "Doesn't the child miss something in not knowing he actually belongs to someone?"

"Children learn that the planet Yargo belongs to them. They learn to worship the almighty leader and to set him as an example to follow. How often do little boys on your own planet set up a father as an idol only to discover disillusionment in early adolescence. Think, my friend, of the disturbances that arise from such a situation. On Yargo the child's idol cannot fail him for he is the most perfect of all men. Thus in patterning themselves after such a god, they in turn will yearn to contribute something that will live on. The child is given a full genealogy of the mother's family. The mother is welcome to visit and learn of the child's progress as often as she wishes. Certainly this is superior and preferable to a mother who is filled with emotional love but must divide her time with cooking, washing, and catering to the husband's demands. This poor soul is so busy that half the time she must say to the little one, 'Don't ask so many questions' or 'Please play with your toys, can't you see mother is busy?' Ofttimes she might even administer a blow if the child performs a misdeed. How many times has a little child heard mother say to a neighbor, 'Oh, if I could just get out of the house for a day, have one blessed day to myself, I would do nothing but sleep'?"

In spite of myself, I laughed aloud. Sanau's mimicry was perfect. I told her so.

"But you forget," she reminded me, "thousands of years back we went through the exact experiences. None of these occurrences can happen today. In our 'banks' and nurseries everyone is there because he or she wishes to be. Everyone is dedicated to tending the child, who learns to feel the world is waiting for him or her to take a role in the scheme of things."

"What happens next?" I was fascinated. "I mean when the child is ready for school."

"The system is very much the same," she answered, "as the children develop, they are sent to live at school. Our theory of teaching works the same way. After all, only a certain percentage of people actually want to teach. I assure you that on your planet over fifty percent of your teachers are poor souls who were forced into this profession through some economic necessity, parental influence, or lack of an offer of marriage. They are unhappy, frustrated, stagnant, and dull in spirit. What kind of people are these to hold the destiny of a future generation in their hands?"

I thought of Miss Massinger and sighed in agreement.

Sanau hastened to explain that the children were not compelled to learn any given subject but were guided along the lines in which they demonstrated genuine interest. Of course, children's minds are not formed and their interests must be guided; but a subject was never forced. If they failed to respond, the lesson was presented with more interest, the teacher was more dramatic. If these efforts failed, the subject was immediately discarded and another proffered. There was no such thing as a child made to suffer the spectacle of public humiliation in failure.

On Yargo, it was not uncommon to find a man a veritable wizard in mathematics, yet almost adolescent in his knowledge of language and art. He was not condemned for this shortcoming; he was given praise for the knowledge he possessed and encouraged to enlarge upon it. In turn, he listened with great respect to the man whose forte was literature and art. They shared a mutual admiration of each other's talent.

Women, no longer burdened with child-bearing or raising, the tending of husbands, and the search for personal beauty, were equally free to continue in their pursuit of knowledge. Since sex itself was also a minor factor, man and woman worked together in complete harmony without any disturbing elements. Complete equality of the sexes was a reality and no laws were needed to proclaim this fact. It was there in actuality.

Some of this left me with countless questions. When I said as much to Sanau she dismissed my objections with a wave of her hand. It had taken the people of her planet thousands and thousands of years to slowly, step by step, come to these conclusions. It would be unfeasible to expect anyone such as

I to suddenly accept such drastic revisions in the social structure.

Although I did have many misgivings on the complete success of these theories, I couldn't help but see some of their basic logic. My own case was an excellent example. I had wanted to be an actress, and now, on this strange planet facing possible annihilation, I suddenly knew it was not just an adolescent fantasy. It had been a very real and honest desire, and for a moment my eyes were flooded with unshed tears for all these unfulfilled ambitions. I wondered if there was a theater on Yargo. I asked Sanau.

Of course there was. And in turn, with surprising interest, Sanau asked me why I had dismissed the idea without a fair trial? Why had it merely been an idea instead of an actuality?

I laughed. "It wasn't just dismissing an idea," I explained, "it was an improbable and impractical whim. First of all, as you are aware, we still have that condition called 'money' on Earth. To become an actress would have necessitated my traveling to New York or California and being staked for a year's trial. This all takes money and it might have taken even longer than a year before I'd even get a walk-on or bit part to try my wings. Meanwhile, who would support me during this period of trial?"

"So you dismissed the idea without ever actually trying it?"

"That's right. It wasn't too hard, either, once I was forced to see the logic involved."

Sanau just stared at me for a moment. Then with an incredulous expression in her lovely eyes she asked, "You mean that's all your life's work became to you—an impractical idea? If there existed this desire from your childhood then that is what you were meant to be. Yet, you overruled and changed your destiny just like that?"

"Well . . ." I found myself floundering. "Yes, I guess you would say I dismissed it. I took a secretarial course and got a job that I liked well enough. I can't say I was ecstatic about it or that it elevated me to higher intelligence. It was a routine job. Then I met David. We're engaged to be married. In fact, we were going to be married in September." I sighed for all the lost pleasure I was now forced to relinquish.

Sanau also sighed, but not from sympathy for my plight. Her sympathy extended to my entire civilization.

"This is most sad. In facing this fate on Venus I am leaving a wonderful planet, a superior race, and the most masterful leader of all. I am to be pitied, but you are to be congratulated for the life from which you have escaped."

"I can't say I prefer this beehive to my new apartment!"

"That is an odious comparison," she replied. "The life that was offered to you on Mars was certainly preferable. At least there

you would have had the chance to learn of a
new race and put your efforts into work that
you might enjoy."

"Sanau, I am not that advanced. I'm afraid
I prefer the simple pleasures of my new
apartment and David to any of the delights
of Mars."

She shook her head with violent disagree-
ment.

"My friend, if you could only hear yourself
as you speak. Listen to yourself without
emotion and in a detached fashion. Why, your
entire life adds up to merely one series after
another of escapes, first from yourself, then
from life itself. You would continue to run
until death held out its arms in comfort. For
you, death would offer peace, an end to your
pain and meager frustrated existence. To us,
death merely offers sweet and well-earned
rest to a life well spent."

"It's not as bad as you make out," I
insisted.

"What are you actually doing that you
enjoy. How can anyone find happiness on your
planet if you are a typical example?"

"Sanau," I almost shouted in exasperation,
"I am a typical example, and I am not unhappy. Perhaps by your standards my life is
stagnant, but remember everything is rela-
tive. Your life would not exactly appeal to
me."

She looked into my eyes. "You have told
me from your heart that you wanted to become an actress, or at least have a chance to

try. That was your paramount desire, yet now you admit to it almost with a sense of shame because you were forced to discard it as an idle dream, without taking time to discover if within your heart and mind there was actually a genuine creative talent. Next you are forced to study a course—shorthand, I believe—that you have no real desire to learn and, upon completing this course, you are next forced to secure a position that also does not fill you with real enjoyment. You slip deeper and deeper into the quicksand of unhappiness and dissatisfaction, but you manage to escape with the discovery of David. You quickly convince yourself that this relief you feel in escape of a sort is love; even though I am not capable of this emotion I am aware that this is not love, my friend."

"You're wrong," I argued hotly. "I didn't have to marry David. I knew other men, but I chose David—above them all. Why, all my friends envy me and . . ."

"Yes, you love him and chose him above the typing and drudgery you were forced to accomplish in this office, but that is all. In comparison to this unwanted job, David was quite a prize. Perhaps, even in comparison to some of the mates of your associates, this David is a prize. Perhaps his features are more symmetrical. Perhaps his earning capacity is superior. So you tell yourself all is well, that you are indeed fortunate. What is next? The anesthesia of excitement prior to your wedding climaxed by the wedding itself.

A few brief months to revel in the new luxury of your emancipation from the reins of your family before you learn you have been bound with less freedom by the reins of matrimony. You bask in this false security. You survey with pride the few meager possessions that you now call your own, enjoying the experience of displaying them to less fortunate friends who might still be imprisoned in the office which you escaped. Next comes your fulfillment, as you put it. You find you are about to bear a child. You believe you have done something extraordinary, something no other has done before, unmindful of the fact that dumb animals throw off several litters every year. You watch with horror as your body swells to grotesque size and shape. For months you lumber about, alternating between mysterious pleasure and dismay and doubt. Will you die? Will the child die? Will it be normal? Will you, yourself, ever be lovely and desirable again? Does your husband still love you with that first admiring passion? Will you ever again recapture that wonderful romanticism of thrilling to his touch? Will he ever forget this misshapen creature you have become and recall the ethereal bride that once he worshipped? Will you have the capacity to be a good mother along with being a good wife and lover? Will this David be successful and make enough money to give this child the necessities it requires?"

"Stop!" I said this with such force that it

brought on the appearance of the creature who stood guard outside the cave. It crawled in and looked at us both, its huge antennae fanning the air as if listening to determine that we were safe; then it turned and crawled away, but we saw its shadow against the ground.

"I'm sorry," I said, chastened. "Sanau, you put such a dreadful connotation on the only wonderful things in life. Sure, you can make white look black. You are taking our life and looking at it through your eyes, devoid of emotion. Without the feeling behind these occurrences, I agree they would appear as distasteful as you make them out to be. A solitary walk in the desert can be a long hot tiring walk. But take that same walk with someone you love, it becomes an experience to remember, and even a desert becomes a lover's lane. I think it's not really just for you to give an analysis of our life as such an impersonal spectator."

"Not as impersonal as you believe," she answered. "You seem to forget we also have gone through these experiences. We once lived with emotions. Not I nor my mother, nor my grandmother, but we have histories and even novels that record these emotions and facts just as you have documents. You have been taught the customs of the natives of your African jungles, of the Indians, even their marriage rites and ceremonies; therefore, I speak from knowledge when I blast the soul-burdening customs of your planet."

I shook my head. "Blast away. Had I been left on Earth, I would have been able to enjoy experiences and emotions such as you will never know. You dwell on the bad things, the swelling of the body, the doubts, but you omit the wonderful experiences that make all the worry and fear well worth enduring. Sanau, maybe it's worth it all for the one wonderful moment you completely overlooked. To lie back after those long months of worry and anguish and then experience the joy of having a baby placed in your arms. To know it is of your blood and bones, united by the blood of the man you love. To know that everything it possesses it has drawn from your body, and you revel in the joy of being permitted to give to this life. It's a living thing, living because of you. I'm fully aware that an alley cat throws off a litter, but her litter is more comparable to the twenty-seven children you have produced, for they are only the afterbirth of a moment of bodily pleasure. If I had been fortunate enough to marry David and have a child, it would have been concrete and living proof of the culmination of real love."

"Real love that would last exactly, as you put it, for a day, a month, a year." There was an undisguised sneer on her face. "But what is one week or one year of selfish happiness, added against years of toil and dispelled ambitions? You are forgetting all the hopes and dreams you were forced to discard in trade for this short-lived ecstacy. You forget

your desire to become an actress. You forget
the boredom of learning a trade for which
you had no use. Think of it, an entire year
spent in uninspired effort. Janet, you can
lose worldly riches and regain them, but you
can never win back a moment of time. And
what happens after this great moment where
you lie back and revel in the miracle of
bearing this child? You will spur your mate
to work at a faster pace than ever and he
will comply, thus meeting a far earlier death
than nature intended. You will spend your
life scrimping for necessities and luxuries for
this child, and will be forced to take on
added chores that give you neither joy nor
inspiration. Before long, you will have com-
promised every idea that in your mind once
spelled happiness. Then, after a life of working, worrying, and striving, your child will
reach maturity. If it is a girl she will go off
to the arms of some man and live the same
life as you. If it is a male child he will come
to you and state his ambition in life. Nine
times out of ten it will not be what you desire
for him or it will be against the wishes of
the female he has selected as a mate. Either
he will be an individualist and oppose you all,
living in torment with his conscience for
causing you unhappiness and for all he has
lost—no success will give him peace of mind
or real fulfillment—or, if he acts like ninety
percent of your civilization and takes the road
of least resistance, he will be thrown into an
occupation that gives him no spiritual grati-

fication and will become one of the automatons you call humans. Thus the cycle continues."

I stretched out on the cool earth. As an orator, Sanau had no peer. Emotionally, I was opposed to her arguments, but mentally I was no match for her rationalizations, so I refrained from further argument. And there was the gnawing doubt that perhaps she was not too far from wrong.

As if to nourish this seed of doubt she continued to detail my own destruction of spirit.

Had I been fortunate enough to have been born on Yargo, I would have been given every opportunity to fulfill my desire to become an actress. When my education was complete I would be placed under the guidance of the Theater Council. Under the wing of the council I would be given a chance to act every conceivable role. The public would act as judge and jury; there would be no critics or press agents that had power to create or destroy an artist. Then, after a time, if it was discovered that my talent was insufficient (which would be improbable since anyone who genuinely loves a craft and works at it without interference rarely fails), I could continue as an actress and strive toward perfection. If I did desire to change, a place would be found in the profession I loved, teaching, designing.

"You see, my friend," she added, "love does exist on our planet, but not love as you define it. Love is for work and creation, not love for one human from another."

"You mean there is no human you actually love?" It seemed incredible.

"I love all my people, though it is not love as you understand it, and respect the work they are doing. In not loving a single human, there can be no jealousy, hate, or intrigue. There is no one toward whom I bear ill will, which I'm sure is more than can be said for an Earth human."

It was completely dark now. A creature lumbered in, bearing honey and water in crude cups fashioned from giant leaves. We ate and drank silently. I had forgotten for a moment the real peril that lurked outside the hive. It was odd, on this night that hung heavy with danger and evil foreboding, that we should talk so rationally of the ways of our planets.

I finished eating and stretched out for the night. I remembered David had a friend who had served time in a prison-of-war camp overseas. Six of their buddies had been mowed down by the firing squad and they were aware that the dawn would bring the same end for them. Thus, on their final night they had all sat around discussing their homes, children, arguing politics and the philosophy of life in general. They talked about everything except the eventuality they were soon to face. Only two hours before dawn the Allies stormed upon the prison camp and they were saved. But Sanau and I had no marines or air corps fighting to rescue us. These were our final hours and there was not even a ghost of a chance upon which to hang a feeble ray of hope.

Just as I closed my eyes, I took courage from the added protection of the dark to ask Sanau the question that had been paramount in my mind all along.

I asked if she was in love with the Yargo.

She expressed no surprise or anger at this question.

With beautiful calm and complete lack of guile, she answered. "Of course I love the Yargo. To love him is comparable to loving one's work or one's planet. For there is nothing that any mortal on this or any other planet can achieve that he cannot equal or surpass."

Then she closed her eyes and probably fell into rapturous meditation of his image.

And so passed the second night on the planet of Venus.

CHAPTER 19

The following morning our monotony was relieved by a surprise flight. No sooner had we finished the ever-present honey than we were lifted in the air by the monstrous creatures and flown across the planet.

The sun broke through the haze with the same infrequency as that of the moon, yet it was bright and hot on Venus. I marveled at the calm acceptance with which I now found myself viewing these little air hops. I floated through the air with no protection other than a pair of giant hairy arms, knowing the droning sound of a motor as only the buzzing of a man-killing insect, yet my only fear was of the events to come.

The trip ended before a giant hive, ornate in structure, that made our dwelling resemble an anthill. I assumed this was the dwelling of the queen. I was correct.

She or it was waiting when Sanau and I were deposited inside the hive. I stood very close to Sanau so she could interpret any fragments of talk she might hear and understand, but to my chagrin and mounting anxiety, Sanau never opened her mouth. It was not for the lack of activity. There was constant buzzing and gyration of antennae, first from the queen, then her staff, then another group who voiced some opinion. The noise grew deafening, like an enormous sawmill. I nudged Sanau and threw her an imploring glance, but she acted like one in a trance, as if she was not capable of understanding me, let alone these strange creatures.

Suddenly the queen raised her great bulky frame to an upright position and made some rattling, buzzing sound. It was a blood-chilling sight: this monstrous insect standing on its hind legs, enormous wings cascading to the ground, tremendous eyes glaring at the room. I turned away.

Obviously, the queen was giving some command and when she had finished, she settled down on her haunches. A tremendous buzz filled the room followed by a sudden hush.

Sanau had fainted!

I think she actually revived herself. The creatures displayed great concern, pressing water and honey to her lips. She managed to open her eyes with apparent effort and pull herself unsteadily to her feet. I held her arm despite my own sudden weakness, for I knew that Sanau had fainted because of something she had heard, something concerning our respective futures. If she had fainted, then I would probably be carried off, a screaming, raving lunatic. It was probably well that only one of us understood at the present.

But I pushed these thoughts from my mind.

My main concern at the moment was that these creatures would not grow aware that Sanau understood them. Fortunately their present concern seemed to be solely with her immediate welfare. They rushed us away and gently returned us to our place of imprisonment.

The moment we were alone I turned a face white with fear to Sanau. She turned away and moaned hopelessly. I kept my voice down as I pleaded to know the facts in their entirety, but her refusal to answer caused me to shake her in frustration.

"I demand to know," I shouted. "I have a right to know!"

She looked at me with eyes brilliant with anguish.

"My little friend, I know nothing. It was merely the heat that caused me to succumb."

She was not well versed in the art of subterfuge. I tried again.

"A Yargonian does not faint under physical handicaps that an Earth person can bear, Sanau. You're not being truthful."

She refused to answer and stretched on the ground, turning her back to me.

I spent a fruitless hour pleading, cajoling, and threatening but she never answered.

When the now nauseating honey and water was brought for our evening meal, I was almost exhausted from lack of success and strained effort. What had she heard that had caused her to faint? That had made her superior spirit wilt to such a degree?

I began to nibble halfheartedly at the honey.

"I would advise you not to eat," she said tonelessly.

I dropped the honey quickly. "Are they going to poison us?"

"That would be a compassionate death," she answered.

I pushed away the food and water and sulked. I remonstrated that I thought her attitude was unfair. No matter what means of death awaited us, the uncertainty that plagued me was more frightening than the truth.

She studied me as if trying to ascertain the honesty of my statement. Obviously accepting my words at their value, she reconsidered and dropped her mask of pretense.

"I was going to keep it from you, my friend, for your own welfare, to allow you at least another night of rest. I can only state that death by our own hand is our only choice."

She began to search the hive for some rough implement to serve this purpose; but the room was empty. Even our food containers were fashioned of soft leaves.

"A branch of a tree would do," she said frantically, "we could manage to pierce our wrists."

All the while I followed her about, helping in the search and urging her to tell me the whole truth. After assuring herself that her search was completely fruitless, she sat down and faced me. There was absolute desperation in her eyes.

"It is not a pretty picture, Janet. I had underestimated them by far. Although they in no way compare with the superior intelligence of the Yargonians, they surpass the inhabitants of your planet in every way. In fact, at one time, they enjoyed the exact physical structure of the humans of your Earth."

These bees were once people? It was impossible to believe, but as Sanau continued, the facts gradually broke through to me. Most of her knowledge had been garnered from the arguments between the queen and her subjects. Our fate was entirely the queen's idea. At first, there had been dissension about it among her people. They wanted to see us go to an instant demise in the way of the leaders and pilot, but today the question had been opened for general discussion and vote. Finally, the queen's alarming proposition had been accepted with vigorous majority.

The planet Venus, Sanau explained, had once enjoyed the same climatic conditions as Earth and Yargo. Following her glacial age, when Earth was mostly an empty globe of water and ice, Venus was the first to grow warm enough to support a race of humans. Then, as millions of years passed, the temperature of Venus grew in intensity and the humans gradually evolved to a race of giant insectlike creatures.

They finally learned to control their impossible climate by building living quarters that absorbed and dissipated the heat and humidity. This accounted for the comfort of the hive in which we were held.

Every now and then a mutation was born, a throwback to the original stock from which they had come. This mutation was often half man, half bee, or a bee with some human characteristics. Fortunately, the mutation rarely survived longer than a few years, but the monsters themselves were a vain lot and did not admire the creatures they had become. They nourished the hope that, perhaps, eventually they could completely return to their former human image.

To add to this spark of hope, the queen had produced a freak mutation that looked almost human. It was a male.

I had been following this bizarre tale with almost a sympathetic interest but when Sanau paused, my sympathy turned to immediate panic. I hardly needed her conclusion. It hit me right between the eyes! She continued to speak. I listened, hoping beyond all reason that my worst fears would not be realized.

"And now we enter the plot," her voice was low. "We are to be privileged to start a new generation. We will bear the offspring of this bee mutation who has somehow managed to survive the age of puberty."

I wanted to faint; I longed for five blank minutes to forget the story she had told.

But I didn't. I merely sat and stared into space. This couldn't be happening to me!

"They are very intelligent," Sanau droned on. "They have entertained this plan for some time, waiting for just such an opportunity as this. They could not land on your Earth or my planet. To risk a kidnapping was too great a danger. They dared not attack our ships. We usually always travel with a complete fleet. In fact, they took great precaution to remain out of our sight as they knew we were superior in force and might and could easily annihilate them. The sight of a lone ship was the vision for which they had longed.

"You were right when you assumed they had no intention to attack. They were waiting for us to run out of fuel so they could force us to land on Venus. By escaping as we did, we played right into their hands."

"But why did they kill Leader Corla and the others? I should think they'd want as many humans as possible."

Sanau smiled. "You forget this is a race of bees. There are no fertile females but the queen. Had the mutation been a queen bee, then Leader Corla, Leader Kleeba, and the pilot would have been spared and we would have met their fate. This mutation is a male so we are necessary. It is their plan that our offspring marry and intermingle with other mutations. In this way, eventually a race of humans will reevolve."

"You said marry, Sanau."

She nodded. "With the race as it is, with one female ruling a race of workers and drones, marriage is impossible. But they are so anxious to recreate their former civilization that they intend to pursue every human custom they once knew.

I didn't answer. We both fell into a bottomless depression, tortured by the visions of our own imagination. I can't remember how we passed those dismal hours. Neither of us slept that night, nor did we speak. I only know that with the first break of dawn came the appearance of the ghastly monsters. They had arrived early on this day of days to bear us to the waiting crown prince.

Our future husband!

CHAPTER 20

We were spirited to the large clearing that obviously operated as their main meeting place and site for all ceremonial rallies.

The queen was perched upon a small stump, her small entourage directly behind her. Massed before her was, I assume, the entire population of Venus. They must have numbered close to a million, insignificant in comparison to the population of Earth or Yargo, but completely overwhelming to Sanau and me. The clearing must have been about three acres but did not provide ample space for this mass turnout. Even the trees were laden with these monstrous giants, eager-eyed spectators in the bleachers.

We were brought directly before the queen. She stood in her clumsy fashion and gave a signal.

The crown prince himself was brought on the scene. In a cage! We faced the monstrosity that with our aid was to propagate human life on Venus.

He was exactly as Sanau had described: half man, half bee. It seemed as if his entire mind and body resented this error of nature for he raged about the cage like a wild animal, snarling, buzzing, and making eerie guttural noises that sounded like the beginnings of words.

He was small even compared to a man, not over four feet. His torso and legs were completely human in form. From the waist up he was covered with a fuzz that resembled fur. Instead of arms he had wispy imitations of bee's legs that looked incapable of doing anything more than angry fluttering and on his crooked back were two large misshapen inanimate wings. But it was his head that was the most grotesque. It was shaped like a human head, but twice as large, and without hair. The same furry substance that covered his body ran through the middle of his scalp and down his back. He had antennae, but his eyes were great faceted bee eyes and his nose was flat. He bared fangs as he raged and snarled.

It was obvious that he did not compare to the other inhabitants of the planet in intelligence. Nature had obviously spent all her energy fashioning this weird body and had forgotten the brain. That he was also violent was proven by the cage, for why else would a crown prince be treated with such disrespect?

I noted a strange mixture of pride and misery in the queen's glance as she appraised her hapless son. I'm sure that secretly she would rather he had been merely another monstrous bee, happy in its flight through the swampland, free to engage in normal activity, equipped with a mind to respect and love her. Instead, the destiny of her race all lay in that warped mind and body.

She quickly turned to her subjects, once again the queen—a mother no more—and quickly buzzed some orders. I saw Sanau stagger against the giant who held her. My stomach dropped, for although I had no idea of what lay in store for us, Sanau's expression was enough to arouse my alarm.

A small army armed with spears fashioned from tree branches immediately marched to the cage and entered. The creature in the cage growled, hissed, and brayed; it sounded as if thousands of wild animals were at bay. The bees who entered held their distance, using their spears as an animal trainer uses the chair to fend off the lion. After ten minutes of blood-chilling screams and snarls, they managed to corner the now livid prince and bind him to one wall of the cage. They left the cage and bowed low before the queen, who once again buzzed some command. Sanau wilted visibly. Two monsters approached and took us from our original captor. They started to lead us toward the cage! I pulled back with a wild scream but those steel arms held me firmly. It was a useless struggle. Sanau and I were pushed bodily into the cage. The door swung shut, leaving us to face the bound and raving creature inside.

Everyone gathered about the cage. It

promised to be an interesting spectacle. Sanau and I pressed together on one side, putting the entire length of the cage between the creature and ourselves. Still snarling against its outrageous treatment, it hadn't even noticed us.

Suddenly it seemed to grow aware that it was not alone and looked up in the midst of a screaming growl. Its bulging eyes met mine. I crushed my fist into my mouth to stifle my scream, fearful I might stir it to further violence. God help us both if those ropes didn't hold.

Suddenly, its fury ended and it became strangely serene. It switched its glance to Sanau, then slowly back to me as if appraising us both. I stood in the dread fascination that must hold the rabbit under the spell of the snake. Then an amazing thing occurred. The thing's saliva-drenched lips slowly parted into a grimace. I'm sure it was intended as a smile, but the yellowed fangs were so frightening that I shuddered violently. Then it began to bob its head, its gaze fastened on me.

Sanau whispered, "Stay calm, nothing will happen yet. Their intent is to put us with it until it gets accustomed to us. It has the intelligence of an imbecile."

I nodded. I even tried to smile. Then it began to flutter those useless little arms and its antennae fanned the air causing a breeze strong enough to blow my hair. Saliva dripped down its chin as it pawed the ground like a colt. I wondered if it was as obvious to the bee monsters as it was to me that the thing had taken quite a fancy to me!

Sanau protectively stepped in front of me, but neither of us had counted on the imbecile's oneness of purpose. He immediately began to snarl and twist, proving with no doubt that he wanted to view the vision of his real love. Me!

Sanau had been completely rejected.

So as not to cause any further commotion, she immediately stepped aside. The thing ceased its angry movements and fixed me with a velvety stare. There were no visible pupils in its great eyes.

"I was testing its intelligence," Sanau whispered. "I wanted to block you out and see whether it would be just as content to gaze at me or whether it actually had a preference."

"Looks like it had," I agreed miserably.

"Perhaps then they will destroy me." There was real hope in her voice.

"I doubt it. They'll probably hold you as a spare." I had no intent of levity, it had just come out that way. "After all, they have to wait and see. Maybe I'll prove barren with that thing . . ." I had to stop as the meaning behind my words brought home my inescapable fate.

Sanau sighed audibly as if the same thought had occurred to her. The thing settled back on its haunches and slid to the ground, watching me with obvious contentment.

It remained calm until they took us from

the cage, then suddenly and violently it leapt
into action. If possible, it seemed more enraged than ever, and for one terrified moment I was positive it was going to smash
through its ropes and cage. Perhaps the
queen was also concerned, for her next command caused the cage to be immediately
borne off, its screaming inhabitant shrieking
what I am sure was the Venusian equivalent
of violent oaths.

Then we, in turn, were flown back to our
former place of imprisonment.

As soon as we were alone and had caught
our breath, Sanau informed me of their plans
for us. Our bridegroom, it seems, was completely unaware of the facts of life. Because
of the obvious inadequacy of his mentality, he
had been kept in captivity. No right-thinking
lady bee wanted any part of him. The queen
did not wish to subject him to any undue
strain, as the strength of a mutant was a
perilous thing at best. So they had kept him
celibate, hoping to capture a true human or
that some other creature would produce a
female mutant. But now fate had made their
impossible dream into a reality. Like insects
drawn into a spider's web, we had intentionally landed right on their planet, and the
mutant had shown obvious delight in the
arrangement. Now they were fully prepared
to proceed.

"I suppose now they'll tell him all about the
birds and the bees," I said in an effort to

force some levity into this impossible situation.

Sanau actually displayed the semblance of a smile. "In a way, yes. They will put him with a volunteer female of their race, a sub-queen. Instead of facing a death battle with the present queen, which is the usual fate, she will be richly rewarded and given a small province of her own to rule."

"You mean there is more than one queen?" I was surprised.

Sanau's brow creased in an effort to order her findings. "From what I can observe, they do not behave exactly like the bees of Earth or my planet. This queen obviously rules and propagates the race. In the insect world of the bee, when another queen is born, she fights the old ruler in a death battle and the victor rules. But, obviously, since their planet is so large, the new queen can merely travel to another province and will only cause war if she thinks she can be victorious. This queen is sole ruler at the moment. Also, I believe that they do not lay eggs, but bear their young as mammals do."

There was a moment of silence. I finally broke the awful stillness with the question we were both secretly asking ourselves.

"What do we do? Certainly we don't just sit around and wait for this revolting thing to happen?"

"I think we must starve ourselves to death."

Sanau had answered quietly and almost matter-of-factly, and I nodded my acquiescence in equally serene fashion. Suicide is a violent action; it should be accomplished quickly as befits the desire behind it. But starvation did seem the only alternative at the moment in spite of the fear of self-destruction. The awareness of what living would bring made death a welcome thought.

When the food was brought to us, we made a pretense of accepting it. The second the creatures disappeared we scooped holes in the earth, filled them with the honey and water. We refilled them with earth, smoothed the ground, and returned the empty containers.

We dutifully followed the same procedure the following morning. I was disappointed that neither of us experienced any hunger pains or felt any weakness. I felt sure we'd both be alive when the prince was ready for the experiment. To add to this mounting fear, the creatures must have anticipated our plans for they remained with us during our evening meal. Sanau motioned to me to consume the food. We could not arouse their suspicion, so I obeyed. The moment they had gone she pulled me to the corner of the hive and there we both forced ourselves to regurgitate. When this sickening procedure had been accomplished, we buried the traces.

I actually began to feel faint. I am not sure whether it was caused by the forceful ejection of the food or the actual lack of it, but my head grew light and I felt violent pains in my abdomen. Sanau agreed she too was not feeling particularly fit and so we enjoyed a macabre moment of hope. With each pang of nausea our spirits lifted. We were beginning to die!

I grew so weak I was forced to lie flat on the ground, my face pressed to the coolness of the earth. I had never really thought about death. I had always secretly hoped that when my time came I would be blissfully unaware. Death couldn't be terrifying if you didn't know it was there. It would be like going to sleep, shutting your eyes and drifting into unconsciousness, never to waken again. After all, the unhappiness associated with dying is not actually the uncertainty of what will become of you, but the misery of leaving the ones you love and the joy of your present existence.

In reality, as far as leaving the pleasures that made life worth living were concerned, I had died the moment the beam from the Yargonian ship had grasped me from my own Earth.

Even on Yargo there was no life for me. The ruler, splendid as he might be, was not actually real. The exhilaration caused by his presence was inspired by my own imagination. The charm that radiated from him was not for me; the smile that made me choke was not even directed to me. To love and admire him would be as emotionally fulfilling as loving a beautiful painting or any work of art, comparable to worshipping and dreaming of a mountain peak or sunset. Beautiful and unreal and equally inanimate.

Yes, I had died on the sand dunes of Avalon. Now I was merely waiting for it to take effect.

CHAPTER 21

I was so weak the following morning I could barely pull myself to a sitting position. I managed to open my eyes and through the slits in the crude door saw that it was daylight. I was thoroughly awake and no longer desired sleep, yet my eyelids fell together and I slumped back on the floor without the desire or ability to arouse myself.

But Sanau was created of stronger stuff; she knelt beside me in concern.

"Are you all right, Janet?"

I stirred slightly to prove that unfortunately I was still alive.

"Wake up. Force yourself to sit," she commanded. "Sleep rebuilds the body. Unfortunately, I feel quite fit this morning. From now on we must not sleep."

I forced myself to obey. My head was light to the point of nausea. My throat cracked and demanded water.

"We must walk," she insisted.

She dragged me to my feet. "We must pace this room to use up our remaining energy. That is half the trouble. Starvation alone might take days and we may have only hours.

We must help to weaken our resistance with physical action."

And so we walked to die. Somehow I managed. It was like sleepwalking. Sanau was actually envious of my lowered resistance as she towed me around and at the same time I think she was grateful for the added burden it forced on her too-durable structure. Finally, it proved too much for both of us and we sank to the ground. I was bathed in dank perspiration.

"How long do you think it will be?" I was gasping for breath and my heart seemed ready to explode in my chest.

She measured me with a long glance. "There is no doubt that you will be the first to die. Your strength is failing rapidly. For once I desire the inferiority of an Earth person." Her tone was genuinely wistful.

"You keep walking," I urged, "don't sit and console me."

Obediently she complied. Her pacing was exactly that of a caged animal and she did not stop until two of the creatures appeared with our food.

Once again they remained while we forced ourselves to eat. Whatever the mixture lacked in taste was certainly made up for by its supply of vitamins. I could almost feel new strength forcing itself through my body, but I wasn't alarmed. Naturally we both intended to repeat the distasteful but necessary occurrence of the previous day.

But to our consternation, only one giant departed. After a short consultation between themselves, one settled down close at our side.

"What will we do?" I whispered to Sanau.

She shrugged. "It is too late, my little friend. It seems the mating of the young prince was amazingly successful, and what he lacks in intelligence he makes up for in virility. Now that his appetite has been whetted, he is eager for us."

"N..o..!" The word choked in my throat. I only needed to see the expression in her eyes. I turned away.

"Strangle me," I pleaded. "I'll be first, I know it. Please kill me, Sanau."

"I only wish I could." There was compassion in her voice. "But even if I attempted such an act, our guard would prevent it."

I slipped behind her. "Now," I demanded in a whisper. "It can't see me. Reach out, choke me. Please!"

She actually made the attempt. Her hands slipped behind and gently gripped my throat. I offered no resistance. I prayed for death to come. She pressed her fingers, soft but firm . . . harder . . . harder . . . I felt the wind go from my chest; water seemed to fill my lungs and against my will and desire my body violently objected to this attempt at destruction. I struggled and when I began to choke, the creature immediately leapt forward. Sanau instantly released her grip and turned to me in mock concern. Although it

had no idea of the action we had tried, it chose
to remain at my side in almost paternal
concern.

I regained my breath and soon felt none
the worse for the experience except for the
pain of remorse over the failure of the
incident.

Soon we were greeted by a committee. The
actual offering was about to proceed.

Once again we were airborne to the large
clearing and once again the entire population
had amassed. Sanau and I were brought
directly before the queen. She, in turn, gave
a hissing command and with no warning, two
monsters began tugging at our space suits.

Obviously the occupants of Venus did not
think them suitable for bridal attire.

Sanau's outfit was the first to be removed.
I was obligingly helping my monstrous guard
with some stubborn clasps when I stopped
and gasped with rage and embarrassment.
They were tearing off the remainder of
Sanau's clothes. She offered no resistance but
stood naked and beautiful, her head held high,
her eyes staring scornfully ahead. It was as
if she was trying to offer me an example.

Then I too was stripped. The creatures
took no obvious interest in our bodies. This
was purely a clinical experiment.

To my surprise, Sanau was selected as the
first to go. She was led before the queen, who
nodded in agreement, and the cage was
brought on the scene. The prince stopped all

movement when he saw Sanau; the whiteness of her body seemed to hypnotize him. I shuddered with horror when I realized that this time there were no ropes to hold him at bay. For a moment he stood motionless, staring at Sanau, then he screamed and extended his shriveled arms through the bars, groping toward her. Now that he had enjoyed a taste of life, he was obviously less particular. He did not even waste a glance in my direction.

They led her to the cage. I screamed and tried to dash toward her but two steely arms dragged me back. I don't know exactly what I intended to do; it was merely the unconscious reflex that exists in all of us to save someone from destruction, to reach out and break the fall, not a true show of courage.

I turned away. They were leading her to the cage. It was too horrible to watch. I sobbed for Sanau as well as myself and through my screams I heard Sanau's voice.

"Janet! Stay calm! Nothing can hurt either of us anymore, except our fear. Force yourself to rise above it. Pretend it is not actually happening. Think of Yargo, of your planet, of your David."

That was the last I heard. The thing snarled a hyenalike laugh. I opened my eyes. Sanau waited before the cage, as one of the creatures crawled to open the door. She stood erect, the whiteness of her skin impossibly beautiful against her black hair falling down her shoulders. I marveled at her unflinching bravery. She resembled some pagan goddess proudly going to a fiery sacrifice.

A true Yargonian to the end, practicing the primary rule of her belief. Not a flicker of emotion. Not even by a droop of a shoulder did she in any way betray the panic she was experiencing. Coldly and almost defiantly she faced that buzzing, drooling beast. Just the bars between them, just a few seconds of time separating her from this horrible fate, and still she did not flinch. With full admiration I bowed to her superiority. It was easy to preach, yet in this final moment, she was living out her most fervid declarations. I longed to emulate this bravery yet knew when my time came I would be dragged screaming hysterically.

And now everything was ready for the final act. The guard stood at the door ready to open the cage. He turned to the queen, awaiting her command, but she chose to fall to her knees and perform some small ceremony prior to the rite itself. All of her subjects followed. This delay only served to prolong Sanau's agony. She stood motionless before the cage, staring at the thing that awaited her inside. I prayed for her. I prayed for myself and tiers and tiers of monstrous bees also prayed, possibly for a favorable outcome to this fantastic experiment.

I watched them in horror. Their black shiny bodies making the ground glisten like ebony. It seemed incredible that they too were praying. I wondered to what kind of deity. Could it be possible we shared the same? I looked toward the heavens as if seeking an answer. The sun had filtered through the maze, a poor, weak, pitiful sun, as if embarrassed to witness these grim proceedings.

And then I saw it!

At first I thought the sun had played tricks with my vision, or perhaps it was my imagination. I shut my eyes to allow the brightness to fade, then reopened them for a more positive look. But there it was—a small round silver disc! I fell on my knees and began to sob. It might not be too late. My sobs rose above the buzzing chanting of the praying insects. Sanau heard me and turned.

"Janet," her voice was low and composed, void of the panic she must be feeling. "Janet, don't cry for me. It will be all right. Save your strength. This is something we both must face and accept."

"Look up, Sanau!" I sobbed. "Look in the sky . . ."

Then she saw it. I could tell by her eyes and the sudden constriction of her throat. Then she erased all expression from her lovely face and turned rigidly to the frenzied inmate of the cage.

I kept my eyes riveted to the sky. I knew it was dangerous but then I wasn't imbued with the fortitude of Sanau. I was me—Janet —a frightened girl from Earth who prayed for the hope in sight.

Our ship was not alone. I counted six, all the size of small apples. They were coming for us all right. The pilot who had remained with the ship must have escaped somehow and gone to Yargo for help, but it would be too late to save Sanau!

The ritual was over. They were now leading her to the door. Once again I screamed.

"Don't say anything, Janet!" Her voice was a command. "Your only chance is a surprise attack."

I kept staring at the sky. It was too incredible, this bravery of Sanau's. She was no longer thinking of her own fate, she was thinking of me. Placing my hope before her own doom.

"I'm going to shout and point to the sky!" I called to her.

"I forbid it!" She was at the door of the cage. The creature had sprung to it, waiting.

"Say nothing!" she insisted, "else they will man their ships and attack. Not one Yargonian must lose his life needlessly. I am not worth it."

I bit my lip to keep from yelling and tasted blood. Somehow the queen's glance had wandered to the sky and she also saw our ships. She screamed and it sounded as if a thousand saws were cutting through wood. Bedlam broke loose. The guard still remained with Sanau just outside the cage, looking to the queen for further orders. To add to the mounting hysteria, the frustrated beast was roaring its disapproval at the delay and almost bursting the bars of the cage in its fury.

Sanau, the enraged crown prince, and I were temporarily forgotten in the midst of this new challenge. Masses and masses of angry bees, transformed in this rage of disappointment and fear of invasion, surged to command posts. Several squadrons flew over the treetops to man the tiger shark planes. Through the din, the queen constantly buzzed orders.

Sanau and I were still held in the viselike grip of the two guards. I could sense their bewilderment. They stood there, fearful to release their prey, yet unwilling to remain out of action during this counterattack. Several times they buzzed their queen for orders but she was too immersed in her efforts to organize her warriors to pay them any heed. I heard the roar of motors; the takeoff of their ships.

A full air flight was now in progress. Flames tore through the murky heavens. The queen remained on the ground watching the battle. Twelve sentries stood by her side, acting as messengers. In the center of this dreadful arena stood our pitiful group: Sanau, myself, the two sentries, all of us looking heavenward, each praying for our own cause. Only the monster in the cage remained disinterested in the action all around. Outraged that his treasure was being denied to him, his roars could almost be heard above the motors of the ships and bursts of flame that fell to the earth.

The roaring overhead continued. One of their ships crashed nearby, killing two of the creatures. Their comrades dragged their bodies from the ship and I was amazed to see the color of the blood gushing from their wounds. It never occurred to me that it would be red, like my own.

I waited tensely, my heart actually pounding so hard that in my nakedness I could see my breast rise and fall. I prayed that no Yargonian ship would meet disaster. I prayed for Sanau. I prayed for us all.

I could see that we were winning. More and more cigar-shaped ships crashed or came limping down for forced landings. The guards with the queen were completely occupied with attending to the wounded. The queen was left alone, shouting orders, waving her great antennae in rage at the impending defeat. Our ships came lower. There was a vast fleet of them, almost a hundred in all. I could still count about ten tiger planes that darted in and out of their grasp with insect fury, but the fight was well in hand. I wanted to shout in victory, yet Sanau and I still remained captive. Neither guard showed any intention of releasing us, although their eyes were constantly shifting from us to the action overhead and the screaming creature was still reaching through the bars in Sanau's direction.

Suddenly the queen leaped from the tree stump that served as her throne. She came to the center of the clearing and looked to the sky, then at the vast destruction on the face of her planet. She knew our complete victory was at hand.

Quickly she issued some hissing command which caused several thousand limping monsters to emerge from the forests. Some were obviously wounded, some carried the less fortunate, but all wore an expression of abject defeat.

She gave one final command. Our guards released us and followed the queen and her herd in quick retreat to the dense forests beyond. For a moment Sanau and I merely stood rooted to the ground. Our freedom was too unbelievable. Then in a surge of emotion I rushed to Sanau. Her relief was so intense that she backed away and put her hand to her head as if to ward off a sudden faint.

It happened so fast that it was over before I could even cry out. I can only remember that screaming laugh of victory! We had both forgotten about the thing they had left behind, still in its cage. As Sanau had backed away one of those seemingly useless arms had reached out and grabbed her.

She leaped away instantly but it caught her by her arm. She pulled with her last bit of strength until she was white with pain but was powerless to get away.

I rushed to her, careful to stay free of the

monster, took her free arm, and pulled with all my might. It was useless.

"Don't worry," I panted. "We can both hold you off from it. It can't pull you into the cage with our combined force. Our ships will land and kill it."

She nodded and looked toward the sky. One of the ships was circling about, preparing for a landing. It hovered above us then shot down a beam of light. I understood immediately. We were supposed to stand in the ray and be lifted to safety. I shook my head, I yelled, I pointed to Sanau. Obviously the ship could not actually see the disturbance, but it dutifully rose and prepared for a landing.

It was only a matter of minutes now, but Sanau's arm was getting blue. The monster's grip was viselike, preventing the flow of blood.

"It won't be long," I comforted her. She remained motionless, her bland face belying the pain she felt.

I was also suffering from the strain. True, it was two against one in this macabre tug-of-war, but the thing was displaying remarkable strength. Stabbing pains shot through my neck and back, yet I knew if I relaxed my grip for one second, Sanau would be dragged through the bars of that cage.

I began to cough. At first I thought it was from the smoke of the battle. Then I realized that all active fighting had long ceased and most of the fires had been extinguished, and turned to find the cause of the smoke.

My hopes suddenly dropped to the pit of my stomach. From the forest, seeping slowly toward us was a black, oily substance, searing everything it passed over. It was like burning oil or tar, yet from the way the trees and foliage shriveled and perished, I knew it had the power of some superpowerful acid.

This then was their final secret weapon to prevent the planes from landing to save us. They probably had not poured it over their entire planet, just on landing sites and on the square mile around us. It was all over now, just when hope had been so near.

One of our spaceships returned and hovered above us. It saw the creeping peril and the futility of attempting a landing. It was instantly joined by two more ships. I knew at that moment all the brilliant Yargonian minds aloft were working together, frantically trying to formulate some scheme to save us. Of course, there was the beam of light, but it couldn't help Sanau and I couldn't leave her.

"They'll send the beam down, Janet. They're probably communicating with one another now. It's hopeless for me. When the beam comes, let go of me and leap into it. The creature will not get me. The burning oil will reach me first."

I shook my head. "I won't leave you." I was sobbing now, sobbing for both of us.

She smiled but the pain was naked in her eyes. Her arm had doubled in size beneath the monster's grip. The blood had stopped flowing.

"Go, Janet, when the beam comes. I am not afraid of the burning oil. It is not the worst way to die. Just tell Yargo I was not afraid. Tell him I died with his holy image before my eyes."

The oil was slithering toward us. It was not more than fifty yards away. I could hardly breathe through the smoke. The spaceship was directly overhead, hovering, as though gripped by the same indecision that overpowered my own emotions.

Then, in the midst of this horror and destruction, I witnessed the most primitive sight of love and devotion that I had ever been permitted to see. Through the smoky forests, oblivious to her own peril, flew the queen. She must have been completely aware that she was a pathetically easy target for the silver ship above, but if thoughts of danger or self-preservation were in her insect mind, I will never know. I do know that in the last moment, her only concern was to save that monstrous freak that was now raging and choking in the cage. She obviously did not notice the stranglehold it had on Sanau's arm. She swooped on top of the cage, attempting to lift cage and inmate and fly above the destruction to the hiding place and security of her other subjects. She might have made it if it hadn't been for the added weight of Sanau and me pulling at opposite poles.

All the while the oil was creeping closer. It was not more than six feet away. The queen buzzed in fright and pulled with desperate strength. Her son screamed like the infuriated animal he was and Sanau and I fought with our remaining strength.

There was not a second left. I felt Sanau relax; she had stopped fighting.

Then the beam shot from the sky. Nervously it skirted about trying to locate a direct angle on us. It settled inches away, waiting for me to step into the safety of its ray.

"Go on, Janet!" Sanau's voice was weak as she pleaded. "Leave me. Take your safety, I beg you!"

I hesitated. I might have obeyed if only the peril of the searing oil awaited Sanau. But I knew if I released my grasp the queen would no doubt manage to rise in the air with the cage, the creature, and Sanau. Then she would be alive, at the mercy of this thing and the rage of these monsters.

I stepped toward the light, and, at the same time grabbed Sanau's free arm with both my hands and pulled with every ounce of strength I had left. I pulled until her arm became loose in its socket. Still I held fast, my determination suddenly no less than the creature's in the cage.

I was directly in the beam of light now and it began to lift me. It proved an added ally, pulling me as I pulled Sanau. Then with one great wrench, Sanau was free! I held her weightless body in my arms as we lifted in the air. I shut my eyes but not soon enough to miss the sickening tableau on the ground below. The queen lifted the cage with its ugly, inmate screaming its wrath as it stared in disappointment at its meager trophy—Sanau's lifeless white arm, which it now held cradled in its grasp!

CHAPTER 22

The return trip to Yargo was a nightmare. We were wrapped in blankets and given brandy. The pilots left me and immediately went to work on Sanau's arm. I scrambled into a coverall that was on board and stood by, ready to lend any assistance that might be needed, but it took most of my strength merely to remain conscious. Each time I so much as glanced at Sanau's gory wound a wave of nausea came over me.

They worked feverishly on Sanau. Her arm had been torn clean from the socket, but somehow they managed to fashion a tourniquet on the shreds of her shoulder. I was grateful that the loss of blood of this enforced amputation had finally stunned her into unconsciousness.

She lay on the bunk, a blanket covering her perfect form, an ugly vacancy where her right arm should have been. Although the ship was equipped with a full medical kit, and all aid had been administered, they had given her nothing to kill the pain that would soon be tearing through her. For after applying the necessary bandages, the pilots motioned for me to keep vigil while they returned to the engine room. Did their desire for complete supremacy encompass physical perfection as well?

Five minutes passed and then I noticed the first flicker of her eyelids. I wanted to run but I held my post. She had to learn the truth. If only I didn't have to be the one to tell her.

She opened her eyes. She didn't speak but the expression on her face said many things and above all it expressed her gratitude. Then a sudden swell of pain drew her glance to her arm. With a start she tried to release her hand from mine and struggled to pull herself to a sitting position to see the damage that she sensed had happened. By this time my strength won out and she fell back on the bunk, exhausted by the effort.

She closed her eyes. After a moment she said, "It isn't off. It can't be. I still feel pains in my fingers, in my wrist."

I didn't answer but the tears came to my eyes.

Then she looked directly at me. "It is off, isn't it, Janet?"

I didn't need to answer. The tears that slid down my face told her the worst.

She turned away. Her teeth bit fiercely into her lip, I didn't know whether this gesture was from physical pain or the pain of her loss. After a few minutes, with her eyes still closed, she said softly, "I am sorry I neglected to thank you for saving my life, little Janet."

"Don't worry about your arm, Sanau." My words stumbled over themselves childishly as I tried to comfort her. "On Earth we have wars where men lose both arms and legs. They survive and live happy useful lives. We're inferior to you and we manage, so someone like you, completely superior. Why, you don't even need two arms."

I know I sounded pathetically adolescent in my efforts to comfort her but I was speaking from my heart, not trying to turn a phrase. Until our brief allegiance on Venus, I had weighed most of my statements, fearing ridicule, but the past on Yargo and Sanau's previous scornful attitude had long since been discarded from my memory. I held nothing but admiration for her courage and strength. I'd never forget her stern attempt to console me as she walked to her own peril to the thing in the cage. Now I felt it was my absolute duty to do everything in my power to help her through this grim experience.

As if acknowledging my feeble efforts, she managed a smile and touched my head in a rare gesture of affection. Her voice was soft and heavy with pain. "For an inferior being you acted in a most superior manner. I doubt if any Yargonian could have shown more courage."

Then, after a brief pause, she spoke again, slowly, painfully. "And as for my arm, I shall indeed miss it, but I shall manage. I only wish I had lost it in an accomplishment for my leader and my planet. It is sad to have lost it in such a needless fashion." Her last words were lost in a sudden wrench of agony.

"Isn't there anything they can give you to ease the pain?" I asked.

She shook her head and spoke with an effort. "Our anesthetics cannot be administered in outer space. They require too much oxygen."

"What about the needle they gave me to knock me out? Wouldn't that help?"

"No. Our systems do not react to such minor sedation. It would be as ineffective as a shot of water."

Once more again her entire body trembled. I sat there helpless. There was nothing I could do but sit and watch that magnificent woman keep her face immobile and her eyes shut against searing and impossible physical pain.

I found myself praying that she might faint; anything to release her from this unbearable suffering. But she remained conscious and silent, showing only by an occasional grimace or twitch the agony she was feeling. An hour passed in silent pain. The ship was flying in the strange motionless way that only the vacuum of outer space seems to permit. It was comparable to standing alone in a soundproof chamber, as if all sound in the world had suddenly ceased, as if every living thing had suddenly perished, and you were alone in a strange deaf world.

There was nothing but the impossible calm, yet I knew we were traveling with the speed of light. I was alone in a silent world, a dead world, accompanied by the mute face of the stricken woman on the bunk before me.

Faint beads of perspiration broke out on her brow and upper lip. I tore the pocket from my coverall, dampened it with water, and wiped her brow and face. She opened eyes that were brilliant with pain. I wrung her hand in unspoken sympathy. In return, she smiled almost apologetically, as if she was sorry I was forced to witness her misery.

She whispered a request for some water. I leaped to fetch it, holding her as I poured it down her throat. She felt feverish. I also felt a sudden spasm of nausea. She reached out and felt my brow.

"Janet, lie on the other bunk. You are not well."

I shook my head and declared I was fine, but I felt dizzy and was seized with a sudden pain in my stomach. This was no time for me to get sick.

"Get me some clothes," she asked, "I do not want to be carried out on a stretcher. I intend to walk off the ship."

I admired this further display of courage, although I doubted that even she could have the strength to carry it off. Nevertheless, I went to the pilot's chamber and gestured my wants. I returned with a coverall and helped her into it. I was aware that she deliberately kept her eyes from glancing at her severed arm, but neither of us could ignore the empty sleeve.

"It might have been worse," she said with a trace of a smile, "the creature could have had me by the neck."

She fell back on the bunk with a slight moan and this time the perspiration streamed down her face. She was fighting the pain, fighting with all her superiority, but she was losing. I was losing too. Her pain was surrounding us both, crushing us. My throat felt dry and my head ached violently. Several times I actually experienced a doubling of vision. I knew I was nearing collapse. I was no match for this ordeal; the sight of blood from even a minor cut always sickened me. I looked longingly toward the other bunk. The cool pillow invited me to bury my head in it, to hide from the ugliness of pain. Suddenly, I was overcome with a real attack of nausea. I left Sanau only to attend to myself, returning weak but resolute in my determination to stay at her side.

"I wish I could succumb to unconsciousness," Sanau whispered. "It would be easier for us both."

"Stop fighting and relax," I told her. After all, she had fainted before, on Venus. Perhaps she would again.

Evidently she read my thoughts for she answered, "I will not faint. On Venus it happened from horror and shock, then also from lack of blood . . . but now," she smiled ruefully, "I find myself wishing for once that we were not such a superior race. A Yargonian does not faint from pain . . . we merely . . ."

I never heard the rest. It was stifled in a low moan. Suddenly she sat up as if struck by lightning.

"Oh, Janet," she gasped, "I can't bear it! I can't bear it!"

I held her tightly. I held her and muttered all kinds of encouragement. I cradled her as a mother would a child, and all the while I knew that she was violently objecting to the consolation she was accepting. I suppose a Yargonian was not supposed to show pain, that was an emotion, too. But she clung to me against her will, her face still impassive, her breath short from gasping pain.

"Why don't you shout?" I ordered. "Shout, holler, scream, or cry. It might help."

"I can't . . . a Yargonian never shows emo—" I never heard the rest, but I felt the wetness of her tears on my neck. I held her close and pretended not to notice. Then suddenly the dam of impossible pain broke through the dikes of generations of control. Her muffled sobs secreted themselves in my shoulder, and through it all her greater pain in self-deprecation forced her apologies.

"I'm sorry, Janet. I'm sorry to prove so inferior . . . I just can't help it."

She fought vainly for control but the pain was now complete victor. Her sobbing continued for an hour. I comforted her wordlessly and all the while kept an eagle eye peeled on the door. If a pilot chanced to enter, I was determined to shield her. No one would know about this human emotion she had dared to release. Fortunately, we were not disturbed. After a time her sobbing abated, she released her grip on me and fought for her breath like a child. She displayed more fright over this emotion she was revealing than she had over her actual physical loss. I soaked the torn piece of cloth in cold water, and this time I placed it over her eyes. As I did this I noticed she quickly averted her face from mine. Her embarrassment was beyond words.

After a time she regained her composure. Then in a quiet voice she said, "Janet, will you cross the room and press the right panel."

I obeyed, assuming it would summon a pilot for something she desired. To my surprise, the room was suddenly cloaked in darkness, lit only by the faint light of the far-off stars. I sank on the nearest seat, taking this gesture as a cue that she wanted to sleep. Instead she called me to her.

I groped my way across the room and perched on the edge of her bunk. I could just barely discern her features in the faint silvery light. She removed the covering from her eyes.

Her voice seemed to come with great effort. "I want to thank you. Later, perhaps, I will shake your hand and look into your eyes. At present my humiliation is so great, I need the blanket of darkness."

"Sanau . . ." I began, but she put her hand across my lips.

"I realize tears are a normal display among your people, but I have committed a great act of weakness. I have reverted to a primitive emotion that was discarded hundreds of generations ago; I alone, of all the Yargonians, have suffered such a weakness. I do not deserve to be a Yargonian. I do not deserve to be a leader. I have shamed myself and my people."

Once again I started to speak but she stopped me.

"I know you are about to vow a promise of silence. Through my weakness and misery, I was not deaf to your words of comfort. But I will always know that I have showed such a weakness. I have myself to live with, my friend."

When I spoke it was with the loving patience a parent administers to a small headstrong child.

"Sanau, I doubt if any Yargonian in the past few generations has endured the tortures you have suffered in the past twenty-four hours. I doubt if even the great Yargo himself could take this pain without some display."

At the mention of his name, fresh tears sprang to her fantastic eyes, as if she were visualizing his displeasure at her actions.

I searched my mind for every assurance to appease her loss of self-respect. I explained that tears had nothing to do with bravery. That her real bravery had been her strength in the face of actual peril, the way she had tried to bolster my courage. Her great accomplishment in deciphering the language of Venus from some few buzzing noises. To give in to an emotion was not a lack of superiority or mental ability. I explained that on my planet it sometimes took a strong man to cry and that only a strong person could feel an emotion. She listened quietly but I could sense that I was making little headway. Her grief over her humiliation was beyond hope and to add to her torment, her pain was steadily increasing. Several times in the midst of my pleas, she broke down and sobbed anew. After a time I gave up talking and trying to reassure her. I gave up all thoughts other than the effort to try and ease her physical pain, which was now beyond any endurance. I gave her water, I bathed her brow, I rubbed her neck. I shielded her from the pilot when he brought us food. I pretended she was asleep on my shoulder and he merely set down the tray, seemingly oblivious to her welfare. She was a Yargonian. A Yargonian was built to endure pain. He had no doubt that a superwoman such as Sanau could conquer anything.

She offered no objection when I turned on the light so I could feed her and take some food myself. All the while I was fighting off the realization that my own pain was far from imaginary or merely sympathetic. My stomach refused to hold the food and I was running a high fever. Had I contracted some disease from that swamp-infested land or from the monsters themselves? How long had we been flying? Was it all night? Was it a day and a night? In outer space everything is night, and suddenly it seemed as if I had never known anything but these endless hours crammed with pain. I looked at Sanau and fought back the hysteria that I knew was welling within me. Sanau seemed to have taken a sudden turn for the worse. I began to fear for her life. Her face was literally gray and the pain now stretched clear across her back. I wanted to call one of the pilots but she forbade it. I was frightened that some infection might have set in but she assured me it could not be. The wound had been completely sterilized. A Yargonian was incapable of inadequacy.

More torturous hours followed. I must have eventually fallen asleep in a sitting position for when I opened my eyes I was slumped in a chair. It was light in the cabin and it told me we were somewhere within the radius of the sun.

Sanau was awake. Her pain had abated somewhat but her eyes mirrored a hurt far deeper than the actual pain she had suffered: the pain of her own self-disappointment.

"We will land shortly," she said quietly.

"Then what?" I asked.

She looked at me questioningly.

"I mean," I paused, feeling I was taking advantage of our new relationship. Yet the question had to be put to her, and having no alternative, I plunged forward.

"What will become of me? Will I be sent back to Mars immediately?"

She looked at me for a moment. Her answer was quiet and without emotion. "Janet, I have no authority to promise you a thing. I am a leader and my vote counts as such, but we have a true democracy and thus it will be the vote of the majority. But I promise you . . ." she hesitated, then spoke with apparent difficulty, "I would willingly give my other arm if it could help you to return to your planet. I promise you nothing except my wholehearted support."

I nodded. It was enough. I knew how foreign such a speech was, coming from Sanau. I didn't urge her on because I didn't want her to realize she was guilty of committing another unpardonable sin. The sin of expressing compassion for a friend. The unpardonable, abolished emotion of affection.

CHAPTER 23

I remember very little of our actual landing. There was a tremendous crowd at the airport and small fragments of frenzied celebration and cheers broke through to my consciousness. I remember Sanau walking down the ramp, erect and unassisted. I recall the impressive yet unemotional approval bestowed upon our crew by a dignified group of leaders. I heard the deafening shout of acclaim for Sanau, but somewhere—hours, minutes, seconds, I can't say—before our arrival, I had lost hold of my strong resolutions and drifted into the welcome sanctity of semiconsciousness.

No conquering hero, I. My last vestige of newly acquired strength had died a dismal death somewhere in space. I made my descent from the ship in the strong arms of one of the members of the crew, yet I was aware that Sanau had made it exactly as she had hoped to—erect, a perfect Yargonian to the end.

In the murky recesses of my stupor, I promised some unseen witness that come what may, I would never betray what Sanau termed her "weakness." I recall making this vow, and then, obviously satisfied that I had completed some moral pledge, I allowed myself to drift into total unconsciousness with the gratitude with which an insomniac welcomes sleep.

How long I remained in this state I will never know. I was in bed when I opened my eyes and although my surroundings were strange, somehow I sensed I was in the royal palace itself.

It was a magnificent bedroom, enhanced by a wall of glass that afforded a picturesque view of the ever-familiar mountain. Another wall had an open door that led to a terrace. Outside, two female Yargonians were holding a discussion with a serious-looking man.

I pushed myself up against the pillows, following this with a vain attempt to get out of the bed. An excruciating pain in my side prevented any such effort. I fell backward and small drops of perspiration came to my forehead. Something very serious was the matter with me. My movements aroused the group on the terrace, who came directly to my bedside.

Said one woman, in phonetic English, "I greet you good day."

In spite of my pain, I smiled weakly. It had obviously been a laboriously rehearsed speech, prepared for my eventual awakening.

The woman, apparently satisfied with her performance, hurried off, presumably to announce my return to the world of the living.

I lay back, fearful that any delay on her part would make this return a temporary visit, for now I was suddenly frightened for my life. The pain was like a burning knife, and if I hadn't the image of Sanau's bravery to recall, I am sure my yelps alone would have brought the entire palace to my side. With a masterful imitation of the Yargonian fortitude, I bit my lips and allowed only the telltale moisture that constantly came to my brow to betray the pain I was feeling.

Sanau appeared almost immediately. Had I been stronger I would have reached out to embrace her with joy, but after one quick glimpse of her cold green eyes, I was thankful that I had saved myself from further humiliation. She was the old Sanau, unemotional, cold, completely attired in Yargonian garb and poise and immobility. Yes, Sanau was intact. Only the empty sleeve now tucked in her belt served as a reminder that once she had honestly suffered a human emotion.

She bowed low. "I am aware that you are not well."

I nodded. I wanted to shout and beg her to return to the woman I had known for a short, pain-filled day. I wanted to shout, "We're friends, Sanau! I beg of you, don't withdraw into that mechanical shell of protection."

But I didn't say any of these things; I merely nodded. My eyes frantically searched her face for a hint of the friendship we had once shared, but it was totally and irrevocably absent, and somehow I knew it would never return. I felt sick from more than physical pain. I had never had a real close friend on Earth. Acquaintances, yes, but never a real friendship. During our experiences on Venus, without intending to, Sanau had supplied these very emotions that I had been denied.

I had listened to her and accepted her knowledge voluntarily; it had not been crammed down my throat. She had offered me unselfish protection and courage when she was facing complete destruction. Not even a mother could have done more. My own mother had always been anxious about my welfare, but selfish about taking me in her arms or bestowing a pat of affection, and I guess my emotions toward her were a mixture of fear and devotion. I would never forget Sanau's calm voice telling me not to be frightened, any more than I could forget how she had pleaded with me to save myself and leave her to die.

On the trip back I had been allowed in some measure to repay this debt to Sanau, just as I had been allowed to release some of the bursting affection that had been locked in my heart for so long.

David had never been affectionate. He rarely held my hand, and if he did, it was in an attitude of camaraderie rather than romance. In rebuttal to my reproofs for his lack of affection, he had answered, "Look, honey girl, fellows who are overly demonstrative are the fellows who are eying another gal while they kiss the fingertips of their own. Always be leery of the handkissing Charlies. Now me, I may not say a lot of pretty things, but what I feel I'll demonstrate in my actions. I'll take care of you when you're sick. I'll love you when you get some lines on your face and flesh around the middle. I'll love *you*, and that's what counts."

These were the disjointed thoughts that came to torment me as I stared in mute disappointment at the woman who was rejecting my friendship. A short friendship, complete in every way, only to turn to the same rejection I had faced throughout my entire life.

As if suddenly deciding to come to the business at hand, Sanau turned to me almost brusquely.

"You have appendicitis," she stated.

I almost sat up. "I have what?"

She motioned toward the man on the terrace. "The worthy doctor has found this most unusual fact. The small organ on your right side is inflamed."

"Will he operate?" I asked, experiencing the usual panic at the thought of surgery.

"If you will allow it."

If I'd allow it! Did I need it? Was it serious? I put these questions to her.

For the first time her face discarded its blandness of expression, and a real glimmer of interest came to her eyes.

"How serious it is we cannot say. It is up to you to sanction the operation."

"But if you're so advanced, surely you can tell how badly an appendix is inflamed."

"We have never seen an appendix," she answered.

Now it was my turn to stare. But she went on to explain that an appendix was a completely useless organ, so, of course, they had gotten rid of it, along with wisdom teeth, tonsils, and coccyx bones. The appendix had been the first to go, and it had not appeared on their planet in twenty thousand years. It was such a rarity that there was not even a sample of one to be found in any medical center. They had only pictures to go on. Naturally, this had been quite an event, the discovery of such an organ actually existing in my body. In fact, she went on to explain, the Yargo himself would be very much interested to view such an organ.

With great dignity, I waved my hand and told her I would allow the operation. It would give me great pleasure to donate my appendix to the Yargonian culture.

Either the following events happened with amazing rapidity or my drugged state loaned an air of unreality and swift momentum to all the proceedings. I vaguely recall Sanau's signal to the doctor, who presumably was awaiting my consent. I felt the familiar needle in my arm and was even slightly aware of being transported to a brightly lit auditorium that resembled an ordinary operating room on earth, except on a giant scale. I recall, as I finally slipped into complete unconsciousness, that I was slightly resentful of the fact that such a large audience was about to witness what I termed a highly personal operation. Through the light-drenched room I saw tier after tier of Yargonians and I experienced a moment of strength and anger that almost forced me to object to this infringement of my privacy. I believe I even struggled to a sitting position, yet in reality I probably never fluttered an eyelash. Then there was the quick surge of anesthetic drowning as I slipped into final and complete oblivion.

There was a day and night of half sleep and grayish consciousness. A slight pull in my side with each movement I made told me the operation had occurred. I was aware that Sanau lifted my head from time to time and forced some juice down my throat. Other than that, I did little but sleep.

When I became fully aware of my surroundings and free from pain, I saw Sanau; Sanau with the cold expressionless eyes. Sanau waiting to criticize.

"You have come through the operation itself with comparative ease, but the ravages of the Venusian experience have left you in poor physical condition. It will take you several weeks to recuperate."

I sensed the contempt behind the remark. She had endured the ravages of the trip and a shocking amputation, yet her superior nervous system had rallied, allowing her to regain full composure and strength in twenty-four hours. On the other hand, I lay in this pitiful state from a mere operation.

Without much hope I asked, "What happens to me after my recovery?"

"The Yargo himself will relay final instructions." She hesitated a moment as if she had something pertinent to add, and then, obviously thinking better of it, withdrew into her shell. She added. "I am leaving tonight on a trip across the planet. I am giving a lecture tour in each state on our findings on Venus."

She turned and started for the door. For a moment she hesitated, and then, with a sudden and almost gauche urgency she added, "If I do not see you again, I want you to know I am grateful. I want to thank you for everything and I want you to understand I am only acting in the way in which I believe and which I know to be right."

For one fleeting second our eyes met. I'll never know the thousand unsaid things she was trying to say, or the actual thoughts behind those stilted words, for she turned abruptly and left the room.

I lay back and tried to think it out. I tried to pry my own emotions and beliefs from actual facts. I tried desperately to recall her exact words; the things she had said, not what I thought she had tried to say.

I was leaving: that much was definite. "The Yargo himself will relay final instructions." Instructions meant action. But where was I going? Back to Mars? To some other far-off planet? I held out no hope for Earth. They owed me nothing, these people. They were incapable of feeling, therefore they could feel no sense of obligation. Besides, by now any sense of obligation was forgotten, and the fact that I had been kidnapped was in the distant past. They were, in all probability, seething at me. Hadn't I caused them untold annoyances? The loss of three good men, Sanau's arm, the trouble of the rescue party, an all-out war with Venus. Oh yes, I was probably slated for the most remote planet in the entire solar system. One inhabited with nothing but a polar bear and me.

Yes, that was it, and it also accounted for Sanau's strange attitude. She probably felt she had let me down. That was why she was getting out of town as fast as possible. Clear across the planet, in fact. On a lecture tour! She had really taken it on the run.

That crushing blow of defeat weakened me more than my physical suffering. I tried to sleep. I longed for a sedative. Anything was preferable to being awake with my thoughts, but I spent a restless, wakeful day. The sun streamed through my room, spreading a cheer I felt it impossible to share. The handmaidens silently appeared from time to time with food, and when evening finally came I sank into a longed-for drowsiness from sheer nervous exhaustion. Just as I was almost embracing a true slumber, the handmaidens clamored in and fell to the floor.

His Royal Highness was approaching!

CHAPTER 24

Instantly I was wide awake. Whether this wakeful attitude stemmed from my own emotional response to this meeting or from the actual radiation his appearance caused, I am not sure. I only know I struggled to rise to a sitting position, but received a wave of dismissal from His Highness, a gesture meant to inform me that all court protocol was to be forgotten on this visit. He came alone, merely to inquire as to my welfare.

I fell back against the pillows and succumbed to staring at him with open admiration, awe, and suspicion. Somehow I had expected this visit to be endowed with all the pomp and ceremony of our previous meetings. I had expected at least six leaders and an entourage but aside from the fluttering of the handmaidens, his entrance was quite simple. Just like any friend who might come to call at a sickbed.

To add to the informality, he actually pulled a small ottoman to my bedside and sat down. Well out of touching distance, I might add.

"I want to praise your bravery," he said, with a warm smile. His statement was too ambiguous for me to attempt an answer, as I was not quite sure to which bravery he was making reference—the bravery on Venus or my attitude about the operation—so I merely nodded wordlessly. He assumed this was stage fright, and he was not completely wrong.

"Sanau was filled with tales of the more than creditable way in which you handled yourself. I offer my extreme sympathy for the many hardships you were forced to endure."

"Sanau was the brave one," I managed to say.

He nodded quietly. "Sanau merely acted in the manner of any Yargonian. You are the one who deserves the praise."

Again I nodded dumbly, as I was not sure whether this was a compliment or an insult.

Then he added, "A twenty-four-hour celebration was accorded to Sanau. Now she is off on her tour."

Again I signified with a nod that I was aware of her departure.

"I also want to thank you for submitting to the operation. As you may have been informed, an appendix is a rare phenomenon on our planet. We were all eager to have a firsthand glance at one."

This time I was really stumped and I felt it was high time some proclamation other than a dumb nod came from me. But what could I say? He was thanking me for submitting to an operation that I needed to save my life. He was acting as if I had really sprung the entire attack just as a benefit to science. I had to say something. I knew that this was merely a call that stemmed from some sense of propriety and court manners on his part. It was probably the last time I'd see him, and I certainly wasn't doing anything to make the meeting noteworthy or even comfortable.

So in a last effort to contribute something to the meeting, I said, "Sanau came to say good-bye. She's wonderful. She doesn't even seem to mind the loss of her arm."

He seemed to weigh my statement. "No, since it in no way prevents her from carrying on with her work.

"I had hoped she might remain until you were in a stronger condition," he told me. "It might have been comforting to have had someone close who speaks and understands your tongue, but she was anxious to be off to work."

I turned away. It would have been nicer if he hadn't said that. It was one thing to sense Sanau had no affection for me; it was too disenchanting to actually hear it.

He rose. "I am sure you will do everything in your power to hasten your convalescence, for upon the restoration of your strength, you will be returned to your planet Earth."

I didn't gasp. I didn't roll over in ecstacy. I didn't do any of the things I thought I would do. All I could manage was a blank stare.

He smiled at my obviously stunned reaction. "I take no credit for this decision; it was entirely Sanau's suggestion."

"But you all had to agree?"

"There was not even a vote," he answered. "The regard in which the people now hold Sanau . . ." he smiled benevolently. "Her slightest wish is their desire and since it was her wish that you be returned to your Earth, it was not even questioned. However, it is to be understood that you leave with a solemn vow to refrain from relating one word of this entire experience. Sanau seemed to feel your word could well be taken."

"Yes, I promise. But where do I say I've been? I've been gone almost three weeks as it is."

His eyes twinkled. "My little friend, that is your problem. A Yargonian speaks only the truth. On Earth I understand you are quite adept at twisting facts to suit your own purposes. I do not mean 'you' in the personal sense," he hastily added. "I mean the 'you' to encompass the people of your planet."

"Oh, I guess I'll think of something," I stammered.

"I'm sure you will. Sanau also placed the same confidence in you. You have obviously created a fine impression of your character in Sanau."

"But she wouldn't even stay a few days . . ." I hadn't meant to say this, but I wasn't a Yargonian. My emotions still showed.

A slight flicker that came to his eyes almost betrayed annoyance. He had paid his call of duty and was more than eager to be off. Somehow my statement had disturbed him. He had risen but lingered as if loath to leave with some important issue unsettled.

He sat down again. For a moment it almost seemed as if he was groping for the right words, and when he spoke his voice was warm and kind.

"My little friend, I can see that you learned to care a great deal for Sanau."

I didn't answer but my mute affirmation seemed to distress him.

"Although I can understand this emotion, I cannot feel it. I understand it because I know it exists on your planet. My little friend, it is fine for you to admire Sanau, to respect her accomplishments, to want to emulate her in every way, but there your feelings must end. You must cease to expect to receive any affection in return."

"Then how do I think of her?" I demanded. "If I respect and admire a friend, I must also love her."

"Think of her," he insisted, "think of her upon your return to Earth. Let her virtues guide you to a more perfect life. Think of her as more masterful and creative than any woman on any world, but think of her as lifeless as a statue in the attributes of the friendship which you seek."

I didn't answer right away. I was sure there had been moments when Sanau had thought of me as a friend. Her concern for my welfare was not lifeless or unemotional.

"Is everyone on this planet completely free of emotion?" I asked.

He nodded. "It has taken many generations of careful breeding to cause this transformation, but now, fortunately, we are a perfect race. We are free from emotion. We have purged our bloodline of self-love or human love."

This time he walked to the door. Once again he hesitated.

"I am wise enough to understand the existence of this force within you. I extend my heartfelt sympathy. Rest well, my friend. It is well that you leave our planet as soon as possible, or else I greatly fear that your heart may be broken."

He walked swiftly from the room.

CHAPTER 25

I was amazed that he came to call the next day, and the day following. And on the evening of the third day I was almost sick with disappointment when he failed to arrive at the customary time.

Had I said anything out of order the previous evening. I lay back on the pillow carefully reliving every statement and fragment of conversation. No, it had been a very satisfactory evening. He had told me about the discovery of a new star system some three billion light years away and I had listened very attentively, wondering what on earth he was talking about. I was sure I had nodded and "oohed" and "aahed" at the proper times. Then where was he?

I combed and recombed my hair several times. Just as I was about to give up and turn off the light, there was a soft knock on the door. I sat up and called for whoever it was to enter. I never thought that it would be His Highness for he never knocked; he just burst in like the sun.

And there he was in full magnificence.

"It was so late, I was fearful that you might have retired," he explained. He pulled the ottoman close to the bed and sat down. Although there was nothing about his appearance to suggest fatigue, I sensed he was tired. For a moment neither of us spoke and we just sat there, real cozy with the big moon hanging over the mountain. I kind of felt like touching his hand and asking if he had a hard day at the office. Fortunately, I stifled such an impulse, and since I really was at a loss for subject matter, I was content to fall back on protocol and wait for him to open the conversation.

He did with a strange question.

"How many years have you lived, my little friend?"

I told him I was twenty-two.

"I am surprised that with such youth your recuperative powers are so sluggish."

So that was it. He wanted me to hurry and get well and get off his planet.

"Our people don't spring back to action as quickly as the Yargonians," I told him. "But I am sure I shall be ready to travel in a few days."

He nodded as if he scarcely heard me. "Aside from self-destruction, or 'wars' as you term it, what is the most common cause of death on your planet?"

I told him heart disease and cancer.

He shook his head sadly. "Heart disease. The cause and cure are so apparent. Find the cure and no one will ever age, for when one discovers how to retain the elasticity of muscle, fiber, and nerve, the heart will remain strong and the body will not age. I am surprised that some of your scientists have not made this discovery Now cancer, that is a more elusive foe to fathom."

Strangely enough his words gave me courage. Somewhere there was a cure for these diseases, and if there was and if they had discovered it up here, I was confident that some day we would too. But then what happened, I asked. How long did people live on Yargo?

He told me the life expectancy on Yargo was close to three hundred years. He himself was eighty.

Eighty!

Why, he was an old man. He was ten years older than my grandfather!

He caught the incredulous look in my eye and somehow he must have guessed my line of thought, for with something almost reminiscent of vanity, he assured me that on Yargo eighty was not even the prime of life. One did not complete his education until he was fifty.

I gasped. What a nightmare. "You mean you go to school for fifty years around here?"

"Actual formal schooling ends after twenty-five years. Then is the time for the real pursuit of knowledge. Then one's study is self-determined. After all, the mind is unformed for the first twenty-five years. One makes and revokes many decisions pertaining to one's life's work. It is foolish to believe that children in their teens are capable of making a decision for their entire future, or capable of consuming knowledge that will stand them in good stead for the remainder of their lives."

I asked Sanau's age. The Yargo said he believed Sanau was close to a hundred.

I took this pretty well. I displayed no emotion. I just started to choke, that's all. After he offered me some water, I found the strength to come up with another question. Since they had overcome everything else . . . why not death?

I was rewarded with a blockbuster of a smile.

It seemed I had asked a most intelligent question.

"My people," he explained, "are not governed by emotion. Therefore, death holds no fear. Death comes to one on our planet only from the actual wish itself, not from any other cause."

"You mean someone just gets up one morning and says, 'Today I intend to die.' and that's it!"

We both laughed together.

"My dear Janet, when one has lived for three hundred years, three hundred years spent in creative work, one is content to die. The brain becomes weary. He has lived and created enough and at long last wishes to rest. He states this fact to those around him, his associates and friends, and after a time retires. And so it is. Death does not visit one until it is beckoned and when it is beckoned, it is longed for as heartily as a good night's rest might be by one on your planet."

I couldn't go along with this and I said as much. I would never want to die if I had my choice.

He smiled. "Perhaps I can clarify this desire with a personal example. When you were very young, little Janet, you probably thought that if you were permitted you would never go to bed. When the time came you fought against it as all children will with many cunning devices, I am sure. Yet, now when you are more mature and may stay awake as long as you wish there are times that you welcome sleep and embrace it voluntarily. Such is death to a mature Yargonian."

"Yes, but each time I willingly go to sleep, I have the knowledge that I'll awaken in due time," I argued.

"Janet, what actually causes you to want to remain alive?"

I thought carefully before answering. "Curiosity, is foremost, I guess, and the love for the people around me, and, well, I guess most of all, just the love of life."

"And not the fear of death?"

"Well, we always fear the unknown to an extent," I agreed.

"That is so, but on this planet none of these factors exist. After three hundred years of creative life the curiosity that you mention is abated. The love of people, as we know it, has been more than satisfied by our creative accomplishments and efforts on their behalf, for everything we do is for the betterment of our planet and the people who dwell upon it. For us, there is no fear of death. We know the answer. There is no uncertainty, and not being bound with mortal loves, there is no dismay at leaving."

"What is the answer to death?"

"Eternal rest, as desirable as a good night's sleep to the weary."

"What about heaven, hell, an afterlife? What about God?"

He stood up. "We have talked enough for now. You must rest."

And that's how it went for an entire week. Sometimes he would stay for almost an hour; other times his visits were brief. And I always sensed an urgency that I would hurry my recuperation and depart.

One night I was determined to get the conversation on a more personal basis. It was a wonderful night: the lights were low, the moon was orange, I was arrayed in a fetching bed jacket, and he was telling me how he had discovered the cure for cancer. As always I urged him on for I noticed his lengthy stays usually occurred when he was intent on making some explanation.

Somehow it seeped through to my inferior brain that the cure for cancer was as simple as the cure for the common cold. The cancer virus is similar in structure to the cold virus, and equally elusive. Now Yargonian children were vaccinated at birth against cancer as well as against disintegration of their muscle and blood vessel structure.

I listened to this discourse with mixed emotions of admiration and frustration. I had been favored with a nightly visit for a full week; I would return to Earth with little knowledge of him as a person. I would be filled with facts I dare not disclose, but somehow I longed for some personal knowledge of the man, something to store in my memories for those long winter evenings at home. I had to associate something with his overpowering sparkle; I wanted to associate one personal phrase along with his blinding smile. With unpardonable brazenness I blurted out.

"Your Highness, do you have any children?"

Without the slightest hesitation he answered that he wasn't quite sure.

Then, in response to my wild look of incredulity, he enlarged on this statement.

"Prior to my becoming the Yargo, several 'cells' were sent to the banks from women with whom I had had physical association. However, since only the heritage of the mother is registered, there was no proof of the paternity of the offspring. However, now that I am Yargo, the women that I associate with for satisfaction destroy the 'cell' immediately. It is not acceptable in any bank."

Straining to match his own nonchalance, I asked how come.

"Because there must never be a claim to the throne of Yargo through any cause other than merit. If a blood tie existed, and the descendant showed any ability at all, you can easily see that there would be some prejudice in his favor. The honor of Yargo must remain open to all and be claimed by the one who has the power and achievement to be so elected."

"But wouldn't your planet benefit if you passed along your heritage?" I argued. "After all, there is something to passing along the cells for a superior brain."

"It would cause prejudice. One family would consider itself better than another and this would create personal ill will and social status, of which we now have none. No, it is better to allow people to develop their own minds with different bloodlines, offering different creative powers. This makes for an equal and stronger race."

He bid me good night.

A big success this evening had been. An hour's discussion on sex with all the sentiment of a high school biology lecture.

I wondered if he was sleeping. Probably not. After all, some women did associate with him. Why couldn't it be me? What was I saying? It was high time I got to sleep and got off the planet and back to David ... David.

I turned out the light.

CHAPTER 26

Thank God Sanau popped up the following day. She had returned from a victorious tour and planned to stop over for twenty-four hours before embarking on another. Naturally, she had come directly to report to the Yargo.

I was paid a brief courtesy visit. It was painful for us both. Try as I did, it was hard for me not to act reproachful. She remarked that I looked well and suggested that I appeared strong enough for my trip.

Just as she was about to depart I asked about the Yargo's sex life in my best offhand manner.

Her amazement stemmed from the fact that I had shared any discussion such as this with His Majesty. Once assured that I had, she explained in her blandest manner the complicated ritual of His Majesty's love life.

The palace, it seems, was provided with quite a harem, consisting of women who demanded nothing other in life than to serve the Yargo in this capacity. These women were selected for this honor in the same manner any Yargonian was selected for any task on the planet. The household staff was chosen in the same manner from those women who enjoyed tending a home, cooking, and serving a man.

"The physical association," I marveled. "It's actually regarded as a well-chosen occupation, legal and all that?"

Sanau pointed out that a physical urge did not necessarily accompany love, and love, even as I knew it, often did not carry extreme physical desire.

"Some are endowed with glands and hormones that demand a larger amount of physical association, just as some bodies demand more sugar and fat than others. Some women never really enjoy a physical association so there is no reason for them to seek it. Yet on your Earth those women who do not enjoy it must pretend that they do to create children and hold their mate. Instead of it being regarded as a mere physical act, sex is costumed in secrecy and masqueraded as 'love' and is the basis for your entire civilization. It is absolutely senseless. What happens to the woman whom nature has endowed with an abundance of hormones that demand to be satisfied? She is only content if by chance she is mated to a male who also craves this constant association. If the mating is not perfect she must deny her body what it demands. She becomes an unhappy, frustrated female, who raises members of your future generation to mirror her neurosis. If, however, she abandons herself to her natural craving, she is condemned by society and looked down upon. It is a bad situation on your Earth denying the chemical desire, which is real, and portraying it as love, which is unreal."

"And on your earth," I asked, "the women who have this craving are the ones who are selected for the Yargo?"

Sanau nodded. "That is correct. These women state this desire and fill out applications, and from these only the most perfect are chosen. They come to the palace and remain there for life."

"Then the Yargo is not completely untouchable?"

"These women who have associated with the Yargo in turn become untouchable. They remain here in seclusion, their lives dedicated to His Almighty Highness.

"But that in itself is backward," I insisted, "and it argues against your entire theory. If these women are red-blooded and demand enough satisfaction to devote their entire lives to its pursuit, do you mean to say that they're content to stay in hiding to await an occasional whim of a ruler with whom they can't even talk as an equal?"

"You forget these women volunteer for just such an occupation with full awareness of all its hazards. To them this brief encounter is a religious experience. Nothing can be more satisfying to them than the realization that they have been allowed to please and gratify the most perfect of all men."

She turned on me suddenly, as if angered that she had betrayed such information.

"If you will restrain this curiosity and turn your energy toward the restoration of your strength, your recovery will be more rapid."

"But I can't help but be curious about all of you," I argued.

"What good can come from this knowledge? You are returning to your planet, with a vow to remain silent, yet you seem to argue each point."

She went to the door.

"Will I see you again, Sanau?"

Her gaze was direct. "I think not. I shall be gone for seven days. Let me find you gone when I return."

She swiftly left the room.

So now it was up to me. Evidently the Yargo was a polite host and would not ask me to go. If I was still here when Sanau returned, I was sure she would stand on no such ceremony. She was right, the longer I remained . . . the longer I remained, what? I would have preferred to return the conquering hero. What explanation would I give for this disappearance? Well, that I would worry about later. The point was I did want to go home. Of course, I did. There was David, my mother, my own world. I repeated these phrases but somehow they fell flat. What did I want? To remain here? That was preposterous; I had just been away too long. Meanwhile, I'd find out all I could about these people and maybe I'd even write a book about the whole experience, as fiction, of course. The Yargo couldn't get mad about that, could he? It wouldn't really be breaking a promise. And why was he untouchable? What would he do if I asked him such a question? Well, I wouldn't.

But I did.

I took special pains with my appearance that night. In fact, I was out of bed sitting on a large chair when he entered. I rather fancied myself that night. It was the first time I wasn't morbidly conscious of my inferiority to this master race. Maybe because Sanau had been so imperious and strong, maybe it was the nearness of the stars through the tinted glass windows, the breeze that rustled the foliage outside, but suddenly I felt sure of myself as a woman. Very feminine, small, and weak, but a flesh-and-blood woman, not a magnificent machine.

When the Yargo entered and flashed his brilliant smile, I returned one of equal brilliance and plunged right into my opening line.

"I am well enough, Your Highness, to sit on a chair, but not yet well enough to kneel before you."

Somehow I had expected him to say it was perfectly all right and that we were such good friends I wouldn't have to kneel. What he said filled me with high hopes.

"I do not expect you to kneel."

That was fine. My smile increased.

Then he continued. "Only my subjects and my friends and my people kneel. You are from a foreign planet. You have no cause to kneel. There is no feeling between us."

My smile vanished.

He didn't seem to notice. He seemed restless. He made no attempt to pull the ottoman to my side or to sit on the chair that I had dragged to a safe proximity to my own. I had carefully staged the entire scene before his entrance, but somehow it wasn't going according to schedule.

"I am glad you are getting stronger," he offered.

I didn't answer. Was this a hint? Had Sanau spoken to him?

"I understand you were favored by a visit from Sanau. Since today has not been a long and lonely day for you, I will not stay tonight."

So she had spoken to him. She had spoken to him and had probably told him in polite Yargonian talk to stay away from me.

"I bid you good night." That was why he had come to see me—not that he wanted to; he just felt I was lonely and had to have someone to talk to. His good manners had made him put in an appearance each evening. Well it was over now. I made the plunge.

"Your Highness . . ." He was at the door now.

He turned.

"There's one question that I'd like to ask you."

He waited at the door. I was no femme fatale, but what I lack in glamour and charm I make up for in tenacity.

In the most matter-of-fact tone I said, "Why are you untouchable?"

He favored me with a patient smile. "For the good of my people."

I shook my head. "It's not that I'm prying, it's just that I can't fathom the entire procedure. Everyone grovels like a slave before you. It's so medieval in a people so advanced. What good can this do for you or your people?"

If nothing else it brought him back into the room.

"It is the only approach one must have to a ruler," he explained. "We have already gone through what you term a democratic way of life. On Earth you have not even begun to approach true democracy."

"To me a democracy is where everyone is equal," I interrupted, "and not where people fall on their faces before a man."

His eyes flashed but his face remained impassive.

"Let us look into past history," he said in a quiet voice full of hidden mockery. I fell back against the chair. He was absolutely incapable of any emotion. I hadn't even been able to inspire anger in him. Just that one flash of disapproval at my ignorance. I had failed in every way.

With infinite patience, he went on to explain, "If you will recall, my little friend, there was a period on your own planet when rulers were a law unto themselves and people kneeled in respectful worship. There was a gradual recession from this custom and so-called democracy made its appearance. A ruler was created by the people and you were taught to respect him—to a degree. You insisted upon proving that he was not divine. You showed his frailties, kept declaring to one and all that he was flesh and blood like everyone else, endowed with the same faults and weaknesses."

"And you say that isn't democracy?" I demanded.

"It is disrespect! In your search for true democracy you have gone too far, a most natural mistake for an uneducated race. You will find the flaws in your ways, if you do not destroy yourselves in the effort. You are a poor floundering people. One day you will learn that you don't want to be ruled by someone endowed with the same weaknesses that you yourself possess; then you will select a leader, because he is superior to all men on Earth at that time. You will choose him because he is *not* like any other man, and because a man such as he is only born once in several hundred years, you will adore and revere every year of his life. You will know he is worthy the moment he steps before you, and because he is superior to you in every way, you will proclaim him untouchable. Would you shake hands with a saint if he made a visit to Earth? Do not your people kneel to your holy man in Rome? Thus it should be with a leader. He should be a spiritual and political ruler, proclaimed and worshipped by all. That, my friend, is true democracy."

He bowed and left the room, and I made no effort to hold him. I was completely exhausted by this tirade. Why, he spoke as if he were God or a demigod of some sort. Maybe he was right, maybe this is the state that we would enter some thousands of years hence. I was too weary to argue his logic.

Yet I couldn't hate him. There had been no pompousness in his explanation. He merely presented facts, impersonal and calm, as if he was patiently explaining to a child why two and two made four. As I fell asleep it all began to add up to me. Two and two made four, at least when Yargo explained the problem.

CHAPTER 27

He did not visit me the following evening or the next. Had I a bag or toothbrush, I would have packed it, but I had neither so I was now merely waiting to be booted off the planet.

I had expected to be informed through a guard or an attendant. After two long days of silence I had no hope of seeing either the Yargo or Sanau again.

You can imagine my surprise when he strolled in on the third evening. Just strolled in as if he wasn't a god or the Yargo or hadn't neglected me for so long.

I didn't say a word. No more questions about his planet or his way of life. It was probably his last visit; I'd try and make it a pleasant one.

It was a balmy evening.

"I think our patient could stand a bit of air," he said with a hint of a smile.

"The room is air-conditioned so well . . ." I began, but he had already thrown open the door and walked out on the terrace. At first I wasn't quite sure what to do. Would it be brazen to follow him onto the terrace? But, if I remained in the room couldn't that also

be interpreted as disinterest and rudeness?
Well, it was a cinch that whatever choice I
made would be wrong, so I blithely trotted
out after him.

Right for the first time! He turned and
smiled. I stood at his side, careful to allow
three feet between us. It was a funny switch,
a man alone in a woman's boudoir and the
woman forcing herself to keep her distance.

He pointed to what appeared to be just
another star in the heavens. It looked like
any other star to me; perhaps a bit fainter.
It was new, he informed me. A spaceship
had already been assigned to investigate its
origin and to determine if it was a new
planet gone off course, a large roaming aster-
oid, or a prenovae.

"It has also been sighted by your Earth,"
he explained.

"How do you know?"

"Have you forgotten? We keep your Earth
under constant surveillance. There are at
least three spaceships that patrol your planet.
But they are only spotted by your people
when they come extremely low to mark some
site."

"At least we are alert enough to spot you.
You certainly cause a lot of commotion in
the newspapers when we do see you."

"That is intentional," he replied.

"You mean you intend to cause us alarm?"

"No, my little friend. We intend to be seen
by your people. We want to plant the seed of
the idea of the existence of other worlds in

the minds of your people. We want them to accept this theory gradually and without fear, but your Pentagon and air force seem determined to bewilder your people with retractions, denials, and misstatements. However, we can still survey your planet from a distance of fifty miles and remain unseen, and with our televisionic lens can see Earth plainly enough to, well, to spot you walking on a beach in Avalon. By intercepting your radio and television broadcasts, we learn your latest news. All this is relayed to me from a transmitter on the spaceship, allowing me to see the same picture on a large screen right in the observatory of my palace."

"Then why didn't you signal your airmen not to take me? Certainly you could see I was not the man you were looking for."

"You are wrong. We only knew Doctor Blount by reputation, and we had no way of knowing whether or not he was a male or a female. It was not until the ship was well on its way that we learned from another monitored broadcast that Doctor Blount was speaking at a university at the time."

I smiled. "I'll bet all hell broke loose up here."

My humor was completely wasted. He returned his attention to the mystery star. I studied it also. I had moved to the rail of the balcony, breaking the three-foot regulation. I was quite close to him, closer than any

Yargonian had ever stood. What would happen if I reached out and touched him?

The thought actually frightened me and caused me to back away. Yet I could not dismiss it.

What would happen?

Would he roar his disapproval or just stalk from the room?

Perhaps he felt my attention wander or he may have sensed the trend of my thoughts for he turned and looked directly into my eyes.

For a long moment we stared at each other. His strange eyes almost hypnotized me but I forced my gaze not to falter. Then without changing his expression, his eyes holding my own, he said quietly, "I beg you not to speak what is on your lips and mind. It will destroy everything."

Beads of perspiration broke out on my brow, and I could feel my heart thumping, but I never took my eyes from him. We stood motionless, then his face changed, almost as if he was about to ask a favor, but when he spoke it was in a deadly monotone.

"I beg you not to speak."

I knew my entire destiny hung on this moment. I could drop my eyes and ask some trivial question about the new star. The moment would pass; it might even be forgotten. But at that moment it seemed my only chance for happiness, the clarity of it seemed to shout at me this was it! a chance to burst through, to find what I had been seeking, or let it pass and return to the muddled insecurity in which I dwelled.

Almost as if his gaze had cleared my vision and given me new power, I suddenly found myself sure. For once, the first time in my life, I was sure; I knew what I wanted. I didn't have to ask my mother, David, my friends, anyone. I knew!

I said, "I love you, Yargo."

I said it calmly and I said it as I had never said it or meant it before.

He didn't answer. He walked a few paces and turned away. And when he turned back to me, his manner was regal and proud. In his eyes I thought I saw something like pity, and I knew I had lost. I had lost my chance for everything. His pity was for me.

But like an animal clawing at a cage, I spoke again.

"Did you hear me? Do you understand what I said?"

He nodded. This time there was no doubt of the pity in his eyes.

I grew angry. I shouted to keep the tears from my eyes and voice. "Haven't you an answer? Haven't you anything to say?"

"Is there any answer?" he asked.

"Yes," I shouted. "There's got to be some answer. Say you hate me! Say you don't give a damn! But don't just stand there feeling sorry for me!"

"But I can't say any of those things," he answered.

"But you don't love me!" I was afraid to hope.

"Of course, I do not love you." There was no feeling in his tone. It was a statement of fact.

"All right," I fought to keep the hysteria from my voice. "You don't love me. We start on that premise. But please, oh, please, don't go into that dissertation that no one on this planet loves a mortal. I've heard it all before. I've lived with it till it's coming out of my ears. But there's one thing I do know: you do have some feeling for me. You may not be aware of it yourself, but you do!"

I paused for breath. When he did not answer, I took a few steps closer and pressed my point.

"Yargo, you are magnificent and brilliant and unapproachable but you do love me. Maybe you don't recognize it but you do, because I know I love you. I never knew what love was until now and suddenly it's clear to me; everything's clear and it would be for you if you'd only allow yourself, only try . . ."

"Janet!" His voice cut me short. "It is impossible for me to love you. It would be as impossible for me to love you as it would be for you to love the foliage that grows on my planet or the creations that have been brought forth by my people. These are the things I love. I love a single blade of grass more than I love you, for that blade of grass grows for all to see and enjoy. I can love no human. I can only love the accomplishments one is capable of creating for others to enjoy."

As I listened my humiliation at this rejection vanished. When he spoke of love there had been a look in his eyes that I had always hoped to find in someone's eyes. David never had it, yet this man radiated it when he spoke of a blade of grass, the advancement of his planet, the happiness of his people.

A man capable of love for such inanimate things, possessing the highest of all intelligence, must be able to feel. He must learn to feel!

"Yargo," my voice was heavy with desperation. "Please, Yargo, open that brilliant mind of yours. You who can understand everything, try and understand me. Try and understand yourself. It is possible. You could feel emotions and not even realize them. Why else have you spent these evenings with me? Certainly there is nothing I can teach you. You've more than satisfied your curiosity about me and my people. You spent these evenings with me because, deep down, you wanted to! Because you enjoyed being with me."

"I believe I have enjoyed your company." He said it as if thinking aloud.

"Enjoying someone's company is an emotion," I hurried on, "it really is. I can contribute nothing to your planet or to your people, but we have contributed to each other, Yargo, and that's the basis of love."

For the first time he seemed unsure, but

when he spoke, his attitude was as if the entire procedure was an impersonal experiment.

"That would be indeed strange, if an emotion that died within my people thousands of years ago was suddenly rekindled in me. Tell me, what else would I feel if I loved you?"

I was actually sick and weak at this sudden turn of events. The hope that surged through me left me unbalanced. If I could convince him! Suddenly I knew without a doubt that I could never again live without this man. I could never return to David, my Earth, my people. There was nothing but doubt for me with them. I did not love David. I loved Yargo, and I not only had to fight for him, I had to fight to make him understand. But there was a chance, a slim one, but a chance, nevertheless.

I could feel the cords tighten in my neck as I strained to speak. I kept my voice low, knowing the slightest show of hysteria would send him away. I clenched my fingernails through my palms to keep my emotion in check. I had to make sense, my inferior brain must make that superior brain accept my knowledge.

"If you loved me," I almost whispered, "you'd want to be with me. You'd want to show me things. Just as you pointed out that new star tonight. That's part of love, sharing something you've discovered with the one closest to you. There's nothing so complex about love. It's really quite simple. Simple, yet perplexing to the wisest of men, and then ...".

"Then?" His eyes and tone were questioning.

"Then you'd want to take me in your arms, to be close to me in every way."

"What would I do with you in my arms?"

I suppressed a wild desire to laugh. He was serious. The magnificent ruler was almost childlike in his desire to understand me, to be completely fair and honest. I knew if he actually thought he did care he would be honest, for dishonesty was not known to him.

There we stood, both of us trying to understand the other.

I came closer to him. I could see the fine hairs of his brows, my mirrored reflection in his eyes. I could smell the faint perfume that came from his bathing water. I came closer, so close that to keep from touching him I would have to stop breathing.

He never moved away. He stood there, his eyes searching mine, as if he might find the answer there.

Then with a courage born of despair and wild hope, I threw my arms around him and pressed my lips against his.

And then fear changed to hope; he was not pushing me off.

He was doing nothing. He felt like stone. Hope crashed to agonizing despair.

In complete defeat, I broke away and forced myself to look at him.

There was sadness in his smile. "Was that an expression of love, Janet?"

I nodded.

"I did not like it. I do not like being touched."

"Unless you seek physical satisfaction with one of your harem." I spit the words at him.

"That is different. That is physical gratification. When my body is hungry and desires such, I take it. I am not hungry now. When I am hungry there is no thought of love, yet you state this is love. No, I did not like it at all."

"That's because you've never kissed anyone," I argued.

"That is so, but I am quick to grasp new ideas if they appeal to me. Your lips upon mine was a most disagreeable sensation." He paused for a moment, then added as if summing up the entire incident, "It was as if I was being closed in upon."

I gave up. But not entirely.

"All right, Yargo, perhaps you did not like my kiss, but you do care. I know you do. It may take time, a long time before you realize it. Maybe it's my fault because I tried to force you into it, but you will find out for yourself, in your own way, and I'm willing to take that chance. I beg of you, let me remain here, and I promise not to bring up this subject again. I'll be happy just seeing you, talking with you. I'll wait all my life, if I must."

He shook his head. "You say that now, little Janet, but I know better. No, you cannot remain here. You are an Earthborn creature who lives through a state called emotion."

"Yargo," my voice shook with intensity. I was begging now. "Oh, Yargo, I know that you believe everything is motivated by the power of the mind. A mind is a wonderful thing. I admire your brain and the brains of your people. I can't help but admire some of the progress you've made. Down on Earth we admire a great mind too, and we have many of them, though none so great as yours. But there's one thing we do have. We forget about it most of the time and only call for it when everything else fails. Like now, I've failed in every way. I've failed with my femininity, my physical appeal, I've even failed with pure logic, so now I must fall back on that one thing—faith. I won't be alone or unhappy. I'll have my faith while I'm waiting."

His eyes clouded for a moment. "I do not understand. Faith in what?"

"In God," I answered. "I'll pray. I'll pray to God to make you understand. We are worlds and solar systems apart, but that's one thing we share—the same God. And He will help me. He'll help us both."

His answer was precise and shocking.

"That is impossible. I am God."

I backed away, unable to even gasp at such blasphemy.

This time his smile was almost mocking. "Tell me, do you still have religion on that planet of yours?"

"Of course, we do. Don't tell me you've abolished that also."

"Oh yes, long before we abolished other emotions. God is a great mind, great strength, great leadership. Religion is for the weak. We rule our own destiny; we do not need fantasy to fall back upon. I am Yargo. I am the mightiest of the mighty; therefore, I am God."

Anger was my only emotion now, and it flooded through me. "I should have known" I shouted. "You wouldn't believe in anything you can't see, touch, or prove; but God is there, and you are not Him. God is very real, even though you can't bring Him into focus with all your fantastic equations, for He only shows Himself to the very simple in mind and heart. But He's there to guide and care for us all."

"I believe in nothing I cannot see," was his answer.

"Of course, but I can prove you are wrong. If all your most learned surgeons cut me open and examined my heart and brain right now, what would they find? They would find a heart and brain, like any other heart and brain. Could they find the love I feel for you in either organ? Could they see it? Could they prove it? No, because it's something intangible. But it's there. It's there so strong and real that right now my head is pounding and I actually feel sick because I love you so. That love, that intangible thing can cause me real physical pain because it is real and strong and so is God! They're comparable in a way. God is love. God causes love."

I paused for a moment, then turned to him pleadingly. "Yargo, don't turn me away. I've conceded all along to your superior planet and your superior brain. For once, listen to me. Try and believe and understand something that goes beyond numerical comprehension. Who created this fantastic planet of yours? Not you nor any of your people. It was created by God. He created all the planets and the suns—yours and mine alike —just as we are all created in His image."

He laughed in real amusement.

Now I was really angry. I turned on him. "I didn't mean to amuse you. I know I've been a constant source of amusement to you all but before I return to the so-called dark age of my planet, let me offer you one piece of advice. Abolish love, if you will, abolish the natural birth of children, kill all the emotions in yourself and your people, but don't leave them without any faith."

"My people have their faith," he answered. "Their faith is in me."

"And you, who do you turn to?" I shouted. "Oh, don't answer me. I should know. You turn to yourself. You need no one to guide you because you are endowed with that great superior brain. You call this advancement? I call this the dark ages. We have a country down on Earth that has abolished religion also. At least they've tried, but some of their people still believe. But it's a sad country; they too think they're advancing in progress. They're not. They've shut themselves off from the rest of the world behind an iron curtain."

"That is the stupidity of your planet," he interrupted. "No universal language, countries warring against one another . . ."

"We have many things against us," I argued. "But there's one thing we have in common—God. We may not all go about it in the same way; there are different paths to take, but they all lead to the same destination. That's what will keep us together. It keeps us from destroying ourselves and that's what keeps this other country alien. In time they will destroy themselves because they have no faith and without faith there is no love, no happiness, no life."

This time he actually threw back his head and laughed, the way one might laugh at an enraged kitten who had gotten tangled in a ball of yarn.

I don't quite remember when I hit him. But I did.

Perhaps it was because he kept laughing. Perhaps it was because I loved him so much and wanted to make him understand. And perhaps it was because I knew I had lost him in every way.

My hand rang as it went across his face. He stopped laughing.

He stared at me for a moment and again there was no emotion. Not even anger.

"I forgive and understand your rage," he told me. "The evolution and progress of thirty thousand years or more is too much for anyone such as you to face; a greater mind than yours would crack under the strain. Yet in time to come your descendants will think and feel as I. It will evolve slowly, but it will happen, if your people have not destroyed themselves before that time."

I turned away and began to sob in defeat.

He came to me. His voice was low.

"And now, may I bid you good night?"

I turned and slowly raised my eyes. His hand was actually outstretched to me. In dumb amazement I took it.

His strange and wonderful eyes crinkled slightly and with studied solemnity he shook hands, Earth fashion.

"I bid you good night." He smiled and left the room.

CHAPTER 28

I was not surprised the following day when the handmaiden entered bearing my old red linen dress. Wordlessly, she handed it to me. Well, this was it. I was leaving as they had found me.

But I wasn't the same. I never would be. I ripped a seam as I hurried into the dress. This was no time to break down.

I wasn't even surprised that His Highness had sent no official parting proclamation. The sooner I got off his planet, the better, I assumed. Even the handmaiden seemed subdued as she helped me dress.

I was escorted by a small committee. There was no one that I recognized. I was carried to the airport in the same cigar-shaped vehicle that originally brought me to the city.

A dreamlike feeling began to take hold of me. This was the trip I had demanded. I was going home.

But where was "home"? Was it on Yargo? Or was it with everything that had hitherto been dear and familiar to me? My own planet, David, my mother. I thought of them dispassionately and without emotion. David and my mother. It was strange, but

Yargo and Sanau—unfeeling and alien—had aroused more honest emotion in me than had the two people who had previously occupied all my attention and love.

As I stood in the airfield, surveying my surroundings one last time, I stared in an effort to transfix every bit of it firmly in my mind, then resolutely mounted the steps to the spaceship.

At the door, once again, I turned. It was almost as if the planet itself was compelling me to remain, as if it shouted, "Stay with us, Janet, we know you belong here. We know he loves you!"

Tears came to my eyes. Tears that made the far-off gleaming domes sparkle like diamonds under the moon's pale reflection. The quiet mushroom shapes of the sleeping ships that were nestled throughout the airfield aroused my envy. These inanimate things would remain, but I would leave.

I was just about to enter the ship when I saw a figure hurrying toward our ship. Through the moonlight I discerned the bright colors of the Yargonian costume. Perhaps it was a messenger, rushing with some word to me. Maybe he had changed his mind!

The pilots also noticed the approaching figure, and waited expectantly as the trim form and empty sleeve came into view. It was Sanau! She was breathless when she reached the ship.

"I am so glad I reached you, my friend."

"Is something wrong?"

"I merely wished to say good-bye." She stated this as a fact, but the flash of feeling shone in her eyes.

The pilots, sensing that all was well, turned and entered the ship. I stood there staring at Sanau. For a moment we were equally uncomfortable and ill at ease.

After a slight pause, she said, "Have a safe journey, little Janet."

I nodded wordlessly. I wondered how much she guessed, how much she knew.

She threw her arm about me and held me close, then almost roughly pushed me away.

"Go quickly," she murmured, "go quickly or you will destroy us all."

The tears rushed to my eyes. Sanau, my cold-hearted Sanau was actually unhappy because I was leaving. For the first time in her well-regulated life I had made her feel an emotion and she was disturbed and bewildered by it. She would always feel she had committed some unknown crime, had betrayed some weakness. I had to make her understand.

"Sanau." I reached out and took her hand in mine. "This is friendship, Sanau. It's good."

"No, it is not," she answered. "It has caused many conflicts within me. That is why I left your side when you were ill. I suddenly found my values were changing."

"You will forget. And I am going away."

She shook her head. "Unfortunately, the damage is done. How can I return to my right thinking?" Her tone was almost child-like. "Janet, on my travels, on my lecture tour, do you know what I found myself doing? I searched for my children. I was suddenly obsessed with a strange desire to know if they were well and content."

"But that's the right way to feel," I said desperately. The time was so short. I could hear the soft purr of the motors.

"It is not the right way to feel. It prevented me from accomplishing my work in the shortest time possible. I actually wasted time traveling to cities in which no appearance was scheduled, looking for a child."

She hurled the word child as if it was the least desirable object for which one might search.

"Did you find any of them?"

"Some." Her tone was filled with distaste.

"And didn't that give you happiness?"

"I do not know happiness other than work."

"Sanau, you did feel something!"

She sighed. "What does it matter what I felt? They were completely disinterested in me. They barely acknowledged our relationship. Their real interest was in the journey I had taken and the things of learning I could impart."

"You mean they met you as a talented leader and not a mother?"

She nodded.

"But what can you expect? It's the way they've been trained to think. But you could teach them. If I, an inferior being, could teach you to feel emotion, certainly you with all your mental facilities could undo the things they have learned."

"No, Janet. Who is to say your thinking is right? I feel it is wrong. Nothing can be right that causes unhappiness."

"You can only be happy if you know unhappiness as well," I argued. "Nothing can ever go on one plane."

"Janet, believe me, I am right." She spoke hurriedly; the silver discs of the saucers were beginning to spin. "On my trip, for the first time, I was unhappy. I was unhappy at the emotion of leaving you when you were ill. I was unhappy at the disinterest of my children in me as a human. One vice and one thought leads to another. Creative work is hampered by such useless thoughts. No, little Janet, we on Yargo are right. So go, go immediately and luck be with you."

"I'll miss you, Sanau."

"I pity you. It is a sad life you return to, little Janet. A short life filled with wasted and painful emotions. That is your life, this is mine. Go to it. Good-bye."

She turned quickly and ran, yet I was almost sure I had seen tears in her eyes; it had happened so fast I couldn't be sure. My own eyes were wet as I turned and entered the spaceship. I stood and watched the door seal itself together. I was going home. I was leaving everything that seemed to matter to me, not only the Yargo and Sanau, but all those wonderful sleeping people I was leaving behind. A great people that needed only to be awakened.

It could never be. In some far-off day this was the future in store for my own world. Perhaps it was the perfect future, but someone wiser than I would have to make that decision.

Listlessly I sank down on one of the bunks and allowed myself to be strapped in for the takeoff. I felt the needle pierce my arm and almost immediately I slipped off into that familiar soft sleep.

I awoke in time to watch our ship approach my Earth's atmosphere. It was thrilling to see. My Earth, floating in the heavens like a strange round ball. It seemed so remote; it was impossible to visualize as a world of cities, oceans, and deserts teeming with life. A strange little lonely planet populated by millions of people who thought it was the only world in the skies. Populated by people who yearned to rule it.

One of the pilots appeared and beckoned me to follow him. We left my chamber and climbed a small spiral staircase down to a small empty room. He pressed a button on the blank steel wall, which began to slide apart.

I grabbed him for support. The wall was opening and beyond it was sky. Was this a double cross? Were they just going to toss me into space? Return me to Earth in fragments?

The opening grew as wide as a door now—a door into the night below.

"Ready?"

I stared at him in amazement. "You speak English?"

He smiled. "Not well. Just small form of it. Have been taught by Sanau. You ready?"

I gestured. "Ready?"

Suddenly the light caught my eye. There it was, the same beam of light that had lifted me was waiting to take me down, a stairway to the world I knew.

"Go," he ordered. "Light will take you down in safety."

I held back. I did not disbelieve him about the safety of the leap, but this green-eyed pilot was my last link with the Yargo and the world I was leaving.

"Hurry," he urged. "We are close over Earth, can be seen by your airmen, perchance. They might come near; then he will die."

"You mean you'd shoot at them?"

"No, ray from our ship protect us from meteors; same ray will also dissolve metal of your ships. Now hurry, jump!"

I jumped. What was there to fear? Without Yargo, what else was there? I would never see him again, never, and suddenly I was thankful for the onrush of merciful blackness. I was slipping into unconsciousness and I didn't care if I never awoke. I would never see him again or Sanau or . . . and then there was nothing more.

CHAPTER 29

It was dusk and the early winter darkness made the room feel cold and impersonal. Doctor Galens turned on the lamps in his office and brought me a glass of water. The light from the lamps snapped us both back to reality. Back to Earth and away from Yargo once more.

I was emotionally spent after the dramatization of my story. Doctor Galens appeared equally disturbed.

For a few minutes he remained silent. He lit my cigarette, emptied the ashtray littered with the stubs of my cigarettes, then reseated himself and looked at me intently.

"What happened after you came to?" he asked gently. "After the trip to Earth on the ray. Where did they deposit you?"

"On the sand dune in Avalon. It was nearly dawn. I stumbled into the village. I must have looked a sight. My dress looked like I had lived in it for a month. My hair was matted from the wind and sea but I wasn't even bruised."

"What did you do?"

"Nothing at first. I just sat there and looked at the sky. Finally I began to walk.

I guess I was in a daze. I kept walking; as I recall, my mind was alert, but I had no destination. I wasn't sure how much time had elapsed since I had been on Yargo; a week, three weeks, a month. I guess I was afraid to think, afraid if I realized I'd never see Yargo again, I might collapse. So I kept walking. I must have reached the village, sort of headed there subconsciously, I guess. An officer approached me; he had been following me for several blocks. After all, people just don't roam the streets of Avalon at dawn. I guess he thought I was drunk or sick, but then when he looked at me, he grabbed my arm, blew his whistle, and from nowhere another officer appeared. I heard him say, 'Yes, this is her' and then . . .'' I stopped and buried my face in my hands.

Doctor Galen's voice was gently insistent. "And then what happened, Janet?"

"I was taken to the local jail. It seems my picture had been in the papers. Oh, I was quite a celebrity in Avalon. Naturally my family and David had gone out of their minds after my sudden disappearance. The entire New Jersey police force had been working on it for weeks. There was even one poor village thief who had been held in custody because I had been seen talking to him. Naturally everything from rape to a trunk murder had been suspected. They had watched the beach for my body, even dragged the bay. Since I was a nobody and my family was neither very rich nor very poor, the publicity had only been local and even then it was forgotten in a few days. Naturally it was not forgotten by David, my family, and the local police force at Avalon."

"I suppose they questioned you at length?"

I nodded. "I looked so awful, and I had no intention of giving them any inkling as to where I had actually been; I guess I sounded pretty incoherent. I think they thought I was a little insane at first. God, I'll never forget that morning, sitting in that awful police station with everyone hammering away at me! They even called in the city psychiatrist. I just acted muddled and said I was tired, that I wanted to go home."

"I don't recall reading anything about it in the papers here," Doctor Galens offered. "Was there any story?"

"No. In Avalon there were big headlines. 'Amnesia victim found roaming the streets of Avalon.' Made their local police force sound like a regular FBI." I crushed out my cigarette and began to pace the room.

"My family and David immediately hushed it up. They came for me and everyone was so kind. Too kind. They actually thought I did have amnesia. At first I allowed them to think what they liked. It saved me from their questions. Everyone tried to act as if nothing had happened. I had lost a month out of my life, and they were just glad to have me back. And then, when I felt more like myself, well, I decided I'd never tell them. I'd keep my promise to Yargo."

"And did you?"

"I tried very hard to readjust myself to the idea that I was back for good, that I'd never see Yargo or Sanau or a spaceship again. I was also trying to bridge the gap that had grown between David and myself. I should just say 'my gap'—David felt as close to me as ever—so one night I decided to tell David. I figured maybe it would help make things as they were. I was even going to tell him how I had wanted to remain and how I felt about the Yargo. I felt he couldn't be jealous of a man who was on another world, and after all, I hadn't done anything wrong. I wanted an honest relationship. A husband and wife can't start out a marriage with a big secret between them."

Doctor Galens nodded. "But you didn't tell him?"

"I started to. I remember the night, it was a Wednesday about a week after I had returned. We had gone to dinner in the Chandelier Room. Billy Sinns was at the piano playing These Foolish Things. That's David's favorite song. I decided he had to know. I said, 'David, when I was away . . . I didn't really have amnesia. I want you to know the truth. No one else knows and no one will ever know but you. I went on a long trip, David, on a flying saucer, to another world . . .'"

"And he wouldn't believe you?"

I nodded. "Worse than that, he acted as if I wasn't really sane. He stopped me and said,

'Darling, I don't care where you've been. You're back and that's what counts. We are never going to talk about it. Things like this happen to a lot of people and we're going to act as if it never happened to you.'"

"I don't give up easily, Doctor Galens, as I guess you can probably see. So I tried again. I said, 'David this is something we've got to talk about.' And he said, 'You know, honey girl, there's an old adage, sometimes forgetting is more important then remembering. If we forget this completely it will be as if it never happened, but if we keep dragging it out and talking about it, it will always remain as an obstacle. Now I don't want to hear another word about it. I love you. I don't care if you went to Mars or Europe or Siam; we all go into another world at times. You're back, and that's it.' Then I said, 'Please, David, just hear me out' and he frowned. He said, 'Janet, girl, I've been pretty patient. There are very few demands I've ever put on you, but I'm making one now. I don't want to talk about it.'"

"And that was all?" Doctor Galens seemed surprised.

"Well, Billy Sinns came to the table just then and David absolutely insisted that Billy sit down and have a drink with us. He did and they reminisced together about songs and stuff. We never got to talk about Yargo again."

"What about the wedding? Weren't you supposed to be married in September?"

I nodded. "I put it off. How could I marry David? I was in love with the Yargo. He was the only thing that was real to me. David was like a stranger. Even the memory of Sanau brought more affectionate thoughts than the real association of some of my oldest friends. David was sweet; he agreed to the postponement. He felt I was badly shaken and needed a rest, so we postponed it for six months."

"And now the actual wedding day is close at hand?"

"In three days, but I can't . . ." I sat down and began to sob. It was all so hopeless. "Doctor Galens, I've tried! I've tried to forget. It isn't as if I've sat around nurturing this memory. Every time the image of the Yargo's face came to my mind, I pushed it away. I kept busy. I kept thinking wonderful thoughts of David. I even sat down and wrote all the wonderful things that lie in wait for me. But it hasn't worked. That's why I've come to you. I can't marry David. What do I do? Do I marry and hope that eventually I'll forget the Yargo. Or do I refuse David and throw away the only slim chance I have for happiness?"

"Janet," the Doctor's voice was soft and almost pleading, "people do go into other worlds when they suffer an emotional disturbance. These other worlds often seem more real than the one they actually inhabit, and sometimes it is impossible for them to return to reality. You have been successful . . ."

I rose. My voice was harsh with anger and

despair. "If you persist in regarding me as a mentally ill and disturbed patient, we are only wasting each other's time. I do not deny that I am emotionally upset, but only because of the adventure I experienced. I did not experience the adventure because I am emotionally upset."

I sat down. Nothing was beginning to make sense. I had to get hold of myself.

"Doctor Galens, I don't mean to get overwrought, but you must believe me. This actually happened. I must think calmly and unemotionally, like the Yargo would want me to, this can all be worked out, maybe then I'll be a superior being, too superior for this world, but not enough for . . ." My voice broke. This time Doctor Galens was almost angry.

"Janet! Stop this kind of talk. You are beginning to sound like that impossible imaginary superruler you have dreamed into being."

The tone of his voice forced me to attention.

"Now then . . ." he paused, his tone once more that of the sympathetic advisor. "Have you any tangible proof that you have been to such a world? Did you bring back any evidence? A small piece of metal, a fragment of material, any object that can prove such a civilization exists?"

I shook my head. "You know the state I was in when I left. Proof of the trip was the last thing on my mind."

"You mean that never once did it occur to you to bring back some concrete evidence of the trip? Even as a keepsake for yourself?"

"Doctor Galens, I told you about my last night on the planet in the Yargo's palace. We had that awful scene. I cried myself to sleep. I was leaving him! Do you know what it's like to leave the only person you'll ever really love? To know there is no possible way you'll ever see him again? It's worse than death because at least death, as we know it, offers the promise of an afterlife, of the soul existing forever. But Yargo doesn't believe that way, perhaps he has no soul. This was the end of everything for me. No, Doctor Galens, a souvenir was the last thing on my mind."

For a moment we both sat silent, each battling our own doubts. Then suddenly his eyes lit up, as if he had found the solution.

"Your appendectomy!"

"What about it?"

"The scar. You have the scar as evidence. Certainly if one of our leading physicians..."

I shook my head. "There is not the slightest sign of a scar. I told you that. They never took any stitches. They seal it with some sort of device. There is no scar." I repeated the words as if they were a death knell.

"But there was an incision, you say?"

"Yes, for about a week. There was a pencil-thin line like a scratch. Then it completely disappeared."

"But your appendix is gone."

I nodded wearily. I wasn't here to prove it had happened. I was here to find out how to continue living in peace.

He stood up smiling as if he had discovered penicillin.

"Suppose we take an X ray."

"As you wish," I answered tonelessly. "I know my trip was not an hallucination. When you take the X ray and check with my family physician and prove that two months before my trip I had an appendix, and now I am without one, and without a scar, you will know it, too. Where do we go from there?"

"First things first," he said almost gaily. He made a phone call.

I was to go to the X-ray laboratory as soon as I left his office. In the morning he would have the results.

I rose dutifully. I was as dismal as the early evening rain that had begun to beat against the window. The X ray would prove nothing but the authenticity of my story. Nothing had been accomplished and tomorrow was one day closer to the wedding.

I went out into the damp night and took a taxi to the X-ray laboratory. There I let the man take a series of slides. I gave him my family doctor's name so he could check on the previous history of my insides and went home.

Another night without hope, without sleep, without Yargo.

CHAPTER 30

I reported back to Doctor Galens the following day.

He was smiling when he greeted me. His desk was covered with large X-ray plates. He offered me a cigarette and waited until I seemed settled.

The doctor was not unlike an actor in his sense of timing. I waited patiently. I could sense he had some important news.

He cleared his throat as if he was addressing a large audience.

"Janet, this problem is going to be easy to deal with, that is, if you are cooperative and accept certain facts."

I nodded and wondered what was coming.

"Janet, here are your X rays, X rays taken from several angles. Janet, I want you to know your appendix is completely intact."

For a moment the enormity of his statement did not reach me.

He repeated it. "Janet your appendix is intact. It is healthy and very much in its proper place. In your body."

Now nothing made sense. I had had the operation. But my appendix was still in me. Was I mad? Was I really mad? Perhaps I

was, then the Yargo wasn't real . . . I must
have fainted.

I was lying on the cold leather couch when
I opened my eyes; the nurse was offering me
a drink. I took a long swallow and spluttered.
It was brandy. I sat up and pushed the hair
from my eyes. I had to think. I had to listen
to Doctor Galens now or all was really lost.
He had to help me or I'd end up in a mad-
house.

He began to bombard me with questions.
Questions that you ask a nut, I guess, because
that was me: a real nut.

I tried not to think. I tried to answer the
questions honestly. Had I always been imag-
inative? Had I read a great deal about the
flying saucers? Had I been frightened by
them? Overly curious about them? Had I ever
suffered from a loss of memory before? Had
I ever been in love with a man who was
unattainable in some way? Superior in intelligence? Did my father in any way resemble
this man?

I tried to answer sanely and logically. Yes,
I had a vivid imagination. Flying saucers? I
had displayed no more nor less interest than
the average reader. Mingled scepticism at
first, then a vague feeling that perhaps they
were some secret weapon of our own. No,
I had never been in love with anyone who
even faintly resembled the Yargo. A teacher
in school once, the history teacher. Yes, he
had been tall, superior in intellect, but he
hadn't been bald with aquamarine eyes. No,

I had never had a loss of memory and my father in no way resembled the Yargo.

But I couldn't believe it hadn't happened. As I answered his questions, I knew all was real.

Doctor Galens was wonderful. He canceled all his appointments and for two days we were closeted together. Perhaps my case interested him, or perhaps he felt genuine compassion for me. For two days we worked unceasingly, trying to mold the fragments of my life together. For two days I accepted and rejected his helpful suggestions, fully aware that he made complete sense.

He explained that perhaps deep down I did not want to marry David. My love for him was genuine, but I was fighting against the actual idea of marriage. This subconscious fight was caused by the frustration of relinquishing the theatrical career for which I had longed. The fact that I had successfully stifled the impulse only served to make it more paramount than ever in my subconscious. I had mentioned it constantly throughout my imaginary trip, in my fanciful discussions with the now mythical ruler. I had seen to it on my dream planet that no one else would be thwarted as I had been. Everyone would be allowed to do just as he wished. It was obvious that I was afraid of love so I banned it on my new planet, so that no one would be allowed to enjoy it unless I participated.

Marriage to David presented another problem, he explained; it meant permanently discarding all my childhood dreams. My fervent desire to go to Avalon, to revisit the place I had enjoyed as a child, was an attempt to recreate the happy, carefree days of childhood when my dreams were still waiting to be realized. This attitude proved I was withdrawing only from the present and retreating into the past.

Sanau represented my mother, whose approval I was constantly seeking, whom I longed to love. Her superiority was the disapproval I constantly felt from my mother. The Yargo was born to show my mother that I was definitely a great person. He was a superior man for me to love, a man different from all others. That I could break through obstacles and attract this superior man meant that I was a person to be reckoned with. But even in my hallucinations I met with defeat. My entire problem, Doctor Galens explained, was my feeling of inferiority and my search for approval in the eyes of my parents. I was loath to accept David because my mother had selected him for me. I was settling for a nice wonderful average man, a man that my mother thought I deserved. If she thought I deserved him, I felt he was not good enough, because I felt she held me in little esteem. I felt she was thankful I was marrying anyone.

Avalon merely brought these thoughts to my consciousness. It was my last hope of fulfillment. When Avalon proved a disappointment, I had remained to search, hoping against hope one dream could be restored. On that final night even my childhood pastime of seeking shooting stars failed to recreate the feelings of awe and delight. Vestiges of broken dreams, forgotten hopes, and the uncertain and unwished-for future returned, and I probably experienced a sudden clash of the subconscious and the conscious. Thus, the breakdown occurred.

The person who wanders around as an amnesia victim *is* in another world, Doctor Galens explained, but rarely does the victim recall the thoughts and fantasies that occur while he is in this other existence. My case was very rare, and my problem was that all three stages were intact.

Now I had to make the real real and the unreal fantasy, Doctor Galens insisted. The longer I dwelled on the Yargo the more I was receding into a dream world. And there lay my real danger.

It took me quite a while to even half-heartedly believe that I had been away in mind only. When my own doubts became too insistent and the memory of the Yargo too real, I only had to look at the X-ray plates. What could be stronger proof of Doctor Galens's arguments than an operation that had never occurred?

Then where had I been for a month? Where had I eaten, and slept . . .

Doctor Galens went on to explain that amnesia victims often led double lives. They took jobs in strange cities; some victims had even been known to commit bigamy.

We returned to the present and its very real complications. He forced me to ask myself if marriage to David was something I did not want. I had no feelings against David, or marriage as a whole, I simply loved the Yargo. But there was no such thing as Yargo, and there was David. Time was too short for a definite solution. Doctor Galens said I needed two years of hard analysis in which I would work into my subconscious and ferret out all my insecurities and grievances.

His final advice was that I ask for a second postponement of the wedding. Once my obsession was defeated, and we started my analysis, I would, no doubt, find a happy future with David.

I left Doctor Galens's office late in the afternoon with a slight sense of hope. After all, he was a brilliant man. He could help me. I would postpone the wedding and would get my old job back. Somehow I would manage to get the money required for a complete analysis. Soon everything would take its rightful place: David would reassume the prime role in my life and the Yargo would recede into a fanciful dream.

CHAPTER 31

Only it wasn't as easy as that.

I stated my intention for the postponement over a quiet dinner that very night. Since I did not mention Doctor Galens or the reason behind my visit to his office, David proved an obstinate opponent.

Another postponement, he declared. Didn't I love him? What would people think? He'd be the laughingstock of town.

I pleaded that I wasn't really well or equipped for marriage yet. He argued me down. I was fine, and once I became his wife all my troubles would disappear.

The pain and doubt that began to be mirrored on his features added to my own insecurity. My mother presented herself as a strong ally on David's behalf. Postpone the wedding, indeed! There were far too many preparations that had already been settled. Poor David's whole life was planned around the wedding. Even Mr. Finley, his boss, was coming. His vacation was set and the tickets were purchased for our boat trip to Bermuda. He had several law cases coming up that had been pushed ahead to allow ample time for the wedding and honeymoon.

And so it went until he reached for the final male weapon. "What is it darling? Don't you love me? What have I done?"

Several times I bit my lip to keep from shouting out the entire miserable truth, but a latent sense of self-preservation made me hold back. If I did tell the truth, David would undoubtedly cancel the wedding permanently. He was too unimaginative to understand about the subconscious or unconscious mind. To him I'd be crazy. That would be fine, just fine. It'd be all over town, poor Janet Cooper, that nice David had waited for so long. It wouldn't do my family any good either. They'd be anxious enough to hush up the whole thing. I'd be labeled the village idiot; I'd never even get a job; how could I go to Doctor Galens then? I'd be worse off than ever, sicker than ever, with no job, no friends, no David.

And because I saw no alternative, I agreed not to postpone the wedding. It would take place the following day as planned.

I sat surrounded by my loved ones—David and my family—on the eve of my wedding, thinking of those other ones so far away, so far away that they never really existed.

I roused myself from such thoughts and even rallied enough spirit to drink a toast to our future. In fact, I seemed so restored to my normal self that David departed filled with male optimism that my sudden fit of near hysteria was nothing more than prenuptial jitters.

No bride-to-be was more disconsolate than I after David departed. My high spirits vanished like the mask they were, and I sat immersed in my self-made gloom. My mother and my aunt bustled about with traditional "family of the bride" excitement, too busy to even notice me. I watched them sort out and pack my filmy undergarments with sighs of admiration. They sprinkled liberal tears on the wedding gown, the trousseau, and me. Finally everything was ready, the new clothes for Bermuda safely packed in the fortnighter and the small overnight bag ready and waiting.

I watched them and tried to restore that brief cheerful mood I had put on for David. I even managed a smile as I watched my mother flutter from excitement to tearful sentiment as she gossiped and reminisced with my aunt. I smiled at their too-careful hairdos that told of today's trip to the beauty parlor. I hadn't even thought about my hair or my nails. I went to my room.

I washed my hair and rubbed it dry with a great big towel. It was losing its luster; it wasn't shiny and wonderful the way it had been on Yargo, but I hadn't been there so, of course, my hair was the same. I did my nails; they were chipping. On Yargo even my nails . . . but there was no Yargo. The house was finally still. It was midnight, time to go to bed. Tomorrow at this time I'd be married . . .

I put out the light and got into bed.

I was running down the street and I was cold. I stopped. It was late. When had I gotten out of bed? I was dressed in a polo coat and the red linen dress. Was I going mad again? I must stop running. When had I gotten dressed? I couldn't remember that. Maybe I wasn't running at all. Maybe my mind has just gone blank. Maybe I'm really mad, maybe I'm still home in bed. But this is real. I can feel the cold and my breath is coming in short gasps. I can even see the fine mist of smoke my warm breath causes in the night air. I am running.

I kept running.

Maybe this is the beginning of another amnesia attack, maybe I'll collapse and dream that I'm back on Yargo. I'm still in this world, on a city street, a street I know so well and still I keep running. Where am I going? I can't even answer myself. Somehow I seem to know where I'm going . . . maybe it is my subconscious directing me. My feet seem to be leading the way down the street, across avenues, on and on . . . the park!

The park! Where I played as a child! Doctor Galens was right. I am trying to go back, searching for memories. Yes, there's the hill; we used to call it Wishing Hill. You ran to the top of it and made a wish, then spit in the wind and it came true. Oh, yes, Doctor Galens is right. I must turn back, back to my home, back to my bed, to David. I need help, I need so much help. But am I really on this hill in the cold night or am I still in bed?

It's dangerous in the park at night, dangerous for a girl to be alone. You read things about it in the paper.

But I kept running, climbing to the top of the hill. I stood there panting and sobbing. Maybe this was madness, maybe I'm not really here, I told myself. Maybe I'm actually going insane. But what of it? For the moment I am here. Make a wish! Make it! What harm can it do?

I looked toward the sky. The stars hung so low they literally screamed at me.

"Yargo! Yargo!" I was screaming but I didn't care.

"Oh, Yargo." I sobbed. "You said your spaceships are constantly watching our Earth. If there is one, relay my message. Yargo, come and get me. Come and get me!!!"

I fell to the ground in exhaustion. The brown stubs of the dead grass scratched my face. I lay there for some time. Nothing happened. Of course, nothing happened. I was mad, sick . . .

Then I remembered the spitting part. Of course, you have to spit in the wind; that's part of making the wish come true. With a sob I pulled myself from the ground and faced the wind. I spit into the night. The wind hurled it back in my face.

For a moment I stood alone on that bare hilltop reaching to the sky as if I expected some miracle, bathed in the wintery light of the moon and pale cold stars.

Oh, Yargo, Yargo! I fell to my knees and prayed to God, to Yargo, but only the stars seemed to hear me. They actually seemed to dance as if they were laughing, mocking me.

And then I saw the disc!

It was there! Small and round, the familiar platinum apple in the heavens. It was there circling its way to me, growing larger . . . larger . . . it was coming!

They had heard me, or now I was actually mad. Maybe that was it. I was mad, mad. But I didn't care.

I stood as if transfixed, staring at the object in the sky. It was over me now, round and still. The wind stopped, the earth seemed to stand still. Now the ray, Oh, please send the ray. *Yes!* No longer eerie and frightening, but warm, a path to the stars, to heaven, to Yargo!

"Oh, God, I'm really mad," I sobbed. "I know I am, I know . . ."

And then the ray lifted me.

Up . . . up . . . up . . . and then the merciful blackness.

When I opened my eyes, he was beside me, smiling.

"Oh, Yargo" the tears streamed down my cheeks. "Yargo, I know you're not really here, but I don't care. If this is insanity, I never want to be sane."

He didn't speak but his eyes never left my face.

"I know this isn't true, because of the

appendix," I babbled. "Yargo you see, I still have my appendix, so I know you're not real . . ."

He took me in his arms.

"I've been searching for you, Janet." His voice was soft. "I've been flying over Earth for months now, always searching. I love you."

"Now I know I'm really mad," I answered blissfully.

"No, Janet, you are not mad. You must come back to my planet. You must save me, and my people."

"Save your people? You who are thousands of years ahead of us?"

He nodded and spoke, all the while holding me close.

"We are the most advanced of any planet. But which is the planet with the most wisdom? I do not know. That we have succeeded beyond all beings in science and progress there is no doubt. But as people perhaps we have retrogressed, for in comparison to you, little Janet, we are not people. How well I understand what you were trying to say. Perhaps there is a time where science must end and emotions, hope, and faith must begin. Who has the most wisdom? You, who have a short time dotted with many illnesses and needs, but feel love and hate and have faith and bear your young; or we, who have conquered all of the world's fatalities, and in doing so have placed ourselves beyond the realm of living?"

I understood and my happiness was that it was he who was pleading now.

"Come back to my world. Help us keep all that is good and . teach us what we have forgotten. Teach us to love one another, to realize that even petty vices that come along with emotion are better than no emotion at all. Teach us the meaning of faith, such as you know it. It is your faith that brought this miracle. It moved a world. Teach us about the God we have long forsaken, a God that caused our great minds to make the mistake of capturing you instead of a man of science so you could show us the way."

"You are a great man, Yargo," I told him. "It takes a great man to realize such a weakness, and I'll try, we'll try . . ."

He held me in his arms and I knew true perfection in that moment. The feel of his strong body close to mine, the purr of the motor, the darkness of the night outside.

He broke the silence and smiled into my eyes. Then in a voice that hid a smile, he said, "And, Janet we never did take out your appendix. I'm afraid our learned surgeon was just overanxious to view such an organ. For upon cutting you open and satisfying his curiosity, he changed his diagnosis and announced that you merely had a good old-fashioned Earth-type stomachache."

I laughed. We both laughed together and I clung to him and told myself I didn't care whether it was happening or not as long as it never ended.

"Maybe this isn't real, Yargo, maybe I'm out of my mind, but don't ever let me come out of it. Don't ever let me go back to Earth!"

He answered seriously. "No, Janet, you will return to your Earth one day, when your people have more understanding, when they can accept the knowledge of other worlds. Then you must return and warn them that there are some things that man cannot and must not master. That there is a limit to advancement, but there must never be a limit to faith and love. If Earth becomes a world of people who no longer know how to love there may be no Janet from another planet to show them the way. Yes, you must go back some day, but only for a visit."

Then he held me in his arms and kissed me and his lips were not like stone.

The following day, the newspapers carried a brief story about the groom who was left waiting at the church. The bride had suffered an amnesia attack the previous summer and, it was feared by her family and doctor, was once again the victim of a similar episode. Newspapers in adjacent areas advised their readers to watch for her.

Especially in the vicinity of Avalon, New Jersey.

ABOUT THE AUTHOR

JACQUELINE SUSANN was one of the most successful writers in the history of American publishing. Her first novel, *Valley of the Dolls*, published in 1966, holds the bestselling fiction record in the *Guinness Book of World Records*. *The Love Machine* was published in 1969 and became an immediate #1 bestseller and held that position for five months. When her third novel, *Once Is Not Enough*, was published in 1973, it also moved to the top of the bestseller list and thus established Jacqueline Susann as the first novelist in history to have three consecutive #1 bestsellers.

A novella, *Dolores*, was published posthumously in 1976, and also became a #1 American bestseller. However, her first book to be published, *Every Night, Josephine!* was to remain her own personal favorite. Little has been written about her writing career prior to 1963, the year *Every Night, Josephine!* was published. Until the discovery of *Yargo*, *Josephine* was thought to be her first full-length work. In fact, Jacqueline Susann coauthored a play, *Lovely Me*, which was performed on Broadway in 1946, and she wrote several magazine articles and short stories in the 1940s and 1950s. Today, the Susann books are to be found in more than thirty languages worldwide and are estimated to have sold over 50 million copies in all editions. And now, added to this body of work, is *Yargo*.

Jacqueline Susann was born in Philadelphia. Her father, the late Robert Susann, was a noted portrait artist and her mother, Rose Susann, is a retired public school teacher. Jacqueline Susann was an actress before becoming a writer (of her career in the theater, she liked to say that the plays she appeared in broke all records too—the track records for opening and closing.)

In private life she was the wife of television and motion picture producer Irving Mansfield for almost thirty years. Jacqueline Susann died on September 21, 1974, after a courageous and privately fought struggle with cancer. With the exception of her husband and a few close friends, her twelve-year fight to overcome the disease was not known until after her death.